Old Sins

Charlie Cochrane

RIPTIDE
PUBLISHING

Riptide Publishing
PO Box 1537
Burnsville, NC 28714
www.riptidepublishing.com

Old Sins

Cover art: L.C. Chase, lcchase.com/design-portfolio.html
Editor: Carole-ann Galloway
Layout: L.C. Chase, lcchase.com/design-portfolio.html

ISBN: 978-1-62649-873-0

First edition
February, 2019

Also available in ebook:
ISBN: 978-1-62649-872-3

Old Sins

Charlie Cochrane

RIPTIDE
PUBLISHING

Dedicated to those who kept asking me when the next "one with the dog" would be coming out. Including my daughters, who were loudest of all.

Table of Contents

Chapter One

Adam Matthews yawned, stretched, and wriggled back down into the bed. If he'd been able to purr, he'd have sounded like a contented moggy, which would have annoyed his dog but summed up his feelings perfectly. Summer holidays, having the best part of six weeks without pupils to teach: bliss. Even if reality meant he still had lesson planning and the like to do, he didn't mind. Not having to listen to the constant drone of ten-year-olds meant he could let his brain go through its annual recovery process. His partner, Robin Bright, was enjoying his fortnight or so of holiday as well, although in his case the break was from chasing villains and listening to the prattle of his constables.

They'd had ten days in a villa on the Med, enjoying sea, sand, Sangria, Spanish food, and a smattering of the pleasures of the double bed. Now they were home, with a few more days to make the most of before Robin had to report back for duty. The house was neat as a new pin, Sandra—the miracle worker who came into their house daily to clean, wash, iron, care for Campbell's needs, and sometimes provide cake—having been in to keep everything in order, garden included.

So they'd nothing planned other than being lazy and making it up to Campbell for their cruelty in abandoning him into the care of Adam's mother. Despite the fact that he'd been spoiled rotten, the dog would take a while to forgive his two masters for not taking him with them. *A while* being, in Campbell's terms, until he'd had sufficient quantity of treats to compensate for the extreme mental hardship his facial expressions would suggest he'd undergone.

"Are you awake?" a bleary voice sounded at Adam's side.

"No. I'm fast asleep."

"Pillock." Robin turned, laying his right arm over Adam's stomach. "Am I dreaming it or did you volunteer to cook breakfast today?"

"Yes. It's my turn." Which was why Adam had been lying in bed thinking, putting off the inevitable. "Although I can't do so unless you let go of me."

"Shame." Robin kissed Adam's shoulder. "I need to clone you so you can be cooking breakfast and romping about here with me at the same time."

"If I were a woman, I'd accuse you of being a sexist pig. As it is, I'll call you a lazy sod." Adam threw off Robin's arm, rolled him over, and slapped his backside. "Don't lie here too long or I'll give all your bacon to Campbell."

"I'd fight him for it."

They both got out of bed, Adam heading to the bathroom for a quick relieving visit before his partner got in there. On a work day, Robin showered and shaved speedily, but on occasions like this when he had the opportunity to take his leisure, he enjoyed lingering over his ablutions. And why not? He worked hard, so he should have the chance to enjoy life's simple pleasures. As long as he didn't linger too much and risk being presented with an incinerated sausage.

When Adam got down to the kitchen, Campbell greeted him with a rub against his legs, followed by a dash for the kitchen door. Lie-ins were great for the workers in the household, but not helpful for canine bladders. Opening that door took precedence over everything else first thing in the morning. Once that was done, Adam could get the kettle on, fish out the bacon—always best done while Campbell was otherwise occupied—put on some music, and potter about the kitchen content in the knowledge that the two creatures he loved best were happy. And long might that state of affairs continue.

Over breakfast, talk turned—inevitably—to their imminent return to work, although Robin insisted that shouldn't be discussed for at least another twenty-four hours. He'd even banned them from watching crime shows over the holiday period, so as not to remind him of what awaited at Abbotston station.

Adam changed the subject to their regular discussion topic. "Am I allowed to mention work in the context of moving house to somewhere slightly more convenient for commuting?"

Given that both of them had relocated to new jobs since they started living together, the comfortable little cottage in Lindenshaw—that had once belonged to Adam's grandparents, as had the infant Campbell—wasn't quite as well located as it had been.

"Campbell says you can mention that all you want." Robin grinned. "He wants a bigger garden to lumber about in. And he keeps reminding me we can afford it, maintenance and all."

"That dog should get a job as an estate agent." Or maybe a registrar. There was also the small matter of a civil partnership to sort out, which they'd decided on earlier in the year but not got any further in terms of planning.

"Mum was asking again," Robin said when he'd finished the last bit of bacon.

Great minds were clearly thinking alike again. "Asking about what?"

Robin gently tapped Adam's arm with the back of his hand. "Don't pretend you don't know. Have we set a date? Will she need her passport? Should she buy a winter hat or a spring one?"

"What did you tell her?"

"That what with the demands of school life and the unpredictable villains of Abbotston, it wasn't easy to fix a weekend."

All of which was true, but wouldn't have mollified Mrs. Bright one bit. "And what did she say in response?"

Robin shrugged. "That she understood the predicament we were in, which I suspect was a lie because she then pointed out that other policemen and teachers manage to tie the knot."

That was also true, although their case was complicated by having feet in both camps.

The real reason they were making no progress was the simple, prosaic one that they were struggling to sort out what type of do they wanted and who they'd invite. They'd both have preferred something small, discreet, classy, and a guest list limited to their mothers, an aunt or two, and Campbell. But was that going to cause ructions among family and friends? Should they invite their cousins, and how could they not include some of their friends and colleagues? And if they invited only one or two each, whose nose would be put out of joint that they'd not been included?

When they'd sat down to do a theoretical-maximum guest list, they'd given up when it hit one hundred, and had then parked the matter entirely. One day they'd have to start it up again, although at present the real desire they felt for entering into that partnership, the official statement that they were a couple and intended to be until death they did part, kept being destroyed by the stress surrounding making arrangements.

"Let's not spoil today thinking about it," Adam said. "We'll grab our diaries later, and set a date—not for the event, so don't look so panicked, but for sitting down and deciding what we want to do. Once and for all and no arguments from anyone not already living in this household. Does that work?"

"Yeah. Got to bite the bullet sometime." Robin grinned. "And I can relate that progress to Mum the next time she rings. She'll make sure we actually do it and don't renege at the last moment."

"Deal." Adam pushed aside his plate and mug. "Right, let's not waste the rest of Sunday. What are we going to do with today?"

"The weather forecast is good. We should get some fresh air."

"Sounds spot on."

"Where do you fancy getting said air?" Robin asked, en route to putting his dirty crockery in the washing-up bowl. "And I assume we're taking *himself*?"

"We wouldn't dare leave him behind. He's still not happy about us going away to that villa."

"He can lump it. He's on holiday all year round."

Holiday time or not, Sunday morning was their favourite time to walk the dog, weather and jobs permitting. Campbell could run off some of his energy, Adam and Robin had the chance to talk, and they could all work up a healthy appetite for lunch. Today they were having beef casserole, which Adam had already got out of the freezer to defrost. The Yorkshire puddings needed no such preparation, being able to go from freezer to stomach via a hot oven in a matter of minutes. Accompany that with a beer and follow it with some sport on the telly—what more could a man want?

"What about going somewhere different today?" Robin asked. "There's the towpath along the old canal. We've not been there for ages, and Campbell loves the smells."

"He loves getting smelly, you mean, which is why we avoid it. Remember last time?" Campbell, being a Newfoundland and thereby convinced that water was his second home, had found the most disgusting stretch of canal to go swimming in. He'd needed hosing down and the car had required a professional valeting to get rid of the stench. "Anyway, isn't there an event on at Rutherclere Castle?"

Rutherclere was a large stately home, the pride of the county, which was said to house a remarkable—highly eclectic—collection of items which various owners had accumulated, mainly during Victorian times. The route from Lindenshaw to the canal would pass close to the grounds.

"Oh, yeah. The one day a year they deign to open the estate to the public."

"You old cynic. It was supposed to be a cracking affair last summer. Everyone at school was raving about it. People say the first year wasn't so great, but they've got the hang of it now, maybe?"

"Whatever they've done, it's grown bigger than anyone anticipated. Every special constable in the county's been drafted in. Please God it'll only be for traffic duties." Robin shuddered. "What did you do when you were little and didn't want something to happen? Go out of the room and turn three times?"

"We were far too civilised to do that, but if performing that action, or anything equally daft, stops you getting called in, it would be worth a go." Robin had only dealt with one murder case so far this year, which was one too many for all involved. If it was time for another serious crime to come along, the damn thing should wait until he was officially back in the office. "Those specials will have their work cut out with the traffic. Last year they only avoided gridlock by the skin of their teeth. The road near the canal's a standard rat run, so we'd be better off away from the place."

"So where can we go to avoid the traffic? All the best walks are over that way."

"What about Pratt's Common?" Adam suggested. "That's nowhere near Rutherclere."

The common was a large area west of Lindenshaw, much beloved of dog walkers, courting couples, and anybody else who wanted fresh air, space, and some trees to either climb in or indulge in less wholesome activities. Adam hadn't been there for years, but today seemed the ideal day—with the piercing blue sky, bright sunshine, and likelihood of dry ground beneath the feet—to become reacquainted.

"Ah, hold on." Robin frowned. "Am I dreaming this, that they have cattle grazing there? Ones with dirty great horns?"

"So I've always assumed, which is why I've avoided taking *himself* there, but one of the learning support assistants at the school told me they were taken off and relocated last year." And if one of that redoubtable group of ladies stated the fact, it had to be true. "Done their job for the environment, whatever that might have been."

"Probably related to grazing or fertilizing. One end or the other." Robin chuckled. "Let's give it a whirl, then. Campbell can run about to his heart's content."

The drive over to the common was pleasant enough, especially when the radio kept cutting in with extra travel news bulletins warning locals to avoid the Rutherclere area. The big event must have been proving a bigger attraction than the police had predicted, although apparently it wasn't simply the volume of traffic causing problems. There had been a three-car shunt on one of the approach roads and rumour of the air ambulance having to be sent in. Adam tried not to feel smug at having made the right decision—pride goeth before fall and all that—although he was grateful when they reached the car park to find it almost empty rather than stocked with people who'd come there to avoid the traffic. There was another parking area on the Lower Chipton side, and if that was equally quiet they'd have the common pretty much to themselves.

This parking area, previously little more than a muddy patch of grass, had been properly surfaced since Adam had last visited, and the space available for vehicles had been expanded. The two cars already present were at either end of the tarmacked area—very British behaviour to be as far distant from other people as possible—so Adam slotted his car slap bang in the middle. As he opened the driver's door, he caught sight of the distinctive yellow air ambulance flying over, and sent up a silent prayer that nothing else would go wrong at Rutherclere and Robin wouldn't have to be called in.

Campbell sniffed the air tentatively as they let him out of the back of the car. He would know this wasn't his usual stomping ground and he'd be naturally wary about what delights or disappointments it would hold in store for him. It didn't take long for him to decide he liked the place, though, and begin to bounce about enthusiastically. They managed to get the lead on him and would keep it on until they could, quite literally, get the lie of the land, then they'd be able to let him romp where he wanted. He was a well-behaved dog, not one to approach strangers, whether canine or human, and generally he'd not stray outside of shouting distance. Clearly, he believed that part of his role was to keep half an eye on his owners while he let *them* have a walk.

Once off his lead, he initially walked no farther than a few paces ahead, although as soon as they started throwing his ball for him to fetch, his confidence and need for exploration both grew. Adam and Robin eventually found a fallen tree to perch on, sun warming their backs, where they could repeatedly hoick the ball over the scrubby grass, watch the dog go scrambling after it, then see him return triumphant with his treasure.

Adam shook his head. "Next time I say that Campbell's an extremely intelligent animal, remind me how he takes such pleasure in performing the same actions time and again."

"I can never work out if he's really bright or really thick," Robin observed. "Or maybe he flips between the two."

Adam grinned "I'd say he's good in a crisis. That brings out the best of his limited mental resources. Otherwise he can't process anything other than food, pat, or favourite toy."

He'd proved his worth in a crisis at least three times, though—and in two of them he'd probably saved a life. Despite the reputations of Newfoundlands, none of these crises had involved water, but death by gunshot or blunt instrument was as definitive as death by drowning.

"That's typical of dogs, though, isn't it?" Robin picked up the ball Campbell had deposited at his feet and lobbed it in the direction they'd come, for variety. "*Wow, a ball! That's my favourite thing. Wow, a biscuit! That's my favourite thing. Wow!* You get the picture."

"Yeah. And that's himself to a T. Look at the idiot."

The Newfoundland had retrieved the ball and was carrying it back in his slobbery jaws like he was carrying the crown jewels. He dropped it in the same place he kept placing it in front of Robin, who'd only just finished wiping dog saliva off his hand from the last time he'd handled the thing.

"He's a disgusting idiot, to boot." Adam grabbed the ball, stood up, and ran to the ridge to fling the thing as far as he could and give them a bit of respite from continual throw and fetch. The ground fell away sharply before levelling onto a plain, so the ball would roll farther than on the flat where they were seated. He lobbed the ball, then plonked himself down next to Robin, taking a deep breath of the bracingly pleasant air. "I'd forgotten how nice it is here. Better than that place with the goats."

"The cells at Abbotston are better than the place with the goats." While holidaying, they'd gone on an expedition to a supposed beauty spot that had been anything but. They spent the next few minutes reminiscing about how ghastly the experience had been, until they risked depressing themselves. "We'll come here again. It's so peace—" A sharp report cut Robin off, and sent rooks and pigeons into the air from the nearby trees.

"What's that?" Adam jumped up, a sickening tingle flying up his spine.

"A rifle, by the sound of it. Not that I can tell much from gunfire." Robin scanned from side to side as he got up, then they both broke into a run. "Where's Campbell?"

"He went off after his ball." *Don't panic. That shot and Campbell's nonappearance is a coincidence.* "Maybe it's only somebody shooting rabbits in the woods?"

"If they are, they shouldn't be doing it so damn close to where the public are. I should have a word."

"You can take Campbell to help 'persuade' them. Where the hell has he—" Adam stopped, sick to the stomach. He had kept his eyes down once they'd got onto the slope, aware of how easy it would be to take a tumble. Now he'd looked up again, the flat western part of the common came into full view and—lying a hundred yards off—a large, black, furry mound. "Campbell?"

Adam sprinted, scared witless. The closer he got, the more the mound resembled an animal, the size of a big dog. One that might be a Newfoundland.

"Hold on." Robin, voice tight, grabbed his arm. "Let me go and see. It looks like Campbell's hurt himself."

"No. It should be me that checks." Adam slowed his pace, though, eyes drawn to the thick black coat that had to be the Newfoundland's, surely. And that shot they'd heard could only mean one thing. "He was my dog before he was ours."

"I know. Sorry."

"I can't believe this is happening." Adam could barely control his voice. Whichever bastard had done this, they were going to pay. He knelt down, tears blurring his eyes as he laid his hand on the dog's flanks. "He's gone."

Robin squatted beside him. "I'm so sorry."

"I . . . It's so unfair. He wasn't an old dog. He should have— Oof!" Adam jolted as something heavy smacked into his back, almost going headfirst into the dead dog.

"Not as dead as we thought he was, then." Robin's voice was shaky, somewhere between tears and laughter. "Where have you been, boy, scaring us like that?"

Not chasing his ball, given that the thing was nowhere to be seen. Campbell had probably heard the shot and either taken fright or gone to investigate; they'd have to solve that puzzle later, though, there being a more urgent matter to hand. Adam wiped his eyes, then properly examined the corpse. Shock must have deluded him, because this wasn't even the same breed of dog. This was a Saint Bernard, one that was still warm, and bleeding, so the chances were that the shot they'd heard was the one which had killed it. He'd certainly not been aware of another discharge.

"What happens next?" Adam asked. "This isn't a case for calling in Grace, is it?" She was Robin's favourite crime-scene investigator and would no doubt quickly work out—or get somebody else to work out—how long the dog had been dead, what weapon had been used, what he'd had for breakfast, and whether his owners loved him with the passion Campbell's owners had for *him*.

Robin, already getting his phone out, replied with, "What happens next is ringing in to report there's a nutter on the loose with a gun. And we'll do that while we get back to the car, as quick as we can."

"Good thinking. Heel, boy." Adam speedily clipped on Campbell's lead, ensuring the dog would keep close by. "Nothing we can do for the Saint Bernard, and it'll upset this lad to hang around a corpse."

"That's the least of my worries," Robin said, picking up the pace.

Adam shivered. Of course. Campbell was a potential target. "Ah, yeah. We don't want two dead dogs on our hands."

"I wasn't just thinking about Campbell. He's not the only sitting duck out here."

Adam gulped and broke into a trot, eyes and ears alert for any untoward movement or noise. Arriving at the car park couldn't come soon enough.

Chapter Two

Robin got Adam and Campbell into the car, reminding them they weren't safe yet. They'd have to keep their eyes peeled and be ready to drive off at a moment's notice. He'd not been able to ring out on the common because of the lack of signal, something all too widespread in this area. There had still been only two other vehicles in the car park when they'd got back there, although one was different. A bright-green Saloon had gone while a people mover had arrived recently, so he advised the owners—as strongly as possible without panicking them and calling on his rank to get the message home—to take their dogs somewhere else for their exercise that morning.

Once that was all done, he called 999; the phone signal was weak but better than the almost nonexistent signal there'd been out on the common.

Thank God he connected with the call handler without the signal fading. He explained exactly what had happened and where, and suggested a suitable response unit was geared up. When asked if there was a remaining risk to life, he answered that he didn't know. These things could get nasty quickly or just fizzle out.

He then got onto Abbotston station and informed them of what he'd done, so they were aware of the situation first-hand as well as second. He toyed with promising to stay on scene until backup arrived, but self-preservation—or, more properly, preservation of the two most important creatures in his life—overrode that. There was a café with a car park about a mile away, so he suggested that as a place to meet the response car if he was required to. When the sergeant told him to simply enjoy the rest of his holiday, he couldn't resist pulling rank, insisting that it would make sense his briefing the responding officers as he could give them valuable information. The sergeant relented, although he still made Robin promise to get himself to safety straight away.

Get out, call out, stay out. Good advice to follow in any emergency.

Before they made their escape—which wasn't too strong a word for it, given how anxious Adam was looking—Robin noted the registration number of an empty Vauxhall Vectra, the only other vehicle in the car park.

The drive to the café seemed interminable, Robin keeping an eye out for anything suspicious and Adam driving with the exaggerated care Robin had seen exercised by drunken drivers. Once they'd pulled into the café car park—delighted to see the place open and so offering the prospect of a big injection of much-needed caffeine—they could at last feel some degree of ease. They'd barely got the drinks ordered when a police car drew up, blues and twos going like mad. Robin toyed with getting out his warrant card and flashing it about among the other customers who were having a good gawp to prove, *See? They haven't come to arrest us.*

"Here we go again." Adam gave him a rueful smile.

"Not my case, this time. I'm just passing it all on. And leaving it to the ones who aren't on holiday." It was hard work letting go, though. He'd been in on the start of this—whatever crime it turned out to be—and part of him itched to see it through. Still, he owed it to Adam and Campbell to pass the buck, to make sure that *off duty* meant exactly that.

He waved at the officers, grabbed his coffee, and went to give them as full a briefing as he could manage. In the hope, naturally, that they wouldn't notice how shaken up he'd been by the experience.

Once Robin had described the events out on the common, the older of the two attending officers asked, "Do you think the shooter might have been aiming at either of you, sir?"

"Unless his or her aim is useless, I doubt it. We were a good couple of hundred yards away and at the top of a slope." Sitting—literally—ducks, if they had been the target. That brought a sickening jolt to his stomach. Instances of random gun crime rarely happened in Britain and certainly had never happened around here. He had to believe there was some logical reasoning behind why the dog had been shot.

"It's probably kids arsing about and they went too far," the other officer remarked. "Probably from Stanebridge."

"If kids have started killing dogs, they'd better hope they don't have me to deal with in the interview room," Robin snapped. "And less of the digs at Stanebridge. This is no joking matter."

"Didn't mean to joke, sir. Sorry." The constable stared at his feet. "But it could have been kids, couldn't it?"

"It could, but don't jump to conclusions." When would officers all learn to keep an open mind? "Has an armed response unit been called in?"

"They want to have a look at what we're dealing with first. The helicopter's been scrambled so we can scan the area."

Robin instinctively glanced skyward. This sounded a typical Chief Superintendent Cowdrey approach, caution married to action. The boss would never assume that this incident was either trivial or treacherous, until he'd accumulated the necessary information. But, and of this Robin had little doubt, the man would be en route to the station, keeping in touch with all the parties involved until he was sure of the bigger picture.

"Sir?" The younger officer's voice startled Robin out of his thoughts, and reminded him that this wasn't his problem. Unless it turned out to be still going on come Tuesday when he returned to work.

"Can you show us roughly where the shooting happened?" The other officer had produced a large-scale map, which he spread on the patrol-car bonnet.

"Hold on. I know the man to consult." Robin gestured for Adam to come across. "You know the area better than I do. Where would you say the dog was?"

Adam studied the map, placed his index finger on the car park, then traced a line to a location that Robin wouldn't have been able to pinpoint.

"Roughly there," Adam said. "I'm going by the contour lines as much as anything, trying to replicate our steps from the car park, so I can't be one hundred percent sure."

The officer nodded. "I reckon we might be able to get this thing out there." He patted the side of the police car, which appeared sturdy enough to tackle any terrain. "I used to play on the common when I was a nipper. My uncle used to take me and my cousin out in a Land Rover, and we'd go all over the area."

"You'd know where somebody taking pot-shots would hang out, then?" Robin asked him.

"I might have done thirty years ago. We knew all the dodges then." The officer grinned.

"Still, it probably hasn't changed that much."

The younger policeman refolded the map so that only the key bit was showing. "Best get going."

"I won't keep you." If there was an idiot with a gun on the loose, then they needed to be caught quickly. "Best of British luck."

"Thanks, but I hope we don't end up needing it." The officer shook his head, then got back into the car.

Robin watched the police vehicle screech out of the car park, torn between the desire to be in on the chase and staying well out of things. His copper's nose was telling him that whatever the outcome of the helicopter search, this situation had the capacity to turn nasty.

Home, sweet home—shutting the front door on the rest of the world had never felt so good. Campbell had been a bit whiny on the way home: he must have registered that something hadn't been right with the other dog, maybe from the smell of blood or the atmosphere of stress emanating from his owners. Campbell might have been daft, but he wasn't stupid.

Robin had sat in the back with him the entire journey, Adam joking that he always had to play second fiddle to a pooch and that was why Robin wasn't in the front with *him*. Adam was clearly worked up though, because twice on the drive home his hands had started to shake on the wheel, no doubt as the realisation of the danger they'd all been in had hit him afresh. Time and again Robin's mind replayed the sound of the gunshot and the sight of the dog. Who'd been using a gun up there, and why? Given the wide, open nature of the terrain, it was unlikely this had been an attempt to kill a particular target—whether man or beast—gone wrong.

Robin had seen the police chopper pass over and then circle back not long after they'd left the café, but there hadn't been anything on the local radio news, which they'd listened to all the way, despite the awful Sunday morning choice of music in between the bulletins. The newsreader made a passing mention of the Rutherclere event and probably the locals would have assumed any police activity was connected to that.

Conversation had been scarce, Adam evidently concentrating hard both on driving and on stilling his fears. He'd made the odd comment along the lines of, "Everyone all right in the back there?" but otherwise their usual comfortable buzz of chatter had been curtailed.

Once home—without further incident thank God—Robin rang in to the Abbotston station to get an update. Not solely his idea: Adam had insisted, no sooner had he pulled the car up on their drive, saying he was burning to know who the intended target had been and whether anybody was still at risk. Robin had soothed him, saying it would be far too early to get any clarity on that, although the same questions plagued him too.

He didn't get much of an answer to them, though, when he got through to the officer on the desk. The helicopter had apparently not spotted anything untoward, although they weren't declaring the incident over yet. The officers *had* managed to get out onto the common and yes, there was a large black dead dog there.

Robin felt a ridiculous sense of relief at having that confirmed. Despite the evidence of everyone's eyes, he'd retained an illogical worry that he'd dreamed the whole episode. Or somehow cocked it all up. A psychologist might have said that was a factor of his childhood making itself known again, the long dormant effect of bullying rearing its head, although Robin preferred to call it typical British anxiety.

"Any idea whose dog it was?" he asked, switching into rozzer mode, the holiday mood dissipating.

"Some chap named Britz over at Lower Chipton. Luckily, the dog had a tag on his collar with a phone number. Or maybe that's unluckily for the owner," the sergeant added, ruefully. "I'd hate it if it was my dog."

"Tell me about it." Robin could hear Campbell snuffling around—how quickly he'd got used to that background noise and how awful it would feel to be suddenly robbed of it. "I guess it's better than your pet disappearing, leaving you not knowing what's happened."

"Maybe. Anyway, you're well out of this. Mr. Cowdrey's got his work cut out explaining to the powers that be why the helicopter's been called in."

"I wouldn't want to be the person grilling him. He'll fight his corner all right." And who could blame him for reacting so strongly at the present time? Terrorism wasn't confined to big cities, so it was no good saying these things didn't happen here. Unfortunately, they could. "I guess I'll hear all about it on Tuesday. If there's anything I can do to help in the interim, let me know."

"You just enjoy the end of your holiday, sir. We need you back in peak condition and at your brightest." The sergeant chuckled. "Excuse the pun."

Robin rolled his eyes. "I've heard them all before. See you in a couple of days."

He ended the call, then headed for the kitchen. "You okay?"

"As well as can be expected, given the circumstances. I'm making lunch."

Robin broke out some beer to have with it; he also broke out Campbell's favourite dog biscuits as a treat.

Adam pointed a fork in the general direction of Abbotston. "Do they want you to go in?"

"Nothing for me to do." Robin gave Campbell a pat. "The helicopter's still scouring the area, but there's no sign of anyone with a gun."

"He—or she, I suppose—would have been long gone. I'm guessing they'd have legged it as soon as they took that poor mutt down. There's another parking area on the other side of the common, so they might have had a car there, or they could have had a quad bike with them on the common itself, although I don't remember hearing one."

"You should be on my team. I like the way your brain works. You'd be too distracting, though."

"Flatterer." Adam gently poked him in the stomach with the end of a wooden spoon. "I'm happy to simply share my thinking here. And the other thought I thunk was that there used to be some cottages in the woods when I was a teenager. They could have gone to ground there."

Robin, who had slipped his phone out with the intention of seeing whether the local media had at last got hold of the story, glanced up at that. "I didn't know that. Were they occupied?"

"A few. May well still be. One or two were derelict but might be standing. We used to hang around there when I was a teenager." He poked Robin again with the spoon handle, this time in the shoulder. "And I got up to nothing worse than trying a ciggie and climbing trees, I hasten to add. I was a good boy."

"Methinks your other dad protests too much," Robin said, addressing Campbell. "Good point, though. I'll text in and suggest the team go and check over any ones that are close to where the shots came from. Somebody might be using them for less innocent purposes."

"Feel free to share my bright ideas. Only make this the last contact from our end. You're still on holiday, remember?"

"Yes, sah!" As soon as the message was sent, Robin's stomach started to rumble, the delicious smells from the oven sending the noise level to earthquake.

Adam smiled, wooden spoon still in hand. "I was worried you wouldn't feel like eating. Seems I'm wrong."

"I've got my appetite back." Robin cast a glance at Campbell, who was tucking into *his* lunch. "Looks like himself's back to normal too."

Adam chuckled. "I only need to do the Yorkshires, and they won't take long. I'll get them on before you leap in his bowl and fight him for his nosh."

"I might too, given how my stomach's complaining."

"Be patient, man. Here, while you were on the phone earlier, I saw this on Twitter." Adam passed over his phone to show where the county police feed baldly stated that their helicopter was attending an incident and asking people to avoid the area.

"Any replies?"

"Only from a couple of people asking why they're not being given any further information. Usual arsy stuff."

Robin puffed out his cheeks. "That's one of the things I hate about social media. Everyone wants to know *now*. Even if we don't yet know ourselves, or we're too busy trying to deal with an incident than tweet about it."

"Remember that plane crash?" Adam asked.

"All too well." They'd been about to go out for dinner when news had broken about a plane going down in the Med. Adam had gone mental at the radio presenter who'd grilled some aviation expert for answers and had been unnecessarily unpleasant when he'd kept pointing out—quite reasonably—that there was no point in grounding other planes or having knee-jerk reactions until the cause of the crash was clear.

Adam peered through the oven door. "Right, these Yorkshires are done. No more speculation until after lunch."

It was after lunch, a beer, and half an hour of kip that they actually got around to discussing the morning's events again. Robin hadn't received any further messages and nothing definitive was featuring on either the news or social media yet, so they'd made themselves comfy on the sofa, with Campbell stretched out on the floor like a living rug.

"I hope himself's asleep and can't hear what I'm about to ask," Adam said. "What's the law on killing dogs?"

"Long story short, if you're a farmer and a dog's trespassing on your land, worrying your sheep, you can kill it, preferably in one clean shot. You'd need to prove you were justified in taking the action, though. Long story longer, if you asked your pal to come over and he brought his dog and it starts worrying the sheep, you've lost the right."

"That's sounds straightforward enough."

Robin grimaced. "It isn't. You're supposed to try to contact the owner first, and only shoot if absolutely necessary. You're supposed to report it, afterwards, too."

"And do they? Report it?"

"Not always. If you dispose of the evidence—the corpse—then how would anyone know?" Robin cast Campbell a glance but the hound was still asleep. "If the dog's a sheepdog, or a guide dog, or any other official working pooch, you can't shoot them at all."

"That can't apply in this case, can it?" Adam absent-mindedly rubbed Robin's arm. "The common's not private land, and there are no livestock up there now."

"Exactly. There's some act—I'd have to look it up to tell you which one and how it applies in this case—that prevents cruelty to animals. I guess the culprit's liable to be fined or even imprisoned."

"Good."

Robin snickered. "You'd prefer they were hung, drawn, and quartered?"

"Not quite. But I'd hope they'd never be allowed to own a gun again." Adam took a deep breath. "I can understand a farmer shooting a dog that had got on his land and was attacking sheep. I can understand him wanting to beat up the dog's owner while he was at it, but what happened this morning's beyond my comprehension."

"Same here." Robin ran the back of his hand across his forehead. "Let's take the emotion out of it and consider this like any other case. Maybe that particular dog had attacked somebody in the past and said victim was determined to get their own back. Doesn't ring a bell with any cases I've heard of, though."

"I've heard nothing like it on the dog-owning grapevine, either." Adam's mother, expert on all local matters of gossip, also had a fund of knowledge concerning other representatives of the canine family. "What if they'd meant to kill the owner and somehow cocked-up?"

"Pfft. It would have to be a right royal cock-up, then. The owner was nowhere in sight. I didn't see another soul anywhere around before or after we saw the dead dog. Unless the owner could run faster and farther than Usain Bolt, and had managed to get over to the copse of trees, they couldn't have been anywhere near where we were. You can't hide in scrub."

"Unless you lie flat like a commando. The other dog must have been doing something similar, surely, or wouldn't we have seen him earlier?"

"I guess so. He might have been hunkered down behind one of the bushes." In which case a human could have been hiding there too. Maybe the shooter themselves.

"Oh God." Adam, face drained of colour, must have had the same thought. "I don't want to think about those bushes. Okay, back to speculating. The person who shot the dog might have hurt the dog simply to get at whoever owned it. For whatever reason they balked at attacking the owner himself. Or it could be a herself. Mustn't jump to assumptions."

"Come and tell some of the new constables that." Robin chuckled. "You've got a point though. Some folk would take an injury to their pet more to heart than suffering a good hiding themselves."

"It's like their children—people feel protective of dependants." Adam idly scratched Campbell's back with his foot.

"They'd have had to know the beast was going to be there at the right time. I assume people don't routinely lurk around Pratt's Common with a rifle on the off chance."

"Maybe they do, just wanting to get their kicks by hurting something—anything—at random. The dog was in the wrong place in the wrong time."

Robin nodded. "That could fit. There are people who get their kicks by mutilating horses or cats or whatever. Like the crowd who watch dog fights. They'd be queuing to get into bear baiting or cock fighting if it were still legal."

"Ever been to Caerleon? The old Roman fort in Wales?"

Where was this line of thought going? "No, although I bet Pru Davis has."

"Yeah, I think it's in her neck of the woods." Adam waited as Campbell readjusted his sleeping position, then gave him another scratch. "Anyway, there's a load of Roman remains in and around the village, including a well-preserved amphitheatre. It's tremendously atmospheric. I visited a couple of summers back, before I met you, and it struck me that even nowadays if you put on a spectacle featuring two blokes fighting to the death you'd not have any trouble selling tickets. There are some nasty people around."

"You don't need to tell me that, sunshine. I meet them every day." Robin rubbed his partner's arm. "Lucky for me I found a good 'un in you."

"You're softer than Campbell." Adam gave him a kiss, though. "So, following this chain of logic, whoever killed the dog might simply like imposing suffering on an innocent creature. In which case, I hope you find him—or her—before they start taking pot-shots at people too.

Or targeting other dogs. Is it wrong of me to say I think that would be worse than aiming at humans?"

"If it's wrong of you, it's wrong of me too. Been wrestling with that one ever since it happened." Robin had seen his share of corpses by now, and while he wasn't entirely immune to emotion when he came across one—not like some of the hardened coppers he'd known when first in the force who seemed to regard a dead body as a butcher might regard a piece of meat—he didn't react in the same way as he'd had with his first.

But that dead dog had really affected him, producing an anger and disgust he'd not felt in a long time. While no human deserved being killed so mercilessly, the investigators could usually, after the event, put together a trail of what had happened in terms of victim or killer that had led to the death. Sometimes it was random, but often there was a horrible logic to what had occurred, including perhaps a point where the victim had said or done something which had produced the most disproportionate and devastating of reactions. What could a dog have done to contribute to its own death?

"Would you like another beer?" Adam asked. "A hug? A slobbery kiss from Campbell?"

"Yes, all three, although maybe not right now. I'd like to know who did it."

"Then you'll have to rely on your colleagues finding out for you."

"Assuming they can work it out before I get back from holidays. Although maybe that would be the best outcome. I'm not sure I could trust myself dealing with the culprit." Robin had been angry enough at the murderers he'd encountered, although he'd kept himself professionally in check; he was irrationally livid at this one.

"You need to calm it, Kermit." Adam grinned. "You don't normally get worked up like this."

"No, I don't. You're right." Robin leaned over to give him a kiss.

"That's better. Get the telly on, and find a bit of cricket. I'll fetch the beers, and you persuade Campbell to get up on the sofa. Not that he'll take much persuading. We'll have a three-way hug and another kip. Things will seem better after that."

And surprisingly enough, the teacher was right yet again.

Chapter Three

Tuesday morning: Robin was back to work at last.

Adam had left the house at a similar time, heading for Culdover, but he wouldn't have his nose entirely to the grindstone yet, given that the children weren't due back for another week. The lucky sod would be able to get himself into gear gradually rather than having to hit the ground running. At any rate, Robin had been able to avoid a Monday return, having booked an extra day of holiday so he could have a day doing boring but essential things like having a filling replaced and getting a couple of new tyres on his car.

So, he was in a pretty chipper mood when he arrived at Abbotston station, mentally prepared to pick his way through the anticipated barrage of welcome-back-type remarks. There'd no doubt be questions on whether he'd had a good holiday, which he'd deal with as effectively and good-humouredly as possible, more interested in getting to his office and seeing what had landed on his desk or inbox. He was almost looking forward to what news Chief Superintendent Cowdrey would have when briefing him on events of the last few weeks. He crossed the car park whistling and entered the building with something like a spring in his step. He'd not got halfway to his office—and only had to field two questions about his holiday—when he bumped into the boss.

"Robin!" Cowdrey extended a hand to shake. "Good break?"

Robin gave him a firm handshake. "Excellent, sir. Raring to go."

"Liar. About the second bit, anyway." Cowdrey chuckled. "My first meeting of the day's been cancelled, but I'm not complaining. Fancy grabbing a coffee and having your briefing now? I'll get word up to your team that you've not been kidnapped."

"Works for me."

Instead of heading down to the canteen, Cowdrey led the way to his office, explaining that he'd been given a filter machine for his birthday earlier in the month and there was no room for it at home. "Already got one, so might as well get some use out of the thing here."

It turned out he'd got a mini fridge too, with a supply of milk and what was evidently his lunch in.

Robin whistled, impressed. "You're not thinking of moving in here permanently, are you, sir? This is comfier than my room was at uni."

"Privileges of the job. Used to be perks like thick carpets." Cowdrey poured the coffee, used to how Robin liked it. "And I see work couldn't keep away from you."

"I know. I didn't go out of my way to find that poor mutt, I can tell you. Thanks." Robin took the mug. "Any developments on that?"

"Nothing as far as somebody running round with a gun is concerned. As for the dog, thank God it had the tag on the collar."

Which was as much a legal requirement in a public place as the chip was, although not everyone complied.

"He'd been out walking the dog earlier that morning," Cowdrey continued. "He said it had got spooked by something and ran off."

"Then why didn't he stay there? We didn't see or hear anyone about, calling for it." Although Britz might have been the owner of one of the cars. "Did you— No, stupid start to a question. Was he linked to one of the vehicles we saw in the car park?"

"No. Apparently he'd gone home—it's only three or four miles as the crow flies or the dog runs. Britz assumed the dog might take himself home. The mutt's got previous. He ran off once before, and after Britz had driven round for an hour searching for him, he found the dog waiting in the front garden."

"Ah. Right." If that had been Campbell who'd run off and not returned, he and Adam would have searched high and low until he appeared, wagging his tail behind him. "It must have been a hell of a shock for the owner."

"He was distraught, it seems, poor bloke." Cowdrey swirled his coffee. "No sign of whoever did it. We've put a notice up at the car park asking for witnesses, but I'm not holding my breath. Kids arsing about and it went too far, is my guess."

"Could be." That seemed to be the default position for everybody except him. Robin couldn't help thinking there was more to it though, his inbuilt levels of suspicion sniffing out trouble. He focussed on Cowdrey's update—the usual catalogue of domestic assaults, small-scale robberies, some teenagers caught dropping things off motorway bridges, and the like. All relatively straightforward and easily solved. Whoever had shot the dog had been either cleverer or luckier in terms of covering their tracks.

"So it's all been routine stuff," Cowdrey said, getting them both another coffee, "apart from an altercation at the Rutherclere open day, although that would have been more in the uniformed branch's line rather than CID, except that one of the men involved is known to the Metropolitan Police."

"Oh yes?"

"A likely drug baron. Chris Curran. A bloke they're itching to charge once they can make an absolutely watertight case against him. They nearly had him once, then it turned out he'd been stitched up. They suspect he deliberately had himself stitched up to make us wary of going after him in future. Slippery bastard."

"I'm guessing this will help them, then. *Something* to pin on him."

Cowdrey grinned. "For once, Robin, you've guessed wrong. He appears to be the victim."

"Ah." What would Adam say if he knew Robin had jumped so swiftly to the assumption that the baddie always had to be bad? "I guess drug barons are allowed days out in the country as well as anyone else. Are we supposed to be backing off on this case, then?"

"No. Actually, we have to play this with a straight bat, as if we officially know nothing dodgy about the victim. We process this as a straightforward affray—it was an argument over a car parking space that morning, of all things—then let Curran bring charges if he wants. I bet he won't, given the background, although we should try to persuade him to the extent we'd persuade anyone else."

"I suspect you're right. Do we watch what develops?"

"Yep. Then we pass on anything that can help the Met's case but do nothing to hinder it."

Robin nodded. "Any record of this bloke carrying arms?"

"Not that we can prove. And he tends to be associated with knives rather than guns, if your mind's going down the line of the common and the dog."

"Guilty as charged. I'll drink my coffee and shut up."

They got their heads down over the rest of the handover, including where they'd reached in the investigation of the Saint Bernard's death. That was going to nag at Robin until they'd got it clear who'd done it and why.

Although if Curran had been getting into a scuffle at Rutherclere that morning, surely he couldn't have been shooting dogs out on the common at the same time. And what motive could he have to do such a callous thing? What motive could anybody?

"Welcome back, sir!" Ben, one of the constables on Robin's team, was coming out of the men's loo as Robin ambled past it on the way—at last—to his office.

"Not the sort of welcome I could do with. Couldn't you have had all the cases cleared up while I was away?"

"You'd have got bored if we had." Ben grinned. He was one of the better young officers among the patchy crop Robin had inherited at Abbotston when he'd transferred there. Robin and his boss reckoned all the dead wood had been cropped by now, some of them leaving the force while others had been shared out among a variety of police stations, on the basis that they could probably make it into decent coppers given the chance. One troublemaker could be turned easily enough once starved of the collective mindset. "It's odd though, not having a big case on the go."

"You'll regret saying that. Don't tempt fate." Robin strolled into the large team office from which a smaller room led off—his piece of Abbotston turf, albeit not blessed with the luxuries to be found within Cowdrey's four walls. He spent a few minutes assuring his team that he'd had a good break, and it wasn't true he'd missed them so much he'd got mixed up in the business on the common to keep his hand in.

"It must have been a hell of a shock, sir. Finding a dog like that." Trust Pru to be instantly sympathetic. She'd come over from Stanebridge at the same time as Robin, the pair of them getting a promotion in the process. She was proving a good foil for him, sparking ideas, seeing things from another angle. *Like the workings for an old-fashioned stereopticon,* Cowdrey had once described them, which had sent everyone googling the things. He'd been right. Two slightly different flat images of the same view producing a three-dimensional image.

"The worst shock was thinking it was Campbell until we could get close enough to see the breed." Best to get that out in the open. "We won't take him walking there again."

"I don't blame you. Mr. Cowdrey doesn't seem to think there's any remaining risk, but he wants us to keep vigilant. Sorry"—Pru grinned—"he'll have told you all that."

"Yep. But you're right. I'd feel a lot happier if I knew who'd done it and why." A shiver ran up Robin's spine.

"Are you okay, sir?" Ben asked. "You've gone white as a sheet."

"I'm fine," Robin snapped.

Pru shot him a concerned glance, then said, "Do you have any information about the woods at Pratt's Common, Ben? I heard they got themselves a bit of a reputation at one time."

"Yeah," Ben said. "Although that was back in the seventies, so I can't see how it's relevant now."

"Haven't you learned yet that anything can turn out to be relevant?" Robin forced a grin. He was well aware that Ben wasn't the sort of copper to jump to conclusions, and the lad looked scared enough at having been snapped at. "What happened to earn the reputation? Drug dens?"

"No. It was just the go-to place for a bit of outdoor how's-your-father. Dad told me all about it."

"Was he one of those who made use of the place?" Robin took a distinct pleasure at seeing the flush spread over Ben's cheeks.

"Leave it out, sir. There was something about my aunty having a boyfriend who wanted to take her up there and my dad telling him exactly what would happen if he tried it." Ben laughed. "His voice would have gone up an octave."

"Remind me not to get on his bad side."

"Oh, you're all right, sir. He knows you're a good bloke." Ben's flush deepened, and he cracked on before Robin could ask when the family had been discussing him. "Anyway, plenty of girls were happy to go along there so this bloke must have stopped hanging around Aunty and gone off with them."

"So, he told you not to go there in case a fallen woman stole your virtue?" Pru said, eyebrows waggling.

"Something like that. If he'd thought it physically dangerous, he'd have said. He used to warn us about the poachers out at Tythebarn. The old woods behind the battery chicken farm, where they used to go for rabbits and pheasants."

"Do you think it could have been poachers this time, sir?" Pru asked.

"No reason to think so. They tend to do their work at night, and Saint Bernard dogs are hardly hares or deer." Robin's hackles rose; at least a hare or deer would end up in the pot, so there'd be a purpose to its death.

Ben, half turned as though to get back to work, said, "Dad used to warn me about somewhere else too. Being dangerous, as opposed to being full of loose women. Might have been the woods at Rutherclere. That was probably poachers, again."

"Or people after your hard-earned cash." Robin, who'd been edging towards his office, opened the door and stared dejectedly at his in-tray: and that was only the paper stuff. He'd not yet braved what was lurking in his inbox. "Right, I've got work to do. I'm shutting the door so I can have an hour to myself and this lot. No interruptions unless it's something really serious."

"I'll make sure of that, sir," Pru called.

Robin carefully shut the door behind him. Back to work with a vengeance.

Adam turned the car into the compact car park of Culdover Primary School, slipped into a convenient space, stopped the engine, and sat quietly for a moment. This had become part of his start-of-a-new-term routine, taking a minute to simply appreciate the good aspects of being back at work, ones that tended to get lost among the bad. Being among like-minded people, who understood things like the scrutiny that Ofsted put you under. Robin was sympathetic, and they'd developed a strong mutual understanding of the pressures in each other's jobs, but there were elements of police work that Adam didn't "get" and vice versa. The Police and Criminal Evidence Act might as well have been written in hieroglyphics as far as Adam was concerned, while Robin thought the Ofsted framework documents were impenetrable.

He glanced up at the building. The school and grounds always appeared neater without the pupils, even if that came at the price of them feeling a bit clinical; school existed for children and the atmosphere was antiseptic without them. As though the building were longing for their return to classes as much as their parents no doubt were.

Still, without the children he'd be able to get a lot done, not losing time to jobs like firefighting upsets between pupils—something that happened with alarming frequency compared to Lindenshaw—or having to pick up a safeguarding issue when the headteacher was off-site. Some of the poor mites among the Culdover intake would probably benefit a damn sight more from better parenting in their lives than from any amount of good teaching. If he was ever a headteacher, he'd be holding classes in the school for the parents on how to raise children—compulsory attendance if he could get away with it—to try to make a positive difference in their offspring's lives.

Make a difference. He smiled, remembering when he'd had a bingo sheet of such phrases, and used it during the headteacher recruitment at Lindenshaw school that had been instrumental in his meeting Robin. God bless *make a difference* and *focus groups* and all the other lingo for that silk purse of good fortune which had come out of a sow's ear of a time.

A car drew into the car park—another one of the teachers arriving to do some preterm planning—so it seemed the right time to leave off wool-gathering and get into the groove again.

In school, he found an atmosphere that was purposeful but informal, no doubt partly because Jim Rashford, the headteacher, was still on holiday. A radio was playing in the school office, and music drifted out of every occupied room he passed. Soon he'd be joining them in having his own playlist blaring out, helping him work by eliminating background noise.

He'd been in for an hour, making solid, some might say spectacular, progress through the jobs he'd set himself when the sound of "Walking the Dog"—a whimsical addition to his playlist—got him thinking about the events of the weekend.

Had the occupants of the car that had been in the car park when he and Robin had arrived, the car which had gone later, had anything to do with the shooting? He wished they'd had the sense to take its registration number, like they'd done for the other vehicle which was still there, but they'd not thought of it at the time. Why should they? Nobody in their right mind, not even the most suspicious copper—and Robin wasn't quite in that category—would assume that any place was at risk of turning into a crime scene, or that something seen in passing might assume a great significance. No wonder witnesses struggled to get details right, given that the human mind takes in and processes so much information all the time. And in these days where so many makes of car seemed to have the same general shape, it was a challenge to guess at that unless one saw the badge clearly. Although he seemed to remember it had been a vile neon green, the sort of colour that seemed to be cropping up everywhere on sports kits. Maybe somebody had bought a job lot of dye and was good at selling it on.

The song finished and "Kashmir" started up. *Time to get back to work.*

There was a sharp rap on the door of Robin's office, then Pru stuck her head round it, the anxious expression on her usually cheerful face suggesting one thing only. Robin prepared himself for bad news.

"Sorry to disturb you, sir. We've had a report of a shooting over in Lower Chipton. Yes, same address as where that Saint Bernard's owner lives. Seventeen Church Lane. Don't have a name for the victim, so we don't know if it's Britz."

Already out of his chair and grabbing his keys, Robin ushered her out of the door. "Let's get down there. Uniform on the scene?"

"Yes, sir. Armed response unit on their way too, although unlikely they'll be needed."

Robin paused. "Why? I'd have thought we need the place in lockdown until we've got the shooter safely secured."

"Well, we don't have a lot of detail as yet, although it doesn't sound like anyone else is in danger, from what the person who rang in said. He told the operator that he couldn't be sure, but he believed it was a self-inflicted wound." Pru shrugged, then they set off again. "Can't take any chances, though, especially with what happened to the dog."

Robin nodded. Not in these times. Rural seclusion was no guarantor of safety. The Hungerford massacre had taught everyone that. "Okay. Proceed with caution, then. We can't assume it's a suicide, despite the fact that's likely. Who rang it in?"

"We don't know. Anonymous caller, male, who just gave the address and the fact a bloke had been shot, likely suicide." Pru almost skipped down the stairs from their floor to the door to the car park, as always eager to get out on a case. "Maybe he was so upset about the dog he couldn't bear to live without it."

"Maybe." Robin halted, halfway down a flight. "On the other hand, there's a chance he killed the Saint Bernard himself, and he'd been overcome with remorse. Although if you hate your dog so much, and don't want to persuade some vet to put it to sleep properly, why take it out onto the common to shoot? Why not despatch the thing at home?"

"Because people would hear you, sir. The common's pretty quiet, so anyone could assume they'd be alone up there, and that if somebody else heard the shot, they'd think it was someone after rabbits or pigeons."

As he and Adam had. "Then why not take the beast there and shoot it close up? Why let it run free and risk missing it altogether? As an eye witness, I can state there was nobody within either view or close range. He could have done it and no one been the wiser." He lowered his voice. "By the way, I appreciated you stepping in earlier. I did feel faint, but I didn't want the team to know. It's the dog. Too much like Campbell."

"Hey, you're okay, sir. I'd never go dobbing you in to the rest of the team." Pru, as wary as Robin at showing emotion, stared at her feet. "Anyway, we all know how much you love that dog. You're entitled to get upset about him."

"You keep to that approach and you'll go far." Robin set off again. "That holiday's made me slack. No use standing here speculating. Let's get down there and get hold of some facts."

Pru drove, leaving Robin to coordinate by phone with those already on the scene. The police doctor, whose role was mainly to make the obvious but necessary statement that life had indeed been extinguished, promised to wait for them. As usual, he was quite cagey about committing himself to details, but suspected the death had occurred a couple of hours previously, which Robin guessed was a good hour before the 999 call had been made. Death had been by a bullet wound, although they couldn't know if it was the same weapon that had killed the dog, until the forensics had been done.

Robin finished the call, then tried to build up a picture of what had happened over the last couple of days. "Who went out to see this Britz bloke on Sunday, once the dog's body had been retrieved? I assume somebody did *go* and see him rather than use the phone?"

"Yes, one of the uniformed branch. Jacquie Parker, the female office stereotype coming into play, but she's apparently good with the family-liaison stuff. I saw her yesterday, and she said he'd been shocked although stoic. No indication he'd killed the dog himself, and no sign of firearms. No licence for them, anyway."

"Which isn't quite the same thing. Not every gun owner keeps it legitimately. Was Britz's car one of those we saw at the common? I know we didn't provide much detail on them."

"I don't believe it was. Ben handled that bit, and I'm sure he'd have mentioned a connection. You know how keen he is to show the latest details he's rooted out. Like your Campbell with a bone he's dug up."

"Hey, we'll have less of that snarkiness." Robin rarely told Pru off, but this time it was needed. "He's a conscientious officer, and I don't want that knocked out of him. He'll lose the puppy nature soon enough."

"Sorry, sir. It was just a bit of banter."

"Yeah, well think next time, maybe? Not all banter's funny." He was probably being too sensitive, the business with the dog having left him with a lingering agitation, although it didn't hurt to remind people that what started as banter could end up as persecution.

Fortunately they'd no more than half a mile to drive to the house, so the awkward silence in the car only lasted a few minutes before they pulled up on the road behind the doctor's car. Seventeen Church Lane appeared to be part of the rash of 1950s houses that had sprung up in and around Lower Chipton when the village had become a fashionable place from which to commute by rail to Kinechester, where houses were already ridiculously overpriced. The property was well kept, as was the small front garden, where a female police constable stood guard.

"That's Jacquie," Pru said, as they left the car, but before they could make contact with her, a woman emerged from the front door of number nineteen, gesturing with her hand. "Looks like somebody wants to get their two penn'orth in."

"Hello-o!" The neighbour bounded out of the gate and along the pavement. "I'm Elspeth Croydon. Can I catch you for a moment?"

She reminded Robin of his first primary school teacher; to his infant eyes Miss Pfaff had been in her sixties, but she'd probably only been forty something. She'd possessed the same ramrod straight posture, iron-grey hair, and gimlet gaze as Elspeth Croydon did, the only difference being a wedding ring. Nothing had escaped her notice, not the least of any pupil's misdemeanours, and he hoped this witness would have the same tendency.

"Of course," he said, with a smile, "although I'd prefer if it could wait until we've been in there."

"Oh. Oh yes, sorry. Come and knock on the door when you're done."

"Will do." Robin nodded, then turned to give Jacquie a smile. Pru did the introductions, before the constable gave a brief, efficient account of turning up at the house in response to the 999 call to find the front door closed but not locked, no sign of a forced entry, and a dead man sprawled on the kitchen floor. Robin thanked her, suggesting she have a word with the people at the house opposite and at number fifteen. Surely somebody would have heard the shot and could help to pin the time of death?

Before they entered the property, the doctor appeared, saying he was done. The wound might have been self-inflicted, or done by a second person and made to seem like a suicide. Hopefully the postmortem could provide a clearer picture. He waved cheerily and left, at the same time as Grace the CSI pulled up in her car.

She leaned out of her window. "I hope you're getting kitted up before going in there. Especially if there's a doubt that it's suicide."

"Got my stuff here, miss," Robin said, holding his protective gear up as evidence. "Are you psychic? How did you know there was doubt?"

"I heard that you were heading out here, so I had to follow. You've got a nose for these things." Grace shut the window as Pru and Robin struggled into overshoes and gloves. "I'm only winding you up, sir," she added as she emerged from the car. "Mr. Cowdrey asked me to come down. He's as suspicious as you are."

Better to be on the boss's say so—if this was a suicide, it was a waste of precious resources to have a CSI taking samples. "Maybe we'll get a better idea if we take a look inside."

Robin glanced into the kitchen, but all seemed in order apart from the presence of a dead body. As the constable had said, no evidence of a break-in or a struggle. He slipped into the living room, his eye immediately drawn to the piano that sat against one wall, with a row of photographs along the top of it. Always keen to take in the details—what books were on the shelf, taste in ornaments of the occupant—Robin stepped closer to study the faces on show, then froze.

"Pru?" he asked.

"Yes. Here, are you all right, sir?" The sergeant's voice sounded distant.

"I'm fine," Robin said vaguely, picking up one of the photographs in his plastic gloved hand. "Before I make a complete ass of myself, let me check with Mrs. Croydon."

Discarding his overshoes at the front door, he nipped to number nineteen. As he'd guessed she might be, the neighbour was swift to answer his knock, probably waiting in the hall.

"Can I catch you for a moment?" he asked. "We'll be back later to chat properly."

"Oh, yes, of course. Anything I can do to help."

He held out the photograph. "Sorry, I have to ask you not to touch this, in case of obliterating existing fingerprints. Is the man in the picture Mr. Britz?"

"Yes. Isn't it obv— Oh." Her hand went to her throat. "Is the body not recognisable?"

"No, it's not just that." Robin hadn't yet got close enough to answer the question definitively, although his first impression had been that much of the man's face was gone. "I'm making sure this photo really is your next-door neighbour rather than a friend of his."

"That's definitely Mr. Britz. Although funnily enough, he's had a friend staying the last few days. In and out, so he's probably been using it as a base."

"Thanks. Tell me that again when we return, so my sergeant can make a note." He flashed her a smile and strolled away. Once the overshoes were back on—and with a notion that this was feeling less and less like a straightforward suicide—Robin showed the photo to a puzzled-looking Pru. "This bloke isn't called Britz. Unless he's changed his name at some point."

"Who is he, then?"

"Unless I'm very much mistaken, this is Harry Wynter. He used to be my schoolteacher." It had only been for a brief time, but he'd helped make Robin's life hell. Maybe he'd also done that to somebody else. Somebody who'd decided he needed to pay for it. Was the unpleasant nature of Wynter's character enough in itself to justify Grace's presence at the crime scene?

"That could be the dead man, although his face is in such a mess you'll need another means of verification."

"He's had somebody else staying with him here, as well." Robin jerked his gloved thumb in the direction of next door. "We'll find out more about him later. In the meantime I'll inspect the body again."

Not that viewing it produced anything other than nausea; it might have been Wynter, but it equally might have been someone else. Robin mentioned what he'd discovered to Grace, and to Constable Parker, who'd reported back. Both the people across the road and at number fifteen were apparently out; it was a working day, after all. Any further enquiries would have to wait, as she got back to preventing-gawpers duty.

Robin and Pru took a tour of the house, but the only evidence of a visitor was a stripped-back bed and some used towels folded neatly on the chair of what appeared to be a guest room. If the man downstairs was the visitor rather than the occupant, he'd either travelled very light or had packed already and put his baggage somewhere else.

A proper search of the house could take place when they had a better idea of what they were dealing with—and what they might be looking for.

Robin, increasingly unsettled at the long-suppressed memories of Wynter, led the way out of the house with a curt, "Let's go and see what the next-door neighbour wants to tell us."

Elspeth Croydon must have been watching for their arrival, as this time she opened the door before they'd had a chance to knock. She ushered them in, offering refreshments, which Robin declined with a quip about how if they accepted all the tea and biscuits they were presented with they'd be the size of balloons. They did take a seat, however. He wondered if Pru had guessed the real reason for the refusal, that he felt sick at encountering Wynter again, even in such circumstances.

"Thanks for coming. You must get your fair share of nosy neighbours getting in the way of you doing your duty, but I promise I'm not like that."

"We never thought you were. You've been very helpful so far." Robin forced a smile. "What did you want to tell us?"

"About the visitor, for a start, but you know that now." Her brow wrinkled. "I'm afraid I wouldn't be able to recognise him. In his sixties, grey hair, and that's about all."

"Did he have a car with him?" Pru asked.

"Not that I saw, but Harry's—Mr. Britz's—is usually on the driveway, and there isn't always parking on the road, so the visitor may have left it in the church car park. People often do if they're visiting folk along our stretch."

"We'll go and check," Robin said, noting that if Wynter had changed his surname, he'd had the sense to keep his Christian name the same. Less chance of being caught out. "When did you last see him? Britz, I mean."

"First thing this morning. Like a lot of old people, I wake early, and I had a cuppa about six o'clock." She pointed to a seat in her bay window. "There's only me here since Ted died, so I was watching the world go by, not that much does go by at that time of day, when I saw Harry in his front garden, just standing and looking distressed. That's the other thing I wanted to mention."

"Did he normally wander about outside so early?" Pru asked.

"Not that I've seen. But he's clearly not been himself the last few days, as you can imagine. Of course, he misses that dog of his. I can't believe what happened to it."

Robin nodded, giving Pru a glance, hoping it conveyed the message *Don't you dare tell her that I witnessed it.*

Mrs. Croydon carried on. "I've been in two minds about whether to ask him round for a chat, but he's a very private person. You might say he bottles stuff up or you could call it good old British stiff upper lip. Except when he's—" She halted.

"Except when he's what?" Robin pressed her.

"I feel like I'd be speaking ill of the dead." She bit her lip.

"Unfortunately, our job involves having to ask people to do that far too often," Robin reassured her, also noting that she'd assumed he was the dead man, so she couldn't have seen Britz subsequently. "If it's not important, we'll not use it, I promise."

"We-ell, I suppose it's important. All I was going to say was that when he'd had a whisky or two—he was only an occasional drinker—he could be a touch belligerent. He was like that over the dog on Sunday evening. He was in the back garden with his guest, but I could hear him from my kitchen, where I had the window open. He was saying he'd make sure that whoever did it would pay."

"Did you happen to hear anything else?"

"I'm afraid not. I didn't *want* to hear, particularly, so I shut the window."

"Very wise. Most of the time, anyway. A pity for us, given the circumstances." Frustrating, too. Robin asked the witness if she'd seen the guest leave or if anybody else had been hanging around that morning, but Mrs. Croydon had been far too busy—today was her baking day, as the delicious aromas in the house bore witness—so she'd been in the kitchen with the radio on. She might have heard a shot, over two hours ago, but she'd assumed it was a car backfiring and thought no more of it at the time. Oh, and there'd been an unfamiliar car parked up the road, the other direction from Britz's.

"Any idea of the make?"

"I'm afraid not. It was large and black. Do they call them SUBs?"

"SUVs," Robin said, with a smile.

"SUV. I'll remember that." Mrs. Croydon nodded. "It was how I imagine a gangster's car might, although I suppose there are enough of them about. I even see them in the Waitrose car park."

Pru concluded the interview with the usual questions about whether Mrs. Croydon had anything else to add, then presented her card so the witness could make contact if anything sprang to mind. Robin's mind was whirring over the new slant this put on things; had Britz been so upset about the dog he'd killed himself after his guest had gone? In which case, who'd found the body and reported the death? And where was *his* car?

He put his thoughts to Pru as they neared Britz's door again.

"I was thinking along the lines that he'd found out who killed the dog, confronted him—or her—and then got himself shot as a result," Pru said.

"Then the killer rang 999? It hardly seems likely. It makes more sense if this dead body is the bloke who's been staying here. Wynter goes off for a walk, or whatever, comes home, finds the body, and rings it in."

"And then does a runner?" Pru shrugged. "Why leave the scene if you're innocent?"

"Fear that the lunatic with the gun who shot your dog and your friend is still about and you're next, so you hare off in a blind panic? That might explain why the call was anonymous, and also what took him so long to make it. There certainly seems to be a time lag between when it happened and when it was rung in." Robin drummed the door frame. "You'll have to find out what number the call came from."

"Excuse me, sir," Jacquie Parker said, "but you can explain both of those if the dead man is Britz. This door has a Chubb lock, so it can't be accidentally locked by closing it. What if an opportunistic thief came along, tried the handle, and thought his luck was in? He goes to the kitchen and gets the shock of his life."

"Carry on. What happens next?" Robin wanted to encourage her. The idea wasn't so daft: he remembered a similar case, where an old woman had died in her bed of a heart attack and the burglar who'd happened to break in and found her that evening nearly followed suit.

"Said burglar scarpers, but his conscience gets the better of him. Sneak thieving being one thing but dead bodies another." The constable smiled nervously.

"That would fit with some old lags I've met. Still, all of this is just speculation until we know who the dead bloke is, and whether somebody else shot him." Robin drew himself up straighter. "Pru, can you ring in to get the word out for locals to be careful. Usual stuff in the case of a shooting. I fancy stretching my legs as far as the church car park."

He followed Church Lane in the direction of the tall spire that rose over the tree line, announcing the imposing presence of the parish church. The car park had three cars in it, although a quick nip over to the building, where somebody was emptying a bucket down the drain, confirmed that two of the vehicles belonged to flower arrangers who were there to get rid of the weekend's displays. They had no idea who the other car belonged to, but it had been in and out of the car park over the last few days. Robin noted the registration and returned to Britz's house.

There was nothing new to be learned there, so they headed back to the car.

"Thinking about this 999 call, sir," Pru said as she buckled her seat belt. "We could listen to the recording of it, if you think you can recognise your old teacher's voice."

Robin gave a deep sigh. "Unless he's disguising it, I'd know that voice anywhere."

It was one he'd never forget.

Chapter Four

Adam, still hard at work in his classroom, had managed to tear his thoughts away from registration numbers or indeed anything to do with the dead dog. His renewed vigour turned out to be so effective, and the packed lunch he'd brought from home so sustaining, that only a sudden twinge in the small of his back told him it was time for a break and a bit of exercise. He dropped into the school office to let them know he'd be wandering into town for a spot of fresh air so not to go looking for him if the building caught fire, when he heard—with a sinking feeling to his stomach—the main story on the local station's news.

"There has been a shooting in Lower Chipton. Police say that a man has been killed, although identification has not been completed. They don't believe anybody else is in danger, but have asked locals to remain vigilant. His identity will be withheld until his family have been informed. We'll have more on this story in our next bulletin."

The school secretary, Georgie, gave him a sympathetic smile. "Your Robin will be down there, sorting it out, I guess."

"Maybe it's a suicide, if they reckon nobody else is in danger."

"Oh, isn't that what the police say to stop people panicking? I doubt it's a suicide," Georgie said. "Not if it's made the main headlines and the victim's not anybody famous. Somebody will have a hunch it's suspicious."

Adam sighed. "You're probably right."

By the time Adam packed up his stuff for the day, he'd had word from Robin that he might be late home and if Adam had heard the news he'd have a good idea why. Adam had been keeping an ear on the news on and off all afternoon, but there'd been no further information released by the police.

He'd got as far as the car, sticking the key in the ignition, when the message alert on his phone sounded again.

If you heard about an alleged suicide in a local village, wanted you to know it's more complicated than that. Could be connected to the dog killing. I'll tell you about it later.

More complicated? It seemed like life in the Matthews/Bright household would be all over the shop for the next few weeks.

Adam stopped at the garage on the way home, topping up with petrol while they were still in the relatively quiet school holiday time, before the rush hour went back to being manic. He'd put on music, not wanting to hear the local news; he'd be getting an accurate version of events later. Still, his mind wasn't at its most focussed as he opened the door to the kiosk to pay for the fuel, so he nearly bumped into the bloke coming in the other direction.

"Sorry, mate," he said.

"Can't you watch where you're— Adam? Adam Matthews?"

"Yes?" Who the hell was— Oh, right. "Gary. Bloody hell. You don't look any different than you did at uni."

Gary laughed. "It's clean living. I avoid it."

"Old joke. Typical you." Gary had always been the joker in the pack. Adam remembered one hilarious evening when he'd shown everyone a horrendous scar on his upper arm, then related how he'd been bitten by a great white shark when swimming off Nairn. One of the rugby lads—prop forward, not overly blessed with brains—had believed him.

"I hear you're teaching at Lindenshaw," Gary said. He'd been a pupil there, possibly at around the same time Robin had, given their ages.

"You're out of date. I've moved on."

"I don't blame you. I hear there was a murder at the school."

"I know. I was on-site at the time." Adam shuddered. "I— Sorry." They stepped aside as another customer wanted to get in. "I think we're making a nuisance of ourselves standing here."

"Same as at uni. Always causing trouble. Here, find me on Facebook and send me a message. We should meet up for a pint."

"Sounds good." Adam nodded, then opened the door again.

"You must owe me a beer or two!" Gary shouted as he walked backwards across the forecourt, nearly colliding with a Fiat that blasted its horn at him, and stopping by a hideous green-coloured car. "Don't dip out."

"I won't." Adam meant that. He and Gary had been good mates the first year at uni, drawn together by the fact Gary was a local boy even though he had subsequently moved to Scotland, when his parents' marriage broke up. By their final year they'd made new mates and had gradually drifted apart. Maybe Gary was back here for good now. He certainly still had relatives in the area—Adam had a feeling that his old chair of governors at Lindenshaw, Victor Reed, was an uncle or something.

"Are you ever going to pay for your fuel?" a loud but not unfriendly female voice called from the cash desk. Sheepish, Adam left off speculating and went to pay for his petrol at last.

When he got home Robin's car wasn't there, the only occupant of the house being a joyful Campbell, who slobbered over Adam, then made his way to the back door. While the canine bladder got relieved, Adam checked Gary Beaumont's Facebook profile. It said he lived at Kinechester now, but that was all the information it gave. Adam sent a friend request, then left a message saying he was free Wednesday evening if Gary fancied a pint then. This would stop Adam being at a loose end, especially since he hadn't got back into the school routine, so there weren't the usual jobs to fall back on.

He usually needed a distraction to immerse himself in when Robin was occupied with a case, not least because it took his mind off worrying that his partner might end up getting himself hurt. Some days he wished Robin had a job in a bank or at an oil refinery or something equally straightforward and relatively safe. Albeit in that case they'd likely never have met, Robin's job having been the catalyst for that fateful first encounter. And maybe Adam wouldn't have fallen in love with a non-rozzer Robin. You couldn't entirely separate the man from the job; that inquisitive and determined streak needed an outlet somewhere.

An equally inquisitive and determined Newfoundland came bounding over, demanding a bit of love and reminding Adam that *he* was available to provide a distraction at any point.

Robin was home earlier than expected, looking tired but at least present and correct.

"Hiya." Adam gave him a peck on the cheek. "I'm getting my dinner. Hungry?"

"Bloody ravenous. Tell me it's not a salad."

"Well, there is a bit of salad on the plate," Adam teased. "There's also a jacket potato, baked beans, and scampi."

"Epic." Robin rolled his shoulders. "Let me change my shirt and take a piss."

"Feel free. I can't pretend you're pleasantly fragrant. And stop slobbering over your other dad." Adam pushed Campbell away. "Or he'll smell worse."

"So kind." Robin leaned in for a sweaty hug before strolling upstairs, Campbell watching him soulfully.

"He'll be back in a minute to give you the proper amount of fuss, you daft baggage."

It was more like ten minutes, but neither Adam or Campbell minded—a fresh smelling, slightly less raddled-looking Robin always being the preferred option.

Adam gave him a thumbs-up. "Give himself a pat while I finish cooking the beans. Want them sludgy?"

"The thicker the better."

"Just like school dinners, then. I used to love those when I was little. Beans, spam fritters, that chocolate pudding that was like concrete. Hey, what's up?"

Robin, ashen faced, was staring out of the window, clearly oblivious to what was being said. "That death, today. It was at the house of the bloke who owned the Saint Bernard we found. We think it's murder, although we haven't got a positive ID yet on the victim. Chance it's the owner, although probably not."

"Bloody hell. Was he shot in the face?" Adam shuddered at the thought of a body so mutilated you couldn't recognise it.

"Yep. Half blown away, so even his mother would struggle to know it was him." Campbell, no doubt assessing that the comforting influence of a big dog was the very thing Robin needed, hove alongside, rubbing himself against the bloke's legs. "Just as well you didn't see it, sunshine. Put you off your dog biscuits. Might have been faked to seem like suicide. Possibly by the man who owned the house, as his car is missing. The dead man might have been the person staying with him. We're still awaiting all the evidence to be gone through."

"I don't need any further details, thank you." Adam forced away the mental images that kept popping up. Talk about Campbell being put off his food—*he'd* not be able to face dinner at this rate. "Are the two events linked, do you think?"

"It would be a hell of a coincidence if they weren't." Robin gave Campbell another pat, while Adam stirred the beans.

"And what else is bugging you that you haven't yet told me? You don't normally get so wound up about a murder. Is it the dog?"

"No. It was your mention of school dinners, of all things. The owner of the dog, being the owner of the cottage where the dead man was found, is known locally as Britz. But when I knew him he was called Wynter. He used to be my teacher at Lindenshaw. When I was ten."

"Hell." Adam turned the beans down, went over, and stuck an arm round Robin's shoulder. "Want to talk about it? Want a beer to talk about it over?"

"Yes. No. I mean yes, I want to talk about it but no, no beer. Too many coppers find the solution to life's problems in the bottom of a bottle. It never ends well."

"Cuppa, then?"

"Nah. Give me my dinner and a friendly ear and I'll be okay."

"Got two of those. You get the cutlery laid." Adam kissed Robin's cheek, then went back to getting the food ready. Once he'd got it plated up and he'd taken his place at the breakfast bar to eat, he asked, "Was this Wynter bloke involved in the bullying you suffered?"

"In so far as he turned a blind eye to what the other kids were doing and when I complained, told me not to be a snitch and to grow a pair. Only he didn't actually say that, obviously." Robin slowly dissected his potato. "He was one of those dinosaurs you still got in education back then. Would have loved to use the cane—he told us that—but because he couldn't, he lashed us with his tongue. He'd have called it 'character building.' I hated every minute of it."

Adam almost said, *Is that all?* because what Robin had revealed didn't explain why his face had turned so ashen and why he kept his eyes fixed on his plate. Adam knew about the relentless bullying his partner had suffered from the little scrotes around him, but Wynter hadn't been mentioned. Maybe that was because what he'd done had been as trivial as Robin was making it out to be, but Adam doubted it. He settled—at the moment—for saying, "I'm so sorry," and patting Robin's hand.

"I know you are. And you're the only person I've been able to discuss this with and feel better afterwards." Robin smiled. "Let's finish this, then I'll take you up on the offer of a cuppa and a friendly ear. With a side order of a cuddle if that's okay?"

"Cuddles are always okay."

Once they'd eaten, loaded the dishwasher, made mugs of tea, and got into the most comfortable cuddling position—which involved banishing Campbell to the floor as he was convinced he needed to be part of the therapy session—Robin seemed ready to chat.

"Every time I think I've turned a corner I get tripped up. I hoped I'd never run into Wynter again."

"Tell me to mind my own effing business, but is there more to what happened than you've said?"

"Of course there fucking is." Robin leaned closer, eyes shut. "Every day of that school year he belittled me. Whatever he could find to tell me off about, he did. It didn't just hurt me, it gave the bully boys extra ammunition. Looking back, I'd rather he'd belted me one. Better than suffering that continual assault on my self-confidence. Now it feels like my schooldays are going to bug me for the rest of my life."

Adam sighed. He'd heard this before, and would no doubt hear it again. "I'm not going to lie. You might never get over it completely, not if the hurt runs too deep. But it will get better, I promise. It's already got better, hasn't it?"

"Yes. They have. Since the most decent teacher in the world came into my life."

"Big wet lettuce." Adam gave him a kiss. "Have you thought of getting counselling? From somebody who's not simply a sympathetic ear, they've got training to go with it?"

"That's the last thing I want. I'd rather put up with the pain. And before you ask, I'm not being a wimp. I knew somebody at uni who got badly abused by a family friend when she was younger. She had one session of counselling—not NHS, this was somebody private she'd had recommended—after which, she had panic attacks. I know it works for some people but her experience put me off for life. I'll talk to you about it, and that's enough for me. So long as it isn't a burden," Robin added, clearly concerned.

"No burden at all. That's what fiancés are for."

"That's the first time you've called yourself that." Robin seemed impressed and pleased at the upgrade.

"Well, if we're going to start seriously planning getting spliced perhaps I should use it again. Especially when our mothers are about, so they'll think we're making progress."

"Oh, shit. That'll have to go on hold again, I'm afraid. I won't have a brain for anything else important for a while."

"That's all right. I'm glad to hear it's still important, though."

"It is." Robin caressed Adam's jawline. "You're more important to me than anything else, you know. Career, everything. If it ever got in the way of things, I'd—" He got silenced by Adam's hand clamped over his mouth.

"Stop it. No making promises that you might regret later. You and your career are inseparable, like me and mine. Everything else will have to work round them."

Robin, having wriggled his face free, said, "I always knew you were a keeper. All joking—and soppiness—aside, we do need to make it official. Not for anybody else's benefit other than ours."

Adam thanked God they'd at last reached a mutually agreed point about this ceremony, one they could action. Once the murder—if it was murder—was solved. "If you don't mind me mentioning Lindenshaw again, and shut me up if you'd rather we changed the subject, do you remember a Gary Beaumont?"

Robin frowned. "Should I?"

"He was at the school, might have been the same year as you or perhaps the one above." Gary had taken a gap year, travelling, before starting his university course. "I knew him at uni and happened to bump into him—literally—today, at the petrol station."

"Name doesn't ring a bell. You could ask Mum—she remembers all of them. Used to prattle on about what x, y, and z were doing and it all just went over my head. What's he like?"

"He used to be a good laugh. We were pally at uni, oi!" Adam rubbed his knuckles over Robin's head. "I saw that look. Not pally in that way. He likes the girls and anyway he was never my type. He moved when his family split up and his mother left this area. I think he was a bit of a fish out of water, because they ended up in Scotland, where his grandmother lived after *she'd* remarried. Back end of beyond. Aberystwyth?"

"That's Wales."

"Aberfeldy, maybe. Aberwhatever. Mind you, some families are hardly an advert for heterosexual family values, are they?"

"Snarky." Robin chuckled. "And now he's back?"

"Yeah, although I don't know if it's for good. I've a feeling his dad and various relatives still live here. Anyway, that'll probably all come out. I thought I'd meet up with him for a drink, seeing as you'll be working late." Adam toyed with whether to say what was in his mind, plumping for honesty, at the risk of getting Robin's back up. "Want me to see if he knows anything about Wynter?"

"You can if you want, but take care."

Robin's cases had a habit of trying to draw Adam into them, and on one occasion that had put his life at risk. There was no reason Gary should be connected with the murder case but you couldn't be too careful.

"I will, I promise. I don't suppose he knows much that you don't." Adam paused. "This Gary wasn't one of the lads who bullied you, was he? And you're pretending he isn't for some reason? I'll quite happily punch his lights out if you want."

"No, thank you. I've got enough on my plate without you getting done for assault. Gary's name doesn't fill me with dread, although might be best to check. Has he got a picture on Facebook?"

"Yeah." Adam quickly found the page on his phone: better to establish right now whether Gary was in the baddies' camp. Gary had accepted his friend request, so they could poke around in his profile, but Robin couldn't link him or any of his pals to the little scrotes who'd tormented him back then. There were lots of pictures of Gary with his mum and someone who might have been his stepdad, and another bloke, maybe a stepbrother. To all appearances a happy family. "Would Wynter have been Gary's teacher at some point as well?"

"Possibly. Pretty typical school, I'd have thought, with teachers staying with one year group. I remember that when he left the school it was all a bit mysterious—supposed to be appendicitis but he never returned after the operation and nobody talked about it. Mum always doubted the appendicitis bit, but she didn't know what had really happened."

Adam nodded, a horrible worm of a thought having started to wriggle through his brain. "What's up?" Robin asked. "You look like you've seen a ghost."

"Not a ghost, so much as an unpleasant memory. This is probably nothing more than putting two and two together and getting about twenty-five, but Gary's car was the same bright-green colour as the one in the common car park when we got there on Sunday."

"Ah. Well, let's hope that's a coincidence. By the expression on your face you've not told me everything, though."

"Unfortunately, that's true. At uni, Gary was in the rifle club. I think his step-grandfather may have represented Scotland in the Commonwealth games. Might have both learned their craft chasing hares on the hills." Adam rubbed his chin. "Maybe I should conveniently find that I have to pull out of meeting him. And not bother to remake a time."

"Don't do that. There's probably no connection." Robin gave him another hug. "Just be sensible. Choose a busy pub. Maybe you could drag someone else along as well? Safety in numbers and all that."

"I'm going to make a right wally of myself asking him if I can bring a mate." Adam puffed out his cheeks. "Interesting thing is I've a feeling Gary might be related in some way to Victor Reed, though. Remember him?"

"Chair of governors at Lindenshaw? How can I ever forget." Robin, stifling a yawn, rubbed Adam's hand. "Do what appears normal. If Gary has got a connection we don't want him spooked. Does he know that you're living with a rozzer?"

"I have no idea. I don't have it splurged all over Facebook. But if he keeps up with any Lindenshaw gossip, he might be aware. Why? Think he's keen to meet up because he wants to pick my brains rather than the other way round?"

"Something like that." Robin stifled another yawn. "Right, early start tomorrow so early night for me." He eased himself off the sofa. "Tell you what. Why not meet at a pub with a garden, and then you can take Campbell. Everyone's best bodyguard and nobody would take a swipe at him in a busy place."

"Sounds like a good plan, given that I still can't shake off this stupid worry that Wynter made Gary's life hell, and he's come back to get his revenge. First on the dog, then on the man."

"If it's any help, and this is—as usual—strictly confidential, I'm pretty certain Wynter is still alive. Pru and I listened to the recording of the 999 call. I'd put twenty quid on the voice being Wynter's, even though I've never heard him sounding so shit scared. You don't easily forget that sort of thing."

"I bet." Adam gave him a kiss, then let Robin get off to bed. He flicked on the television, turning down the volume so not to disturb the constabulary kip, but he couldn't concentrate on the programme. Surely it was a coincidence that Gary was at the common and then they'd bumped into each other at the petrol station? Adam couldn't imagine anyone less like a murderer than his old mate, although that was probably how lots of people felt when someone they knew turned out to be a killer.

With a sick feeling in his stomach, he realised there could be further deaths. Wynter being alive didn't mean that much if Gary—or whoever had committed the murder—*had* intended to get their own back. There was every chance he'd mistaken the actual victim for the ex-teacher, in which case no wonder Wynter sounded terrified. Once the news hit the media, the murderer would know they'd made a mistake, and they might want to rectify it.

Chapter Five

Wednesday morning, Robin awoke after a disturbed night's sleep, one punctuated with dreams he couldn't quite recall, but which had involved his school days. The only useful thing to have come out of them was the recollection that Wynter had a deformed little finger back then—he used to say he'd got it caught in a gun carriage mechanism, although Robin wasn't sure he ever believed him. He couldn't recall what the dead man's little fingers had looked like the previous day, but he texted the message in to the team who'd be doing the autopsy, before leaving for work.

Ben was already in the office when Robin arrived, and after he'd given a cheery hello, he said he had something to tell once Robin was settled.

"Great. Give me five minutes."

At what was likely five minutes and three seconds, Ben appeared at the office door, holding a sheet of paper and wearing his trademark puzzled expression. "I remembered this from last year. I don't know if this has got anything to do with things, sir."

Robin smiled encouragingly; this officer had shown plenty of promise and some of his leads came up trumps. "We won't know until you tell us."

"The event they've just held at Rutherclere. Welcome to the posh house, or whatever it's called."

"Welcome One, Welcome All, as you well know." Robin grinned.

"Remember all the problems it caused last time?"

Pru, who'd sneaked up behind him, nearly freaked the constable out when she said, "The locals up in arms about the congestion? I was on duty that weekend. It was a nightmare. They sorted the traffic flow better this year, although holding a big open day like that at a location you can only get to down small lanes is asking for trouble."

"And the connection to the shootings?" Robin asked. "Apart from being on the same weekend as this year's event?"

"Threats, sir. The outrage didn't end at letters to the papers or appearances on the local television station. Somebody said they'd be sitting with their rifle ready to take pot-shots at the tyres of anyone parking outside his house and walking the rest of the way."

"I'm hoping, with a big clue like that, people were able to put a name to the 'somebody'?" Surely even the officers at Abbotston—den of iniquity and inefficiency that it had been then—could have narrowed the search down. Not many people lived within walking distance of the grounds at Rutherclere.

Ben grinned. "We're not totally useless, sir. Although we couldn't prove it, the threats seemed to trace back to a guy called Mike Treadwell, who lives about half a mile from the site and has a nice expanse of green outside his place. Nice when it's not churned up by cars."

That sounded like he'd seen the place. "You went and spoke to him?"

"Not on my own. Sergeant Lewington as well."

"Ah." Lewington had been cleared out, with some of the last remaining rotten Abbotston apples, so there was always a possibility that he'd not handled this as he should. "Go on."

"We told Treadwell we knew about the threats and that if we could prove it was him, or anything stupid happened, we'd be straight back round with a warrant to search his place from top to bottom. We also made sure the firearms licensing manager knew. When his rifle licence was up for renewal, it was refused. He didn't appeal against it."

"But did he dispose of his firearms? And how does this link to Wynter? Britz. Whatever."

Any answer got cut off by the telephone. Chances were this was Grace, or one of the forensic team, as they seemed to know when he was in the middle of a conversation and generally took the opportunity to interrupt it. "Bright speaking. Hello?"

Not Grace this time, but the police doctor, about to perform the autopsy on the dead man. While he didn't have any details on the corpse yet, he could say without a shadow of a doubt that it had two perfectly normal little fingers and no suggestion that either of them had been surgically straightened in the past. He'd get Britz's dental records—he had enough jaw to work with—and would do a comparison, but the chances seemed to be that the dead man wasn't the owner of the house.

As Robin relayed the news to his fellow officers, Ben's face dropped. "I think that makes my bit of news meaningless, sir."

"Let me be the judge of that when I've heard it all. Did Treadwell get rid of his guns?"

"I don't know."

"Then maybe you should get down there and find out. Irrespective of a link to the case, we can't have unlicensed firearms lurking about." Robin tapped the desk. "Did he deny making the threats?"

"Yes. And Sergeant Lewington didn't exactly press him on it. He'd no patience for people coming down here in Kensington tractors, blocking the roads." Ben rolled his eyes. "Anyway, that was the last we heard of him. I checked his record, but it's clean as a whistle. Maybe he found something else to get angry at."

Maybe. Although why would his anger head off towards Pratt's Common or Lower Chipton? "You still haven't given me a connection to the Britz-who's-actually-Wynter-and-probably-isn't-dead case."

Ben flourished a Post-it note, like a magician pulling a rabbit out of a hat, only with less enthusiasm now that it appeared Wynter wasn't the dead man. "I went over the original gun licence paperwork. You know how you have to have people vouch for you as referees? Treadwell had Wynter vouch for him. Same address, real name."

"Okay. Pru, can you organise a team to do the house to house stuff down at Lower Chipton, please? Usual who and what did you see and hear and when. Ben, let's go and see Mr. Treadwell." Robin pummelled his right fist into his left palm a couple of times, like an athlete slapping himself before the big race, getting into the zone. "And don't look so disappointed that we're only chasing up a long shot. Everyone has to start somewhere."

"Sorry, sir, didn't mean to."

"Just as well you're not in an interview room, because you'd give the game away. You need to develop a poker face. Then you'll be first in line for the next time I have to interview some hardened gangland criminal."

"Maybe that's what Treadwell will turn out to be, sir. The secret mastermind behind the local drug trade. Growing cannabis in his attic, which is why he doesn't want people parking at his house."

Robin shook his head. "I never thought I'd meet someone who had as many flights of fancy as my previous sergeant, but you're running him close. I'm expecting nothing more exciting than him being able to tell us why Wynter calls himself Britz."

It was a slender connection, almost as thin as a spider's thread, but maybe it would turn out to be equally strong.

Ben, charged with contacting Treadwell to organise a meeting, hadn't hung about. He'd found a number, even more fortuitously found the bloke in when he'd rung, and arranged to see him at noon.

"He's retired, sir," the constable said as they set off for the interview. "So I was surprised that he was available so quickly. My grandad says he's been busier since he retired than he was before."

"Not uncommon, I believe." Good that Treadwell had been able to see them, though. While Robin sometimes liked to simply turn up and catch a witness unawares, thereby not allowing them time to build up a story, in this instance arranging things in advance would save wasting time. Catching people off guard was harder than it seemed, anyway. Anybody who was guilty as sin would have already got their story off pat ready to be trotted out at a moment's notice.

Before they'd left the station, they'd had word that the wound couldn't have been inflicted by the weapon that had been found with the body, that Britz's car—registered in the name of Wynter—didn't appear to be in Lower Chipton, and that door-to-door enquiries would have to be attempted again that evening as none of the nearby houses appeared to be occupied during the day, apart from Mrs. Croydon's, and she reckoned most locals were either at work or on holiday. Robin had briefed Cowdrey, then got an alert sent out for forces to be on the watch for the missing teacher. Mrs. Croydon had also been asked to let them know should her neighbour return.

Robin had also checked whether his boss was happy with him continuing to lead the investigation, given his connection with the missing man. He'd not been as frank as he'd been with Adam—he'd never been as open with anyone else and doubted if he would again— but had confessed how much he'd hated the bloke. Cowdrey reassured Robin that he'd every confidence in his ability to keep professional and personal apart, although he added the caveat that if things came too close to home, he would expect Robin to make the right call on his ability to remain impartial.

The identity of the victim continued to defy any of the usual means of resolution. He wasn't carrying a wallet, nor car keys, and the vehicle in the church car park was registered to a hire company. It was possible the man's wallet had been packed in the boot while he returned to the house for reasons unknown—perhaps something as prosaic as using the toilet, although in that case where was his means of getting back into the car?

As far as Robin was concerned, some certainty in this case couldn't come quickly enough.

Treadwell's house, and the expanse of green between it and the road, resembled a Hollywood version of an English country scene. A beautiful cottage, awash with late-summer flowers and foliage in the garden; Robin could understand why Treadwell didn't want four-by-fours coming and churning up the greensward. However, given the pristine condition of the grass, it was clear that whatever measures the Rutherclere events access team, or whatever they called themselves, had succeeded in keeping unwanted parking to a minimum. Still, the people who'd parked there before must have been pretty desperate or the previous arrangements must have been totally inadequate, because this had to be a good half a mile's walk to the gates of Rutherclere and then presumably a yomp up the drive to wherever the event itself was set up.

Treadwell was waiting for them, and seemed happy enough to be interviewed. He invited them to sit in his lounge, which also resembled something out of a film. The chairs were so deep and comfortable, and the pleasant drone of bees coming from the open window so calming Robin worried they'd be lulled into losing their investigative edge. As a result, he leaped straight in. "How did you know Harry Wynter?"

"Harry Wynter? There's a name from the past." Treadwell visibly relaxed, maybe having expected to be grilled about the threats he made.

"Please answer the question."

"Okay." Treadwell smiled. "We go back years. Went back years, I should say, because I've not seen him in a couple of years. He used to be in the Stanebridge branch of the Lions, before he moved away. He took me under his wing—some of the members there were a bit up themselves at the time. More interested in the kudos than in charitable aims."

"He stood reference for your gun licence," Ben stated.

"Yes. He was perfectly acceptable as far as I know."

Robin side-stepped remarking on that opinion. "You say you 'went back years.' Have you lost touch?"

"Yes. He moved out of the area must be, oh, ten years ago, at least. You lose track of time when you're my age."

Ben cut in. "But he's been your referee since then."

"Yes. Is there a problem with that? Do referees have to live close by?" When neither policeman replied, Treadwell said, "We used to exchange Christmas cards, and then a couple of years ago his simply stopped. I assumed he'd either decided he didn't want to be in contact anymore or something had happened to him."

"So you weren't aware he'd moved back to the area?" Robin asked.

"Has he? Then he must have given me the brush off, mustn't he?" Treadwell didn't seem that bothered. "He always was a bit of a mystery. Kept himself to himself."

"When you say he was a mystery, does that include using false names? Britz, for example?"

"Britz?" Treadwell snorted. "If you'll excuse me saying so, that's the last sort of name he'd have gone by if he wanted to disguise himself. Robinson or Thompson or another equally true-blue-British surname. Not what you'd call politically correct, was Harry."

That didn't come as a surprise. Time to change tack. "You were contacted by my colleague here over threats you'd made concerning the owners of vehicles parked outside your house."

"I was wondering when you were coming to that. I recognised the constable here." Treadwell grinned. "I'm afraid I misled you and your colleague. I *had* made those threats, although I regret them now. You were right to come and see me, and to have my gun licence revoked."

Ben gave Robin a surprised glance, but they let the witness continue.

"It was the best thing that could have happened, taking my rifle off me. Truth is, I was having a bit of trouble with my temper—work worries—and I might have done anything." Treadwell shook his head. "I must have been such a pain to live with. No wonder my wife left. I wouldn't harm a fly now, though. Honest."

"Glad to hear it." Robin studied him for a moment. "Can I ask what caused you to change?"

"I retired, for a start. Life's a lot easier without the nine-to-five. More than that, I saw the light. Not literally, I mean, but I had my road to Damascus moment. On the road to Abbotston, funnily enough, the week after I'd had my firearms licence revoked. I was listening to Radio 2 and there was a bloke doing *Pause for Thought*. He made me, well . . ." Treadwell grinned sheepishly. "He made me think. My family were always churchgoers, have been for generations, but I'd lapsed. Anyway, I went along to church that next Sunday and I haven't looked back."

Ben quickly adjusted his dropping jaw, although he clearly couldn't hide his surprise.

"Anyone would think I've confessed to being a mass murderer, Constable. Don't be so shocked. People do get converted, and we're not all long-haired loonies in sandals."

"I didn't think you were." Ben, evidently flustered, made a note in his book.

Robin resisted the temptation to let Ben dig himself deeper into the hole he'd created. He asked Treadwell, "The vicar would be able to vouch for you being a changed character?"

"He could vouch for my attendance, and for the things I volunteer to help with. Although if you want to be absolutely sure if I'm telling the truth you'll have to consult the Guv'nor."

Ben glanced at Robin then back to Treadwell. "The Guv'nor?"

Robin suppressed a chuckle. "I'll explain later."

"I haven't left it at working on my temper. I've developed a lot of patience too, which is all to the good, given the number of loonies— sorry, the vicar says I shouldn't call them that—who rock up here and want to chat."

Robin, who'd come to the conclusion that the interview was a waste of time, glanced up from where he'd been fiddling with his cuffs. "Chat about what?"

"About that old murder. The one that happened during the war. The Babe in the Wood. I don't know a lot about it, and I'm not particularly interested to learn more, but I know it happened on the Rutherclere estate, the part that's nearest to this road. I keep spotting a loo—sorry, shouldn't call them loonies—people coming along, trying to get a gawp at where it happened. They usually come back disappointed, though, because apparently you can't see the site from the road."

"So they come and ask you about it?"

"Sometimes. Or they simply drive past. It can be like Piccadilly Circus here, with all the cars coming and going for whatever they're holding at Rutherclere. Just as well I don't get cross about traffic anymore."

"Right." Robin made a mental note to get one of the team to follow up the old murder and the people interested in it, although he couldn't see how it would have any bearing on the shootings. "Did you get rid of your guns, by the way?"

"Yes, I did. The day after I lost my licence."

Ben tapped his notebook. "Was that as part of the Kinechester gun amnesty?"

"No. That didn't happen until later. I did an internet search, and there was one on in Manchester, so I drove up there and dumped them at the first station I could find open."

"You carried them in the car with you?"

"Yes. They were locked in the boot when I stopped at the service station. You can check with the police in Manchester because I gave them all the details."

"We can hardly do that if it was an amnesty, can we?" Or check the CCTV from every service station en route. Robin left his chair. "Have you still got the cabinet where you stored them here?"

"I'm afraid that went to the scrap merchants. I wanted to get rid of any trace of them, as soon as possible."

Robin shared an exasperated glance with Ben. All this was achieving was getting them hot under the collar. He gave Treadwell a terse reminder of what his duties had been regarding taking care of his guns, which was probably pointless but made Robin feel better. He also instructed him to get in touch immediately should Wynter resurface.

Back in the car, Robin asked Ben to drive to the main road, then pull into the petrol station with a shop attached. It was time for a sandwich. Once they'd got supplies in, they drove on to a lay-by, stopping there to take their refreshments, like Saturday-morning tourists on the way to their holidays.

"God," Robin said, when he'd got a decent chunk of food inside him. "That's who Treadwell meant by the Guv'nor."

"Oh. Right. Sorry, sir." Ben paused, sandwich halfway to his mouth. "I was being thick. He caught me on the hop."

"I think he caught us both on the hop. Was he like that last time you saw him?"

"I honestly don't remember. He doesn't seem to want to hide anything, now, though. Do you believe his story? All the 'I was saved' stuff?"

"Why not? It happens. People do find faith, or something else that motivates them to change their ways." And Treadwell had struck Robin as being less of a liar than someone caught up in the need to confess his sins. None so righteous as the recently converted and all that.

"Do you want me to check his story with the vicar?"

"Only if things develop to the point it seems necessary, but it won't signify much, anyway. Just because he goes to church doesn't mean he won't take a pot-shot at somebody. Look at some of these fundamental so-called Christians." Robin took another few bites of sandwich, but while the food stopped his stomach rumbling, it was doing nothing to help his brain.

"What about Treadwell saying Wynter wouldn't have used the name Britz?" Ben asked.

"That doesn't mean a lot. Treadwell could have read him wrong, or Wynter could have deliberately chosen something unexpected to more effectively keep up the charade if he were spotted. 'That can't be Harry, he wouldn't use that name.'"

"I'm not sure how reliable a witness he is. He does seem a bit prone to exaggeration. All that stuff about Piccadilly Circus. They've only opened the estate up on those two occasions, and this is known as a quiet road. Unless it's being used as a rat run because of the roadworks they're doing on the bypass."

"Yeah, well, you know what people are like when they have a grievance. Since when did facts get in the way?" Robin paused as his phone sounded with an incoming call from Pru. "Hallo. Got news for me?"

"I think so, sir. We've got a tentative identification on the dead man. The car was rented to a chap called Fabian Saggers. He's a solicitor, from Surrey, apparently. The man at the hire company knew him. The local police are going to drop into his office anytime now, to try to get a photo and the name of his next of kin."

"Given the circumstances, would a photo be much use? The name of his dentist would be. Good work, anyway." Now they might be getting somewhere. "Any connection between him and Wynter?"

"Give me a chance, sir. I'm working on it."

"I'll get Ben back as soon as I can, to give you a hand."

"I'll need both of them. Oh, can you hold on a second, sir? I've got an e-mail coming through from Surrey."

"No problem." Robin gave Ben a brief update, then encouraged him to finish his lunch and get them back to Abbotston.

"Hello?" Pru came back on the line. "You'll like this. The solicitor's firm Saggers works for—*worked*, if he's the victim—is called Pepperell and Purvis. Like something out of Dickens. Thing is, that's the company Chris Curran uses, the odd occasions when he gets called in for questioning."

"Chris Curran?"

"The supposed drug dealer who got into a fight in Rutherclere car park."

"Ah. He didn't get into a fight with Saggers, did he?"

"I don't think so. It's an unusual name so I should have remembered it from reading the case notes, but I'll double-check."

"Great. Can you organise a team meeting in about an hour? That'll give us ample time to get back even with Ben's driving."

Ben, who'd just pulled gingerly into the main road, gave him an affronted look.

"Will do, sir. Chances are we'll be a bit further forward than we were first thing."

"Yep." Robin ended the call, then gave Ben another update.

"It's like finding a handful of jigsaw pieces at the back of a drawer, and wondering if they all belong to the same puzzle," the constable said.

"I like that analogy. I'm going to steal it for the team briefing." Robin grinned. "The pieces I have are a major drug dealer getting thumped at Rutherclere, then someone from his solicitors' firm getting shot a couple of days afterwards, both of them off home turf at the same time. The household dog from where Saggers was staying getting itself shot the same day as the thumping and the houseowner—who's been living under an assumed name—disappearing. Any bits I've missed?"

"Wynter being pally with a bloke who admits to having made threats to people visiting Rutherclere, and people being obsessed with some old murder that happened there."

Robin remembered something Adam had been saying once about cause, effect, and independent factors. He'd filtered out much of the technical statistics stuff, but the crux of the message had been that two or more items might appear to correlate—the amount of ice cream sold on the beach and the number of shark attacks seemed to spring to mind, so that must have been the example Adam had used—which rose and fell at the same time, and so seemed to be linked. Only it wasn't one causing the other. A third variable, in Adam's example how hot the weather was, had affected the other two. Somewhere behind all these apparently barely related facts was there a factor which was influencing them all?

"Penny for your thoughts, sir?"

"Apart from hoping you're concentrating on the road? Thinking of your jigsaw pieces. And wondering what the picture is we're trying to make."

.

Chapter Six

I n the back and forth of Facebook messages on Tuesday evening and again on Wednesday morning, Adam had eventually managed to set up the meeting. Gary had sounded delighted at the thought of sitting in a pub garden—they had to make the most of the weather while it lasted—and hadn't seemed bothered by the likely presence of the dog.

Adam had contacted Robin to say he'd have his protector with him and was there anything he should be asking about? Or equally importantly avoiding asking about? Robin's reply had been both confidential, regarding the likely identity of the dead man, and cautious, reminding Adam that if things started to become hairy, he was to get out of there, canine protector notwithstanding.

With that sobering thought in mind, Adam got to the pub early, grabbed a lemonade shandy and a table in the garden, then sat down for a minute or two's thinking. Adam had sometimes wondered what *his* pupils would be like when they grew up, and surely Wynter would have had similar thoughts back when he'd been teaching Robin. It was easy to fall into stereotyping—this one would be the lab-coated boffin, that one would be in a young offenders' institute—so what would Wynter make of Robin having flown up through the ranks of the police? Surprise, probably. Would Robin's sexuality have brought the response *I always guessed as much*? It was possible the teacher had suspicions, back in Lindenshaw days, which might have been why he'd given him such a hard time. In that case, would he also have expected Robin to have turned into either a thug, because of the bullying, or an outrageously camp character?

Or had Robin simply been beneath the bloke's notice, a soft little boy who'd needed toughening up, one who'd left no real impression on the teacher's memory?

Anyway, Gary would most likely have an opinion on what had gone on at Lindenshaw school and the character of Wynter, an opinion which would prove valuable, irrespective of the connection with the murder.

When Gary arrived, Campbell was his usual charming self, clearly intent on having the man eating out of his paw, no doubt with the ulterior motive that if he played his canine cards right he'd soon be eating out of Gary's hand. Adam had brought a supply of dog biscuits so that there'd be less risk of a *please feed me, my owners never do* type incident and when they ordered food he deliberately went for something—fish—that Campbell would turn his nose up at.

"I have a feeling you're related to somebody I worked with at Lindenshaw," Adam said, as they returned from the bar to where Campbell was keeping watch over their table.

"You're thinking of my uncle Vic."

Adam suppressed a snort at the name Vic. Nobody he knew had ever referred to Victor Reed in such a common manner; they wouldn't have dared.

Gary carried on, clearly oblivious. "My mum was his sister. That's how she and Dad met in the first place. Uncle Vic had come here to work and she was visiting him. There was a barn dance that weekend, and they went along. So did Dad. You get the rest."

Adam nodded. If "Vic" had been a shock, then the man attending a barn dance was a bigger one.

"He's been good to me, especially after Mum died."

"Sorry to hear that." Adam had seen some of the Facebook posts Gary had made at the time. He'd clearly been heartbroken.

"Thanks. It was February of this year, but it hasn't got easier to process. Some silly bitch stepped out in front of her car. Mum swerved, hit a tree, and died the next day. The stupid bint of a pedestrian got away with hardly a scratch." Gary took a swig of beer, apparently not having registered Adam's flinch at the *silly bitch* comment.

"Not fair, is it?"

"No, it ain't. My stepdad was great, as was my bestie Nick. Actually, I think he was as cut up about it as I was."

Adam had a feeling Nick might have been the bloke in the family photos—he was sure he'd seen that name on one of the tags.

Gary ran his fingers across his forehead. "Anyway, Vic's the reason I knew all the inside goss about that murder in the school. Shame nothing like that happened in our day. I can think of one or two teachers I'd have liked to bump off."

Adam resisted saying Gary should try coming across a dead body where he worked, deciding to cut the bloke some slack. He must have taken his mother's death very hard and perhaps he was putting on an act to get by. Laughing at death rather than cowering.

Better lead the conversation onto Wynter.

"I hear there was a brute of a bloke at Lindenshaw, back in the day. Must have been about your time. Robinson?"

"You mean Wynter. Yeah, he was a right bastard. He'd have been on my list of people I'd like to get rid of." Gary raised his hand. "Just joking, by the way. Don't tell your bloke."

"I won't." He would, though. It might only be banter, but you never knew how small pieces of information could add up.

"Uncle Vic told me all about you hooking up with your policeman. Romance over the corpse. He says he's not up-to-date with what you're up to now, since you moved schools. He'd love to meet up for a pint and a chinwag. He'd have come today, but I said I didn't want to sully his ears with stories from uni days."

"Too right. Especially the one about Bill and the siphon."

The conversation turned to catching up on what their old mates were doing now, which included doing time in the case of one bloke who'd been on the fringes of their group, although not the aforementioned Bill, the prop forward of very little brain, who'd seen the light and was currently studying for holy orders. Nothing among that would interest Robin, so after they'd eaten, Adam went back into action.

"Did you see about that awful thing that happened last weekend up at Pratt's Common?"

"The dog? Yes, I saw that on the news. There was something today about the owner being killed too. I bet he topped himself. I'd be upset if somebody shot my pet, so maybe that was the last straw." Gary tipped his head to one side, quizzically.

Adam tapped the table. "I hope you're not fishing, because even if I had any inside information, I wouldn't be able to share it with you. Or anyone."

"You've seen right through me. You've always played your cards close to your chest. Ideal partner for a rozzer." Gary grinned. "Got to be long working hours for him, though. Worse than teaching. And I bet he's never really off duty."

"You could say that. Work certainly seems to follow him around." Adam gave Campbell a pat. "*We* found the dead dog. Didn't see it being killed, thank God, although we heard the shot. Got the shock of our lives because we thought it might have been Campbell that had been hit. The silly sod had run off."

Gary, frowning, shook his head. "I'd been up there, earlier. It'll sound bloody soft, but it was one of Mum's favourite places to go, when we were younger. When she was—" he took a deep breath, clearly composing himself "—you know, in the hospital, I promised her I'd come back one day and say hello and goodbye to the place from her."

Was that a genuine outpouring or simply a clever setting up of a cover story? Adam couldn't tell. No doubt Robin was better at this sort of thing, getting a feeling about whether what he was being told was real, rather like Adam had developed the ability to tell when children were lying.

"She'd have appreciated that," Adam said. "Shame it had to be spoiled."

"Luckily I missed that bit. I must have been long gone by then. Didn't see you two, so perhaps we didn't overlap or we were at different car parks. I wouldn't have recognised your car anyway. I bet it isn't as distinctive as mine."

"I've seen more subtle colours." And now that Adam could think better than he had the evening before, he noticed a whacking great hole in his logic. The vile green car had gone by the time they'd got back to the car park, so unless Gary had hared off from the scene at Olympic pace, and managed not to be seen in the process, he couldn't have been the one who shot the dog. "We didn't see anyone close by after the shot was fired. What sort of range could a bullet carry?"

Gary's brow creased. "Depends on the weapon. Professional sniper's rifle, it could be hundreds of metres. I used to compete over fifty, back in the day, and a dog's a damn site bigger target than what we aimed at. Your shooter could have been hiding behind one of the gorse bushes. There are plenty up there. Unless he—or she—was totally clueless, they must have been targeting the dog, rather than it being shot by accident. Unless . . ."

"Yes?"

"Unless they meant to shoot *him*." Gary jerked his thumb at Campbell. "Was it a similar breed?"

Adam looked at the Newfoundland lying happily at his feet. "Yeah. Worryingly so."

He'd been thinking about whether another murder might happen, but he'd confined himself to thinking of Wynter as the potential victim. What if the same applied to Campbell?

By the time Adam had got home, he'd finally persuaded himself that *their* dog couldn't have been the intended prey. Nobody could have known he and Robin would have been going there, and they'd not been followed. Either the person with the rifle had been just picking prey at random, in which case Campbell had been lucky, or the Saint Bernard was the target.

The light was still on in their bedroom, so he called a cheery "Hello!" up the stairs as he came through the front door, and got a reasonably happy "Hello yourself!" in response.

"I'll be up in a minute, once I've settled Campbell for the night."

When Adam reached the bedroom, he found Robin sitting propped up against the pillows, reading.

Robin flexed his neck. "Can't seem to get off. Too many thoughts whizzing round."

"What's the book?" Adam perched on the side of the bed. "Biggles? Since when have you read Biggles?"

"Used to all the time when I was little. Comfort read. Last time I dropped into Mum's, I picked up my collection."

"That's what you've got hidden in your bedside table." There could be worse things. "Rough day?"

"Not so much rough as busy. Too many different strands. I suppose it's always like this in a case, but this one feels more complicated than usual." Robin laid down his book. "How was Gary?"

"No different to how he was at uni. Searching for a job round here now he's got no roots up north. His mum died."

Robin nodded. "That's rotten. Anything come up to do with Wynter?"

"Plenty. He hated the bloke as well. Said he wanted to bump him off. I think it was a joke."

"Yeah. Probably. Was he up at Pratt's Common on Sunday?"

"Yep. He didn't attempt to hide the fact. Useful input about shooting too. Do they know if it was the same gun—rifle, whatever— used on the victim and the dog?"

"Early signs suggest not, and they think Saggers was killed using a silencer, which is why nobody heard it. But you know forensics, the wheels grind slow at times. We should have the victim ID confirmed tomorrow."

"Moving forward, then?"

"Something like that." Robin yawned. "Too many puzzles, still. Forensics team say the weapon that was found in the dead man's hand is unlikely to be the one used to kill him. Clumsy attempt at making us think it was suicide, maybe?"

"So clumsy you saw through it straight away?" Adam started to undress. "I suppose it might have been a strategy to buy time. The killer having an hour or two extra in which to scarper, while you thought you were dealing with a self-inflicted wound, might have made all the difference to them."

"It may not have been to fool us, anyway. What about fooling Wynter? He said it was likely suicide when he rang 999, so he either lied or believed it."

"The fact he's done a runner suggests a lie. Was he fond of telling porky pies?"

Robin snorted. "I wouldn't have put anything past him. Gary didn't have any inside info?"

"No, although he's related to a man who might. I think it's time I reconnected with my old chair of governors. I bet he'd tell me all sorts of tittle-tattle he wouldn't tell the police."

"I don't doubt it." Robin yawned again. "Usual caveat. Take care. Not that I think Victor's a murderer, but we've been taken unawares before."

If real life followed the pattern of fictional murder mysteries, the least likely person was going to be the culprit.

Chapter Seven

Thursday had dawned bright and looked set to be a cracking late-summer day, not that Robin was going to see much of it. They'd been told that Saggers's girlfriend would be coming down first thing; Pru had offered to guide her through the awful process of identifying the body, then Robin would join them for an informal interview. That was never a part of the job he relished, asking awkward questions when someone was grieving, but experience had told him that grief was often a thin veneer hiding a ton of guilt. The most likely person to murder you was somebody you knew.

This time had been unusual, in that the Surrey force hadn't been able to get a contact for any next of kin, but they'd reported Kerry Holding had turned up claiming to be Saggers's girlfriend.

"*Claiming* to be the girlfriend?" Robin asked Pru, who'd taken the phone call. "Is there any doubt?"

"I don't know," the sergeant replied. "The constable I spoke to reckoned they didn't live together—only been an item for a couple of months, Ms. Holding says, and they hadn't made a big thing about it with friends or colleagues. The officer did feel that something didn't ring true about their being in a relationship. Twenty years age difference for a start."

Robin shrugged. "It happens. We shouldn't jump to conclusions about other people's private lives."

"What about copper's nose, though? You say we should take it into account."

"We should, although I'll qualify that by saying only if we know the copper and can trust their instincts. Ask Adam about the time he did jury service and some of the things his fellow jurors said, based on their instincts. Or maybe don't. It'll shake your faith in the justice system."

They went straight into the morning team meeting, which turned out to be fairly brief, just a matter of making sure everyone was up to speed with Wednesday's news. The most recent addition to the team—an efficient young constable who'd been christened Catherine but who insisted on being called Caz—confirmed that the Vauxhall Vectra Robin had spotted in the car park belonged to an old couple who'd parked there to go picking blackberries from a patch that always ripened early. They had the bramble jelly to prove it.

Not long after, Pru got called away to take their visitor through identifying the body, which she completed with great dignity, according to the text Pru sent Robin afterwards while the woman concerned was visiting the toilet. He made his way to the comfortable, pleasantly decorated interview room that had been designed for these purposes, encountering Ben—who was bearing a tray with coffee pot, mugs, milk, and sugar—at the door.

"Can you open it, please, sir? I've run out of hands."

Robin turned the handle and let them in. "Where did you get that?"

"Can't say, or everyone will expect special treatment." Ben grinned.

"Well, it's much appreciated, and not only for our visitor. Thanks."

Robin watched as the young constable strolled off down the corridor. He needed to be careful that Ben didn't end up simply being the fetch-and-carry and look-it-up-on-the-internet officer. Pru was such a good sergeant, and had become such a part of Robin's working practice, it was easy to forget to give the others the right opportunities to build up their experience, and the interview with Treadwell hardly counted as extending Ben's. He resolved to do better, then busied himself with getting the room ready.

Pru's voice—accompanied by another female one with deep, attractive tones—sounded along the corridor. Robin went out to meet them, finding himself immediately, if pleasantly, surprised by Saggers's partner. Kerry Holding was probably in her forties, dressed with impeccable taste, extremely attractive—and black. His first thought was that her ethnic background was what had rung untrue with the officer in London, the ridiculous assumption that a white bloke wouldn't go out with a younger black woman. His second idea was that he wished he had Constable May with him, an officer he'd been impressed with at the time of the Abbotston Slasher case, but she'd moved on to another division where she was said to be one of its rising stars. His third thought was that he was having just as prejudiced an idea as his colleagues in Surrey, falling for the trap that you always had to pair ethnicity either side of an interview table. How would he feel if he always had to be seen by a gay doctor, for example?

Fortunately, Pru's peerless handling of the introductions and his own actions of making sure that Ms. Holding was settled and served with a coffee had covered over any hesitation he might have shown as he got his muddled mind in order.

"I'm sorry you've had to come down and do the identification. The whole thing must have come as a great shock," he said.

"You have a gift for understatement," Ms. Holding replied, although it was with good humour. "And please call me Kerry. I'll feel less like a suspect then."

Pru seemed mortified. "I hope I didn't give you that impression."

"Sorry, I'm being mischievous. My mother says that I've always relied on humour to get me through tricky times. You've been very kind, very professional." Kerry sighed. "We'd not been together long, Fabian and myself, although we clicked from the start. I never believed in love at first sight, and I wouldn't say that's what this was, but it must have been close. I miss him like hell."

Robin believed her. The simplicity with which she spoke implied deeply felt emotion barely kept under check. Or an acting ability to rival any Oscar winner. "We've questions to ask, of course, which may seem intrusive, but you'll appreciate we have a job to do. Let's get the worst out of the way. Where were you on Tuesday?"

"Finishing off a stay in Bristol, after a weekend conference. Historical novelists."

This interview was full of surprises. "In that case, you'll have people who can vouch for you during that time?"

"Of course, Mr. Bright. I'm not exactly hard to notice at that sort of gathering." Kerry raised her eyebrow. "And I shared a room with a girlfriend. I can give you her contact details. I guessed you'd want them."

"You guessed right. That would be useful." Pru waited as the witness jotted down a name and phone number. "This conference sounds interesting. Are you an author?"

Kerry chuckled. "I'd like to be. At the moment I sit at the feet of giants and learn from them. The interest in history is how I met Fabian. We were at a talk about the lost rivers of London, of all things."

An unusual way to meet, but only slightly stranger than meeting the love of your life across a makeshift interview desk as part of a murder enquiry.

"Fabian wasn't interested in attending the conference?" Robin asked.

"Not his cup of tea. He preferred real history rather than the fictional versions. We only tried going to the cinema once to watch a historical film. He muttered all the way through it. Too many anachronisms." Kerry rummaged in her bag for a handkerchief.

"Take your time. We know how hard it is talking about someone you've lost," Pru said, soothingly. "All we want to do is catch who killed him."

"I know." Kerry dabbed her eyes. "Anyway, as I was off for the weekend, Fabian said he'd have a weekend gallivanting as well. Meeting up with an old mate of his."

"Wynter. You might know him as Britz."

Kerry gave Pru a quizzical glance at her statement. "I don't know really him at all. Fabian called him Wynter, though."

"How were they connected?" Pru asked.

"I have no idea. We don't—didn't—discuss every little bit of our lives. Now I wish we had." Another dab of the eyes, one that seemed genuine enough. Robin guessed Kerry wasn't usually the sort to show emotion.

He waited until she was finished before asking, "Have you met him?"

"Briefly. Have you?"

Robin resisted the comeback, *Unfortunately yes,* even though Kerry's moue of distaste at the mention of the man made such a response tempting. "I have. Several years ago. What did you make of him?"

"Honest answer? Nasty piece of work. Sly. Did he used to be a teacher?"

"Yes," Pru cut in, probably to shield Robin. She alone of the Abbotston team knew that his school days hadn't been the happiest. "Why do you ask?"

"Because I'd have hated to be in his class. Wouldn't have trusted him." Kerry shook her head. "My mother would have been down the school like a shot demanding he got sacked for being a dirty old man."

"You need to remind her that the law says innocent until proven guilty." Pru grinned at the reply, though.

"You try telling her that. I wouldn't have been surprised if somebody had tried to kill *him*. A disgruntled ex-pupil, maybe."

Robin ran his finger around his collar; he knew this case would cut close to home, but he'd imagined he would cope without a second thought. He'd managed investigating the Lindenshaw murder and the memories that unearthed, so why was this proving so hard? Adam would probably say it was because it involved people, rather than places. Thank God Robin had got Pru in the interview with him and hadn't chosen this one to broaden Ben's horizons.

He forced himself to speak. "You can't think of anyone who'd have wanted to kill Fabian?"

"No. Honestly. He was a widower, and I'm not aware of a mad ex-girlfriend hanging around. I also doubt he's got—had—any clients who bore him a grudge, although his colleagues should help on that line. If I could think of someone, I'd tell you. I want whoever this is brought to justice."

"Would that apply if it turns out Wynter was the intended victim?" Pru asked.

"Of course," Kerry snapped, showing anger for the first time. "Sorry. I didn't mean to bite your head off. I'm finding this difficult. Perhaps when I've had time to get my head around this we could talk again? I promise if I think of anything significant in between, I'll get back in touch."

"That's fine." Robin pushed his chair back, aware that they'd come to a natural end of the interview. They passed a few platitudinous pleasantries, then accompanied Kerry to the station door.

"That was interesting," Pru said, as they watched Kerry walk back to her car. "The way she got angry at the mention of Wynter, and the way she made it plain *she* was ending the discussion."

"Perhaps she does need to grieve a bit. Or maybe she needs time to get her story together."

Pru cuffed his arm. "You're such a cynic."

"I'm not. I'm just a realist." Although why Kerry had been so agitated about Wynter, a man she claimed to barely know, he couldn't tell.

Investigations often seemed to move at a strange, syncopated pace: sometimes no new information came to hand despite hours and days of routine work that was seemingly leading nowhere. And then there'd be a frenzy of stuff coming in, almost a bewildering deluge at times, that might take them off in new directions, often several at once. It soon became apparent that today was in the latter category, although the information came in dribs and drabs rather than a flood.

An off-duty police officer with a good memory for registration plates had been walking his dog past a Surrey pub the previous evening and had spotted what he thought might be Wynter's vehicle in the car park. He'd returned today, confirmed that the car was the one they were looking for, although there was no sight of the man himself. The pub had rooms, and while nobody called either Britz or Wynter was staying there, the car registration had been listed for a guest called Thompson. The pub landlord would let the officer know when the guest returned so they'd hopefully have the slippery swine in their hands soon.

Pru had worked through what little had come back from the house to house enquiries, but nobody had seen or heard much the morning of the shooting. Most of the people had been out, at work or on holiday or simply making the most of the last week of the summer holidays, although they'd had one report of a shot being heard at around the right time. The person concerned had assumed it was somebody shooting pheasants, as that often happened at one of the local farms.

"If they're shooting them at this time of year, then it's out of season," Pru added, "but I suspect we've got bigger fish to fry at present than illegal game hunting."

"You suspect correctly." Curse the village for having emptied itself at the crucial time.

"Mrs. Croydon rang me and said she'd remembered something, though."

"I like the sound of that."

"Apparently Wynter used to have one too many glasses of whisky and get garrulous. Once he started going on about having a nest egg hidden in the Lower Chipton church hall. He helps keep the place clean so he can come and go as he pleases. Said that nobody would think of searching for it there."

"Did he give any clue about what *it* was?" Robin's mind went off on a whistle-stop tour of possibilities. Pictures that could be used for blackmail? Stolen high-value goods? A stash of pornography or some equally unpleasant hoard of weaponry, enough to enable somebody to go out in a blaze of what the perpetrator thought was glory?

"Mrs. Croydon had no idea. He was rather secretive about it."

"We should get hold of the keys, run over, and give the place a thorough once over. For all we know, Wynter's hiding there. These halls don't tend to get as many bookings in the summer holidays."

"What about his car being in Surrey?" Pru pointed out.

"I suppose it could have been nicked. By someone called Thompson. Anyway, if this thing he's hidden away really exists and isn't simply a cock-and-bull tale to amuse the neighbour, it could be relevant to why somebody took a pop at his dog and his pal."

"I'll get onto finding a key." As Pru came out of the office door, she almost collided with Ben, who was looking as proud of himself as Campbell did when he'd been in the garden and found a long-lost rubber ball. Hopefully whatever the constable had brought wouldn't be as disgusting.

"I've got some gen on that killing Treadwell mentioned. The Babe in the Wood."

"Sounds like the panto." Pru stuck her head back round the office door.

"Behave." Robin gave Ben an encouraging smile. "Go on."

"Nineteen forty-one. There was a little boy—only nine years old—went missing from the family home about a mile from where Treadwell lives. The row of old cottages that got condemned a couple of years back. He was found dead in the woods on the Rutherclere estate. Official records say he'd wandered off, maybe got scared, and died of a weak heart. Nobody was ever charged or anything."

Faint bells of recollection sounded in Robin's head. In his early days in the Lindenshaw force, he'd had a discussion with a long-serving colleague, who'd mentioned the case and how it still riled some of the retired officers, even those who hadn't direct experience of it. "Treadwell called it murder, and he wouldn't be alone in believing that."

"I know," Ben said gleefully. "There are whole blogs devoted to the killing. Want me to start working through them and seeing if there's a connection to our case?"

"Yes." Robin rubbed his hands together. "Pru, Kerry said that Saggers was interested in true history. I know it seems a long shot, but could Saggers have been here to visit Rutherclere, and therefore the site of the killing, on the one day of the year there's public access?"

"I'll ring Kerry and ask her if he ever mentioned any babes in any woods."

Suddenly Robin felt infuriated at the nickname. Whatever the cause of the child's death—accident, medical incident, or at somebody's hand—he deserved as much respect as Saggers, notwithstanding his having died so long ago.

"He did have a proper name, you know. I'd prefer that we used it."

Pru winced. "Sorry, sir."

"Apology accepted."

"He was called Tommy Burley," Ben said, having consulted his notes. "Do you want me to get back on the computer?"

Robin stroked his chin. "Not yet. We don't want you being tied to a screen. *You* can chase up a key for Lower Chipton church hall, and then we'll go out there." He gave Pru his best smile, not wanting her to think she was being punished for the previous conversation. "Pru, I'd like you to be here in case they pick up Wynter. I'd also like you to go over the incident at Rutherclere with the drug dealer. See if Saggers's name turns up."

"Okay. I'll also ring up Mrs. Croydon and see if Wynter mentioned any interest in the Tommy Burley case. Although if he was walking his dog at Pratt's Common, he couldn't have been at Rutherclere on Sunday."

"True. Unless it wasn't him walking the dog. Which might explain why it had run off."

"He could have gone to Rutherclere and Saggers might have taken the Saint Bernard out," Ben said. "Wynter might have shot him for letting the dog be killed." He looked from Pru to Robin and back again. "Okay, just an idea."

"I've heard worse." Robin nodded. "Right, we've got work to do, let's get onto it."

His job was going to be mentally preparing himself to face Wynter once more.

St. James's Hall, Lower Chipton, resembled every Victorian-era church hall Robin had ever come across, and there were plenty sprinkled about the local villages. Some had been sold on or knocked down and replaced by something much more fit for twentieth-century purpose, although that had become increasingly difficult as people sought to preserve local history. This one gave the impression that it needed a friendly bomb to drop on it and put it out of its misery.

"Cor, this place reeks a bit." Ben flapped his hand in front of his face as he finally managed to get the lock open and pushed the door.

The place not only looked but *smelled* like any other community centre Robin had ever entered: wood, old books, something resembling the stink of distant boiling green vegetables. "I've come across worse. You need to harden your stomach, Constable. You'll smell—and see—worse than this in your career."

The least pleasant part of the aroma was the association with education; this was exactly how Lindenshaw school had smelled when Robin was little. So many aspects of those early days had stayed with him, some of them long buried only to emerge at the strangest times, like when his mother had served up cabbage and he'd not been able to eat it. He'd once had some cold school-dinner cabbage stuffed in his pocket, and when he'd been presented with the lovely plateful of food his mum had dished up, he hadn't been able to get his mind past the reek of greens. He suppressed a shudder.

"Any idea what we're actually searching for, sir?"

"I'm not psychic," Robin snapped. "Sorry. That wasn't called for." God, he was getting tetchy about this case. "I have no idea, but we mustn't forget we could be dealing with a potentially dangerous situation. My money would be something he's nicked and is waiting to fence once people have forgot about it, but given that Wynter is a white male, bit of a loner, of a certain age, and a nasty piece of work to boot—take my word for that—then he's exactly the sort of bloke who walked into that school in Dunblane."

Ben blanched. "I hadn't thought of that. Not on our patch. It's the kind of thing that happens elsewhere."

"Elsewhere is 'our patch' for somebody." Robin wasn't sure that made much sense outside of his head, but Ben appeared to get the point.

"If I was reading this in a book, Wynter would be the prime suspect for having shot Saggers. Can someone put a stash of ordnance in a location like Lower Chipton village hall?"

"I'm sure they could if they wanted to blow the place to kingdom come. Which is probably the best thing for it." Robin shrugged. "People are ingenious. If they want to find a way, they'll do it. Stick stuff away under a stage in an old box marked *Property of the Lower Chipton ladies choir*, and nobody would dare touch it. Although how Wynter could regard explosives as a nest egg beats me."

"We'd better get the sniffer dogs to go over it before we start poking around. That's not overreacting, is it?" Ben's face was still a paler shade than normal.

"Depends what we find. Anything suspicious and we'll call them in, but my guess is it'll turn out to be something totally different. They'd have our guts for garters if we call them in unnecessarily."

He sent Ben off into what was clearly the hall kitchen, which would likely be worst affected by the cabbage smell, then began to search the main part of the building. He'd just worked out how to open the door to what appeared to be under-stage storage when the tip-tapping of heels on the boards made him spin round. Perhaps it was simply some poor deluded pensioner coming along for the Thursday afternoon bingo who didn't realise they needed to be in Upper Chipton. Although given the red high-heeled shoes, what looked like a top-of-the-range lightweight dress, and the general air of superiority, the visitor seemed anything but a lost soul.

"Hello? Can I help?" Robin asked.

"You can tell me who you are, for a start, and what you think you're doing here."

"Chief Inspector Robin Bright." He flashed his warrant card. "And you are?"

"Daisy Lockwood. I run the WI branch." She waved an elegantly manicured hand as though to indicate her domain.

"You don't have a meeting today, though." Unless Ben had cocked up when he'd checked the bookings roster while getting the key; they'd not wanted to go blustering in and scaring a room full of preschoolers having their holiday club.

"No, but I wanted to do some preparation for our next one."

Robin smiled politely. "I'm afraid that won't be possible at the moment. Not until we've finished here."

She frowned. "Can I ask what you're doing?"

"You can but I won't be answering." He smiled again. "Sorry if you think I'm being unhelpful, but that's the state of play at the moment. Now, if you could leave us to our business, please?"

"I suppose I have no alternative." She turned on her red high heel and flounced off.

Ben emerged from the kitchen. "I wouldn't like to get on her wrong side."

"Too late for that where I'm concerned. I guess you were hiding until she'd gone." Robin eyed Daisy through the window. Despite the theatrical flouncing away, she'd stopped outside and was watching the hall. "What's she up to? If I were a betting man I'd have a tenner on her not being here for anything to do with the WI."

"Maybe she saw the hall door was open and wanted to check we weren't nicking the teacups. Nothing in the kitchen, by the way."

"Right. Let's check any other rooms—I'll do the ladies' loo so your sensitivities aren't offended—and then we'll head under that stage. But first you lock the front door. It won't stop her coming in if she's got a key, but the noise should alert us. I'll try to get the blinds down." Robin jerked his thumb over his shoulder towards the windows. "Stop her peering in."

Nothing turned up from their search of the toilets, even after Robin insisted they stand on the seats to look in the Victorian cisterns, which provided an ideal hiding place for anything which was securely waterproofed.

"I don't have to go in there, do I, sir?" Ben said, as they got the doors open to the under-stage cupboard.

"Scared of the dark?"

"Nah. Spiders. Can't stand the little buggers."

Robin sighed. "You put on your phone's torch and help me see, then."

"I can do better than that. I saw a board of switches." Ben nipped over to the kitchen, and soon both the hall and the dark recess were flooded with light.

"No chance of missing anything in here." As Robin crawled through the entrance, he was struck by how well provided for the area was. About four feet in height, well lit, laid with linoleum rather than bare floorboarded like the rest of the hall, and with all the items stacked and labelled efficiently. "I've found Ms. Lockwood's WI things, although it doesn't look like they get dragged out that often."

"There's plenty of storage in the kitchen, and another big cupboard in a recess off it. I bet many groups use that on a day-to-day basis." Ben's voice was distant; clearly he wasn't taking any chances with spiders being routed out by Robin's rummaging. "There was Brownie and Cubs stuff as well as the WI and the Sunday school."

"Same in here. More Christmas decorations than you could shake a fist at. Nothing—" Robin paused, having caught sight of a box labelled *Lindenshaw Memories. Property of church archives. Do not open.*

"What, sir?" Ben sounded anxious.

"Don't worry, it's not a tarantula." Robin, using his penknife, gingerly raised the edge of the box, shone the torchlight from his phone in, then called for Ben. "You'd better come in here and have a shufti. I think this only contains papers, but I want a second opinion. Irrespective of spiders."

Huffing and muttering, Ben slowly crawled in alongside him.

"What do you make of it?"

Ben peered at the box. "Over-labelled, for one thing. Don't they usually keep parish archived material in the church itself or up at the central collection in Kinechester?"

"My very thoughts. And why would Lindenshaw material be tucked away in Lower Chipton?" Robin raised the flap again.

"That looks like old newspapers to me," Ben agreed a touch too readily, phobia clearly overriding caution. "Can we get it into the light?"

They edged backwards, Robin dragging what turned out to be a surprisingly heavy box. Once they could open it properly, Robin started to lift out the dusty newsprint. "There's more than paper in here."

Packed about with tattered copies of the *Express* and *Mirror*, was a metal strongbox secured with a hefty padlock.

"Blimey," Ben said, picking up the box to give it a shake.

"Careful in case that explodes," Robin said, then chuckled as Ben hastily dropped the thing.

"Doesn't sound like it's got jewellery or anything rattling around in there." Ben wiped the dust from his hands. "Shall we take it back to Abbotston and get some bolt cutters on it?"

"Yes. I don't think this is genuine church stuff. Anyway, I know the vicar of Lindenshaw, and he'd forgive us if it turns out this is the church silver and we went a bit too far in the furtherance of our duty." Robin grinned. "I'll put the box back where I found it, though. In case anyone's intending checking."

"You mean that woman who came earlier?"

"It's a possibility. And if we lay hands on Wynter but don't have enough evidence to detain him, he'll probably be down here like a shot."

Laying hands on Wynter hadn't happened yet, though, as they found out when Robin checked his texts. Pru had managed to talk to Kerry, and she'd confirmed that Saggers had mentioned an interest in an old unsolved case that went back to the Second World War and had involved a child.

"Sounds like you'll be welded to your computer the rest of the day," Robin said, once he'd updated Ben on Pru's texts. "We need details on Tommy Burley and any connections he has to the people involved in this case."

Ben nodded, enthusiastically. "Can't wait."

Driving back from Lower Chipton, they passed a sign advertising a wedding fair at Rutherclere, the upcoming weekend.

"Opening up the place twice in little over a week. We *are* honoured." Robin snorted.

"They must be getting hard up for cash, letting in the riff-raff again." Ben snickered "The locals are going to love that, sir. Another traffic jam."

"Are these things so popular?"

Ben shrugged. "Depends. Rutherclere has only recently got a licence to do weddings, so all the world and his wife might turn out to see what they have to offer."

"All the world and his wife-to-be, you mean."

"Pru warned me about your jokes." Ben deftly manoeuvred a mini roundabout; his driving skills were better than the average constable Robin had come across. "Anyway, weddings are big business now, not simply a do in the church and off to the village hall for sandwiches and a glass of bubbly. I bet they'll cost an arm and a leg at that particular venue."

"You seem to know a lot about the subject."

"More than I want to. You remember my sister, Carrie? You and Adam met her once when my lot were at Stanebridge farmers' market."

"I remember." Ben's twin, the pair of them as alike as the brother and sister in *Twelfth Night*.

"She's tying the knot next year, and either Mum or I have spent every other weekend being dragged round some place getting information. I'm supposed to be providing the male viewpoint, as Den—that's her bloke—is on secondment in Norway and she's having to do all the preliminaries." Ben snorted. "You wouldn't believe the options for transport on its own. Vintage, ultra-modern, horse and carriage. I've seen them all, and Carrie's no closer to making a decision on that alone."

under an assumed name. Both Adam and Robin were confident that Victor might tell his ex-colleague things he wouldn't tell the police. People did sometimes labour under the misconception that rozzers were only interested in facts, not in gossip, whereas an old pal like Adam was more likely to want to hear any old scandal that was going. Also, Victor might not sift out things that he wouldn't want to put in an official statement. A chat over a pint hardly counted as an official interview.

Car parked, walk completed, and both dog and owner having worked up a thirst, Adam found a table in the pub garden just as Victor appeared at the gate. The White Hart, on the edge of East Baddesley, which was the next village along from Lindenshaw, was within walking distance of Victor's house, his having moved there after his next-door neighbour had become the second victim of the Lindenshaw murderer. Convening on home ground would surely put the bloke at ease, and the excellent beer—which could be ladled into him as he wasn't driving—might loosen his tongue.

The next half an hour was fallow ground in terms of getting to the crux of things. Food, drink, catching up with the doings of Victor's children and grandchildren, then a long and slightly boring account of him and Gary sorting out a pile of old family photo albums on Tuesday. Adam eased the conversation into local gossip, which meant having to listen to another long and not very interesting story about Victor's new neighbour. She was reputed to have run a brothel in another village about ten miles away, her business being cleverly disguised by locating it in the flat above a hardware store so the stream of male visitors wouldn't be thought out of place. That was the most amusing bit of the tale, the rest lamely petering out in a case of mistaken identity. Adam edged the conversation towards news about any of his ex-colleagues on the Lindenshaw governing body, ones whom he didn't see out and about these days.

"I hear from the vicar that only he and Christine Probert are still on the governing body from our days."

"Yes. There's been quite a turnover. Neil has to be a governor, of course, comes with the parish, although he'd have volunteered irrespective. Not every vicar has the knack of connecting with children the way he does."

"I wish we had him at Culdover. The incumbent there needs a bit of a boot up the ecclesiastical backside." Adam sneaked Campbell—who'd been appropriately angelic—a morsel of bread. "I'm told you stepped down as chair."

"Yes. Unfortunately, the role's grown and my time hasn't grown with it. What with adding in the travelling distance, I felt it was time for a change. Christine's said to be doing a great job."

"So I hear." Adam had also heard that Victor had been eased out rather than stepping down. Clean slate all round. There was an advantage, if that were true, because if he had been got rid of, then he might be willing to trade information that should really stay behind the scenes. Hell hath no fury like a governor scorned.

"You'll be able to put your talents into other things. New challenges."

Victor nodded. "Always irons in the fire, that's me."

"Do you keep in touch with the staff at the school at all?"

"Not really. I suppose you'd have more call to."

"A bit. I'm connected with a couple of the teachers on social media. We may have parted ways but we still remain friends. Like you did," Adam added, hastily. "Not always the case in education. Like poor old Oliver Narraway."

Oliver had been another governor at Lindenshaw, an ex-headteacher who'd blotted his copybook, although not to the extent of being banned from any contact with schools. *He'd* known all sorts of juicy tittle-tattle and would no doubt have been able to dish the dirt on Wynter, but him being Victor's dead neighbour made tapping that source an impossibility.

"Yes. Poor bloke. Maybe it was as well he wasn't around when the whole story behind the killings came into the open."

Did Victor really think that being murdered was preferable to dealing with scandal, or was it simply the usual hyperbole that people used without thinking about what they were actually saying? Anyway, hadn't Oliver known all the backstory and wasn't that what had led to his death?

"Am I dreaming it or was there some teacher at Lindenshaw got into a bit of bother? Ages before my time. Mum told me about him when I got my job at the school." Adam put his hand to his forehead, hoping he was giving a real impression of thinking and not coming over like a drama queen. "Williams? No, not that. Something like it."

"You mean Harry Wynter." Victor rolled his eyes. "That was long before your time. The school was well rid of him. Nasty piece of work."

"Yeah. I heard he used to take his hand to kids if he caught them apple scrumping in his garden." Adam's mum had been the source of that story. "Lucky he didn't try anything like it in class."

"I'm not so sure. About his not trying it in class, I mean. People wouldn't have spoken about it in those days, and the pupils would have been scared to speak up. You don't have to go back that far to find a time when some parents would have positively encouraged it. Keeping the children in line." Victor winced. "My backside can attest to the fact, if you'll excuse my French. You probably avoided corporal punishment."

"I did." Robin had too—his suffering at the hands of teachers had been more of a verbal assault. Adam remembered his own grandfather expressing concerns that the end of reasonable physical punishment would lead to an unreasonable use of sarcasm or other underhand ways to keep order, ones that would have a longer lasting psychological effect than a smack on the bottom might. Adam wasn't sure that *reasonable* physical punishment had ever existed, certainly not in the case of schoolchildren, but he could see the crux of the argument. You had to find an effective way to stop pupils running riot and if there was no stick, what was your carrot?

He'd always been successful with keeping behaviour in his classroom good. Making sure children were interested and kept busy was half the challenge, although you had to know when to impose sanctions and always go through with exacting them. Children liked boundaries, albeit they also liked pushing them.

"So, why did Wynter leave? Mum was always very mysterious about him, and I've spent years dying to know the truth. Trouble is, if people hide the details of stuff, the worse you imagine things were."

"It wasn't touching up small boys or girls, if that's what you're thinking. Like your mum said, he was accused of being a bit too ready to give out six of the best. Not confined to when kids came apple scrumping. Balls knocked into his garden—I bet that was deliberate— or any other behaviour he didn't like, he laid into the culprits.

The headteacher at the time challenged him, some of those being current or ex-Lindenshaw pupils, and apparently Wynter lost his rag. Said the school was full of little toerags who thought they ran the place and they'd be better off bringing back the cane and getting some order into the establishment."

"Bloody hell. I bet the shit hit the fan."

"You might say that. These days he'd have been marched off the premises and been up in front of a disciplinary hearing. Back then, the vicar was chair of governors and he wanted it all hushed up. Church school. Reputation of the Anglican communion and all that nonsense." Victor rolled his eyes and finished his beer. "The parents were told he'd had to retire on ill health grounds, with immediate effect. Some of them might even have believed it. Want another?" He waggled his empty glass.

"Shandy again, please. Got to get me, the car, and the dog back home in one piece."

While he waited for Victor to return from the bar, Adam gave Campbell a bit of fuss and had a think. Wynter must have left a string of boys—and presumably girls—hating him. Had one of them nursed their wrath for so long that it had become a burning rage, culminating in taking their revenge first on the man's dog and then on Wynter himself? In which case they'd have somehow mistaken the victim for their old enemy.

Once Victor was back, and properly thanked for the drink, Adam asked, "Any idea where Wynter is now? Mum reckons he'd left the area, but somebody told me he'd been seen around."

"He did leave when all the scandal broke, but I'd be surprised if he went too far. Stanebridge born and bred, like me, and both of us the sort who'd not want to stray any distance." Victor certainly appeared to know a lot about Wynter, although it was a pity the Lindenshaw gossip machine hadn't run to where the teacher had got to.

"Mum also reckons he's been living under an assumed name back here. Perhaps that's just as well, given that he left under such a cloud." Maybe that was going too far in terms of being a leading question, but if the name change rang any bells with Victor, he didn't show it.

"Doesn't that only happen on the telly?"

"It happened in the last murder case Robin had." That had involved an equally nasty piece of work.

Victor nodded. "I read about that in the paper. Beggars belief."

"Truth's stranger than fiction, as they say. We had something strange happen, this weekend. We were up at the common, exercising Campbell, when that dog got shot. Naturally, we thought it was him at first. Longest minute of my life."

"Hell. That must have been awful." Victor cast a glance at Campbell. "Gary was up there, as well, although he must have missed that happening or he'd have mentioned it. I think he had Nick with him too."

"Nick?" Adam played dumb, not wanting Vic to know he'd done a bit of Facebook stalking. He now knew Nick was the guy who featured in the family snaps, and that the bloke had made tearful and incoherent comments on the posts Gary made around the time of his mum's death. He'd stopped short, by a whisker, of threatening to beat up the person who'd stepped in front of her car. Adam had briefly wondered whether Nick and Gary had been an item, but Gary had always been straight as a die, so they must have simply been the best of buddies.

Vic soon confirmed the theory. "Childhood pal and they've stayed thick as thieves. Charlotte—that's my sister—used to treat him like another son. He's been a real good mate to Gary, going up and helping him through the funeral and afterwards."

Adam nodded. "Gary didn't mention him."

"I've probably got it wrong, then. No, I know what it was. He and Nick went to that Rutherclere thing together. I was getting confused." Victor shook his head. "You'll find that happens as you get older."

"You're as sharp as ever, Victor." Although if he *was* getting confused, that might be another reason for his having been eased out of the Lindenshaw governing body.

"Thanks. Do you know anything about the man whose dog was shot, by the way?"

Adam leaned forward, lowering his voice. "If I tell you this, you have to swear to keep it secret. Robin would have my guts for garters if he knew I was sharing information."

"I promise."

"They reckon it was Wynter's dog."

"But the news said the owner was called Britz. Ah." The penny dropped. "The assumed name. No wonder I didn't make any connection." Victor paused, beer halfway to his mouth. "Here, are you doing a bit of legwork for your boyfriend?"

"You've got me bang to rights." Adam put his hands up in surrender. Rather than feeling cross at being found out, he was strangely relieved. He reckoned Victor would be equally forthcoming with information, now his whistle was wetted.

"Then you owe me another pint." Victor chuckled. "Tell Robin not to believe everything he hears. The rumour mill's been grinding about Wynter for years, and this will set it turning again. You know, back when Wynter left Lindenshaw, I can remember somebody swearing blind the bloke had clipped their son round the ear on a particular day in a particular place. But Wynter couldn't have done because at the time he'd been sitting two rows in front of me at an Abbotston Alexandra game. Folk won't accept it when you try to tell them the truth, though. They want to believe what they want to believe."

"Sounds like people with conspiracy theories." Time to introduce the subject of Tommy Burley, whose death Adam had briefly researched on his phone while walking Campbell. Finding hard facts had been a challenge, given the preponderance of wild speculation. "Which brings me to the next bit on Robin's shopping list. A young boy died in strange circumstances at Rutherclere, during the war."

"The Babe in the Wood. You talk about your mum being mysterious, mine used to clam up tight when anyone mentioned either him or the Rutherclere estate, well into her old age. Said we were never to go trying to get in there because bad things happened." Victor took another swig of beer. "What does Robin want to know?"

"If Wynter had any interest in it. There appear to be whole websites devoted to people airing theories."

"Not that I recall. Young Gary's mentioned it, though. He went to that Welcome One, Welcome All event, and he reckons several people got into trouble for trying to get down into the woods. Rutherclere estate management had it cordoned off, but that didn't stop them."

Interesting that Gary hadn't mentioned going there after he'd been to Pratt's Common, although he *had* been upset about his mum during that part of the conversation, so it might not have seemed important.

"What else does your Robin want to know?"

"Only who shot the dog and then did the shooting over at Lower Chipton, although he's not expecting you to know that off the top of your head." Adam sniggered. "But if there's anything else you can think of that the police should know about Wynter, even if it's just a reliable rumour, then I'd be pleased to pass it on. I promise you won't be charged with slander, so long as you only say it to me."

"I wish I could help but I'm as much in the dark as you are, and what little light I can shed I've done so." Victor's brows knitted. "There is one thing, though. The vicar at Lindenshaw, the one who wanted to cover up Wynter's misdemeanours. I'm sure he was something to do with the Babe in the Wood. Related to him or related to somebody who'd been involved at the time. I doubt it's relevant."

"You're probably right."

He'd report it back, though. With an added mention of Gary having been at Rutherclere, and there having been people trying to get in to the copse where Tommy Burley had died. Given that the Babe in the Wood had clearly been part of family folklore, had Gary himself been one of those trying to sneak a look? No matter how much Adam wanted his old mate not to be involved in this case, he appeared to be well and truly tangled up in it. Although knowing Gary, it was possible he'd simply been in the wrong place at the wrong time.

The conversation with Victor also begged two further questions: why was there a local assumption that the boy had been deliberately hurt, and what had Tommy Burley been doing going into the woods anyway?

Chapter Nine

While Adam was wining and dining in the Thursday evening sunshine, an irritable Robin was making his way to the interview room where Wynter was waiting for him, with Ben acting as watchman. Pru would be riding shotgun for this discussion, although she'd slipped off to the loo before they got stuck into questioning the witness.

Robin's frustrations centred around the strongbox they'd found, and Cowdrey's reluctance to let them open it. Their conversation had started well enough, the boss asking for his view on Wynter's character and receiving as impartial an answer as Robin could muster.

"Sounds nasty. I don't believe leopards change their spots that often, so I guess he's much the same now."

Robin, being of a similar opinion, had simply nodded and let Cowdrey continue.

"Was he the sort of man to kick up a stink about some wrong that had been done to him? Real or imagined?"

"Unfortunately, yes."

"So if it turns out he's totally innocent and we've prized open his private property without a warrant, he'll go apeshit. And if it turns out he isn't innocent, whatever we find will be inadmissible as evidence unless we get that warrant. Have we enough to apply for one?"

"Isn't a murdered man at Wynter's house and his having done a runner enough?" Robin had asked, but Cowdrey hadn't been swayed. He'd apparently had a similar situation early in his career, and it was a case of once bitten twice shy. Opening the box would have to await the outcome of the interview.

Robin took a deep breath. Had he composed himself enough? Would he ever be composed enough, however much time he had to prepare? What if Wynter suddenly confronted him with something like, *Chief Inspector Bright! I'm not sure I can take that title seriously when I have vivid memories of you picking your nose in the boys' toilet at school.*

Deciding he was just being a silly git who'd faced nastier bits of work than Wynter and had the upper hand, Robin opened the interview room door.

The teacher didn't present the daunting sight Robin had expected. That he'd be greying, balding, in his late sixties was as predicted, but it came as a shock that Wynter no longer gave off an air of overpowering authority. Perhaps that feature of the man had been exaggerated by memory.

Robin gave Ben a nod, then began proceedings. "Mr. Wynter."

"I'm afraid you've got the name wrong. It's Britz."

"You weren't Britz when you taught at Lindenshaw." Robin let the words sink in, relishing his old teacher's surprise and discomfort. "But we can discuss that when my colleague arrives."

As if on cue, Pru appeared at the door, which meant Ben could get back to his desk or off home, and they could begin the formalities of the interview. Once those were done, Robin asked, "You've been calling yourself Britz. Have you changed your name by deed poll?"

Wynter spread his hands. "No, Chief Inspector, I haven't officially changed my name. It's simply been easier to ditch Wynter for a while. I haven't done anything illegal, because I've made sure all my official dealings are in my real name."

"Whether you've done anything illegal is for us to decide." Although none of the team's searches had turned up the sort of identity fraud Abbotston officers had encountered before. As he said, all the official stuff was tickety-boo. "You can start by telling us *why* you did it."

"Did what?" Wynter shifted in his chair.

"Use an alias, for a start."

"If you know about Lindenshaw, you'll be aware of the lies that were told about me. Vile stuff. The easiest thing was to ditch the name that was associated with— Hold on. Bright. I remember you. You were in my class."

If only it were possible to control the colour of your face. Robin was sure all the blood had drained out of his, no matter how determined he was not to let his emotions show. He couldn't deny it—would this be the point at which Wynter screamed conflict of interests? Best to make what headway he could now. "I was. And I'm aware that you left the school under a cloud."

He wasn't entirely sure of the details—that was what Adam would be researching right now—but the shot had hit home.

Wynter jolted forwards, grabbing the table edge. "Lies. That's what the cloud consisted of."

"It isn't a lie that a man was found dead in your house. That you said it was a self-inflicted wound. And that you disappeared afterwards."

"I don't deny any of it. I found the body and I panicked, something of which I'm not proud. It occurred to me that if I reported it as a suicide, I could buy some time to get away. Suicides don't get the media interest that murders do. I grabbed a change of clothes and a washbag—literally only that—and went to ground."

"You have a habit of going to ground," Pru observed. "You left the area before."

"It's a free country, last time I looked. Have they created a law against moving house and then coming back again?"

"Not if you've an innocent reason for doing so."

"As innocent as a babe." Wynter, smirking, had relaxed once more: they'd got him rattled but now he was on the front foot again. "I like it here. My parents are buried in the churchyard at Stanebridge, as is my little brother. He died of whooping cough when he was five. I couldn't leave them with nobody to keep an eye on them."

The facts of that could be easily checked, if not the intention. "Nobody could argue with that, although leaving the scene of a crime is another matter entirely. You have to agree this instinct to hide away is the sort of thing a guilty person would do rather than an innocent one."

"Or a persecuted person. They shot my dog!"

"Who did?" Robin asked, not quite believing his luck at getting to a culprit so quickly.

"I don't know." Wynter sat back again, arms folded. "That's your job to find out."

Robin tried to stay civil, though it was increasingly a challenge. Not least because he was annoyed at himself at prematurely counting his chickens. "You said *they*. You must have someone in mind."

"I have plenty of people in mind, but there *is* a law against slander, so I won't mention any of them by name. Not while I don't know for certain." This was the old Wynter showing its face. Blustering, bullying, slippery. "Anyway, is it only the innocent who run? Have you never wanted to go to ground when something happened, despite knowing you weren't at fault?"

That was a low blow. Had it been a deliberate jibe at Robin's past, and how *he'd* wanted to hide away from the bullies who'd made his life such a nightmare back in his childhood? "I wouldn't have gone to ground if somebody had been murdered. In my house."

Pru, evidently worried at the interplay and how it was affecting Robin, cut in. "How did you know Fabian Saggers?"

"He was at school with me, believe it or not. Back in the Stone Age." Addressing Pru, Wynter had turned on what he clearly felt was his charm, a stereotypical old-fashioned manner of speaking to women. "He'd got back in touch and wanted to meet up again. He was going to be in the area and thought he'd kill two birds with one— Sorry, that's not the best analogy to use. Anyway, I realised that he was a bit lonely, and so I invited him to stay with me rather than put up at some awful overpriced bed and breakfast place. He said that all the prices had shot up locally because of this Rutherclere event."

"How could he get in touch with you if you were using an assumed name?"

"Because, my dear, he used the electoral register. I had forgotten to go the stupid website to say I didn't want my details shared."

Patronising git.

Robin had noticed Pru wince at *my dear*; he wished he could have Adam's opinion on the bloke. Adam had built up a knack of knowing which teachers needed an eye kept on them. The thought of his lover had a calming effect, as though he were in the room, saying Robin was doing a good job. Robin took up the questioning again. "And why did Saggers want to meet up after all this time?"

Wynter gave an airy wave of hand. "Oh, he wanted to touch base, as they say. Talk about the old days."

"Eh?"

"You took Saggers's wallet with you. Don't pretend." Robin waited to see what yarn the witness would spin this time.

"I won't. I don't."

Robin was certain that was a change of tack, and that Wynter had been about to deny the fact. How much had he been amending his responses depending on how much they knew, or how accurately they guessed? Wynter, who'd had his fingers pressed to his temples in thought—or in pretending to think—said, "I do remember thinking that if I took Fabian's wallet and car keys then there'd be a chance that people might believe it was me who'd been killed, so I'd buy myself some time. I didn't have the sense to take his car and leave mine. Like I said, not thinking clearly."

"If you wanted to complete the illusion, you should have left *your* wallet in his pocket too," Pru said.

"Oh, I couldn't have done that." Wynter appeared horrified at the notion. "I'd have had to spend *his* money, and that wouldn't be right."

"Oh, for fuck's sake." Robin took a deep breath. He should really leave this to Pru until he'd regained his temper.

Luckily she seemed to be on his wavelength and picked up the questioning. "You could have taken only your credit card with you and left the rest. You don't strike me as being a stupid man, and isn't this a stupid story you're telling us? Buying time to make an escape? How were we, or anybody else, going to be taken in for too long?" She leaned forward, elbows on the table, smiling sweetly. "So, did you shoot Saggers?"

"What? No. Don't be ridiculous."

"Maybe you found out he was the one who killed Buttons and you took an appropriate revenge."

Wynter sneered. "Don't be ridiculous. The person who shot Buttons killed Fabian. I'm sure of it."

"But you still insist you won't tell us who you think that is? Or list the many names you say you've got in your mind?"

"No." Wynter crossed his arms, sat back and stared at them defiantly. "And you can't make me."

"He's a bleeding nutcase," Pru said, once they were out of the interview room.

"You can say that again. Shame you can't keep somebody in custody simply for being a slimy git." They could legitimately hold Wynter on suspicion of murder for another few days, although they might not have enough evidence by then to charge him. No weapon, no apparent motive, no indication from Wynter that he was hiding his guilt, although Robin was certain he was hiding something. Perhaps some item would turn up in his car or among his belongings, once they got Grace poking around amongst them.

"Maybe releasing him would loosen his tongue," Pru suggested. "If he really is so scared for his life that he ran away, he won't want to be back in Lower Chipton."

"He didn't run far from the place, though. Seventy miles, if that." Robin glanced round at the sound of footsteps in the corridor. "Ben! I thought you'd gone home."

"I'm on my way. Just wanted you to have this." Ben handed Robin a scribbled note. "We had the details on Saggers rung through earlier. Medical report says he was shot at close range, probably as close as from the kitchen door. No evidence of a struggle or an attempt to escape."

"Very interesting. The killer was in the house with him, and presumably was somebody Saggers knew well enough to be at ease, even when whoever it was produced a gun."

Pru jabbed her thumb towards the interview room door. "That puts matey back in the frame."

Robin nodded, despite having his doubts. "Right, I'll handle the custody sergeant about getting our pal here a bed for the night. Sleeping in a cell might make him see reason. You two get off. Oh, sorry—" he slapped his forehead "—I'd forgotten. It could be useful to get some inside gen on Rutherclere, off the record. Ben, you couldn't persuade Carrie to go along to this wedding fair this weekend?"

Ben winced. "I'd rather have my teeth pulled out, sir, if it's all the same to you. Anyway, Carrie's away this weekend, so it's a few days free of party favours and centrepieces. Couldn't Pru go along?"

"Me?" The sergeant looked as horrified as if Ben had suggested she have her teeth pulled out. "I'm not that good an actress. What about you, sir?"

Robin cringed. "I'd feel like a spare part."

"Then you'd fit in fine, sir, if you don't mind me saying so." Ben chuckled. "Half the blokes at these things act like spare parts. They should have a groom-to-be creche."

Pru gave Robin a sly glance. "Talking of grooms, I believe you get same-sex couples visiting these affairs."

"That's true," Ben agreed. "Logically, it would be better for *you* to nose around, sir, as you've got a better grip on the bigger picture for this case."

Before Robin could protest, Pru asked, "What about you and Adam going along? He could pretend to be interested in fireworks and video recordings while you could keep an eye—"

Robin raised his hand. "Stop it right there."

"But why? Seriously, you'd be the best qualified of any of us to go undercover on this one. From every angle."

Pru was correct, although that still didn't make a comfortable notion for Robin to get his head round.

"Okay, I'll see what Adam says. Now go, before you make additional work for me."

He eyed the interview room door. Suddenly dealing with Wynter seemed a more enticing prospect than convincing Adam that he suddenly had a great desire to explore wedding venues.

When Robin got home, Adam was still awake in bed, reading a book about World War I fighter aces.

"Sorry if I disturbed you." Robin kissed the top of his head.

"You didn't. Can't sleep for whatever reason, so I'm fantasising about men in uniform. Inspired by your pinup, Biggles. How's it going?"

"Slow. How was your evening?"

"Interesting." Adam gave a potted account of what Victor had told him, none of which surprised Robin. "Not sure if it's worth calling up that vicar. I e-mailed Neil to see if he knew anything about the bloke, but all he had was a name. The Reverend Charles Edmunds.

He said he'd try to find out if they have a contact address for him now, assuming the bloke's still alive."

"If he strikes gold, can you forward the info to me? Although I'm not sure where it gets us. Sounds like Wynter wasn't a pervert back then, anyway, just nasty. He's no more pleasant now."

"Sounds a right charmer. Is he getting a night in the cells?"

"Yep. While I get a night with you." Robin stifled a yawn. "Not that I'll be any use in the romance department. But we'll be comfy."

"Yep." Adam laid down his book. "How do you *know* Wynter wasn't a pervert back then, though? He may not have tried it on with you, but that doesn't mean he didn't molest other little boys. Or girls. Sometimes physical and sexual abuse go hand in cloven hoof."

Robin shrugged. "I've been all over his record, and nothing's turned up apart from a few points on his licence for speeding. Not even a sniff of trouble on the paedophile front, and don't say that could be because he was never caught or never reported. I know about that."

"Glad to hear it. Don't forget, absence of evidence isn't evidence of absence. Sorry, doing it again. Telling you your job."

"I'll set Campbell on you if you don't behave. Remember how he sorted out Stuart?" Robin's ex-sergeant had been an unwelcome guest earlier in the year, one who'd seemed firmly ensconced before the dog had taken matters into his own paws. "Talking of marital matters . . ."

"Oh yes." Adam grinned. "That was what gets called a Radio 2 link. Too strained by half. Go on."

"I've got a favour to ask. It's to do with the investigation, so I wouldn't foist it on you if you're not willing. I'm simply pleading that you hear me out completely before you punch me."

"That bad, is it? Selling my body down Bosie's to fund a wider range of forensic tests?"

"The pinch hasn't hit that much. Yet." Bosie's was the only gay bar in Stanebridge and a constant source of humour.

Adam sniggered. "Go on. I must be bleeding barmy, but you have my assurance I'll listen."

"Okay, thanks." Robin took a deep breath. "At present, this case crystallises into several threads."

"I don't think threads crystallise." Adam sniggered again.

"Smart-arse. It's too late in the evening for you to be coming over snarky."

"Sorry. I promise to behave myself."

"First time for everything, I suppose. See if you can behave yourself this weekend too. Thing is, Rutherclere keeps cropping up, linked to happenings past and present. Nothing clear and obvious apart in terms of the present, apart from that bit of a punch-up on Sunday involving somebody the victim knew, but I've got a pricking in my thumbs."

"That should be good enough for anybody to take seriously. Your thumbs have got a track record of reacting when there's something to react to."

"Thanks." Robin was grateful Adam hadn't pointed out that in the first murder case he'd been allowed to take the lead on, the one which had been the catalyst to their meeting, said thumbs hadn't pricked quickly enough to save someone's life. He'd saved a few since, though.

"So what are you suggesting that needs me to be well behaved and to which I'll object so much that I'm going to take a swing at you?"

"I want to try a bit of undercover work. Get the lie of the land before we go down official channels."

"You don't want me to visit there? I don't think they allow school trips."

"Worse than that. I want you to come with me to a wedding fair they're holding on Sunday."

"Blimey." Adam, eyebrows raised, seemed stunned.

"Now do you see why I was worried about you punching me?"

"Surprisingly enough I don't want to punch you this time. I'm just a bit taken aback." Adam nodded slowly. "Right. So I'm going into this with open eyes, would we simply be attending the event so you can have a surreptitious snoop around?"

"You'd be having a snoop around, as well, if you wouldn't mind. Two sets of eyes and ears being better than one of each."

Adam, eyes narrowed, said, "And would we be casting two sets of eyes at the wedding fair stuff too? Or is it all an undercover op?"

"Of course we would." Robin swallowed hard. He was making a right mess of this. "I'm not going to pretend that this investigation isn't our primary motive, but anything that helps us move on a step or two wedding-wise has got to be a good idea. Hasn't it?"

Adam had a think, then grinned. "Okay. You're on. Only give me a proper briefing beforehand, will you, so I know what I'm looking for?"

"Will do, although it might have to wait until Sunday morning. By then *I* might know what we're after." Robin stifled another yawn. "Right, teeth and bed. I've said a proper goodnight to Campbell. Didn't want him fretting."

"Very wise. Although he's getting so many evenings out he can't complain about a bit of neglect. Hey, should we take him along on Sunday? We could say we were interested in having him as page dog."

"If I thought that was a serious suggestion, I'd be sleeping on the couch. Practice behaving."

Another snigger from Adam, followed by, "We're both so tired I don't have the chance to misbehave," accompanied Robin out of the door.

Chapter Ten

A night in the cells hadn't apparently done much to soften Wynter up. Maybe, as Pru had suggested, he felt the police station was the safest place for him to be, if he thought somebody really was out to get him. Robin resolved to let the bloke stew a bit longer, especially as this seemed to be another day of news coming in thick and fast.

Caz was shaping up well under Ben's guidance, and Robin felt confident he could be trusted to show her the right ropes. It wouldn't harm the lad's development, nor his future prospects, to have somebody under his wing. At the morning briefing, she was first to put up her hand to speak.

"Ben's not the only one who can do a bit of googling." That got everyone chuckling. "I was having a nose around some of our outliers. Treadwell's name turned up on the council site. Seems he was one of those who objected to the Rutherclere application for a licence to host weddings."

"His objection didn't work, then." Pru snorted. "I bet palms were greased to make sure the application got through. Or the old boys' network went into action."

Caz nodded. "I wouldn't be surprised. Although the total volume of objections was small and the grounds for them—increased noise and traffic, alongside historical parking issues—probably didn't cut any ice. Anyway, it wasn't only Treadwell's name that turned up. There were six objections lodged, and one was by Wynter."

"Interesting." Robin raised his hand. "Sorry, that sounded patronising. It really *is* interesting. Any other names on the list we know?"

Caz shook her head. "Not sure how it relates, though. Would you shoot somebody because they objected to your wedding licence? Especially if their objection hadn't stopped you."

"No, but feelings run high about the most ridiculous things. You'll find that when you're as long in the tooth as we are." Pru, sitting on the edge of a desk swinging her legs, looked barely more than a teenager herself. "I can imagine somebody having a blazing row about the subject and getting into a fist fight. Like the punch-up last Sunday about a parking space."

"A fight, yes, but not a shooting." Robin pointed out. "Good work, though. Anyone else got something?"

"Me. Or rather Jacquie Parker sent this along," Pru said. "Our mate Mrs. Croydon caught her last evening, when she was doing a check of Wynter's property. No sign anybody's been there, by the way." Seventeen Church Lane was now trussed up with police tape, like a large and bizarre birthday present. "Mrs. C. says that Wynter had a lady friend who's been coming to his house for the past year. Dora. Dinah. Something like that, she's not exactly sure. She reckons the woman's always expensively dressed, if a bit flashy."

"Penchant for wearing clothing like red high heels?" Robin asked.

"How did you know? Been peeking at my notes?"

"Prior knowledge. I think Ben and I may have met her at the village hall, when we were searching for Wynter's nest egg. Her name's Daisy Lockwood."

"Maybe she was after the same thing, sir," Ben suggested. "If Wynter wanted to make a clean break, then maybe he'd need to cash in whatever was valuable. That would explain why he hadn't got that far. He'd need to meet up with her for a handover."

"I like that idea." Robin pursed his lips in thought. "I wonder if she tipped him the wink that we'd been there? The timing of us searching the hall and his deciding to leave that pub without settling his bill is too suspiciously coincidental. He must have known the risk he was taking in doing a runner."

"Want me to find out about her?" Pru asked. "If she was in and out of the house, she could easily have walked in on Saggers. He might well have known her and not been suspicious. People tend to underestimate women, anyway, so he might not have had his guard up quick enough even if she produced a weapon."

Did that old-fashioned thinking still apply? And if that logic could be applied to Daisy, could it be applied to Kerry, who'd have lulled Saggers further into a false sense of security? "Did Kerry's alibi check out, Caz?"

"For Friday evening through to early Tuesday morning, yes. Unless the pal's lying, which I don't think she is because I checked some of her Facebook posts and there are photos of Kerry at the event. And out on the Monday night lash." Caz consulted her notes. "She left straight after an early breakfast on Tuesday, but she'd have had to be going like Lewis Hamilton to get to Lower Chipton in time to kill Saggers."

"Thanks. And yes, Pru, find out what you can about Daisy. I want to be forewarned and forearmed when we interview her."

"Talking of forewarned, sir," Ben piped up. "I've carried on poking around on the net ever since that Tommy Burley thing first came up. I was working on it yesterday while you were grilling Wynter."

"Don't you have any life away from a screen?" Caz asked.

"Better to kill time doing that than play spider solitaire," Ben said. "Which would have happened back in the bad old days here. Anyway, I've found a Harry on one of the forums, and a Fabian, which I'm guessing are our two, but I've also found a Treadwell there. Might be our bloke."

"Might well. Could be how he got to know Wynter, rather than meeting through charity work," Pru suggested.

"Or perhaps they already knew each other and *he* got Wynter interested. Or Treadwell might simply have been finding out more about the case, given the issues he has—or says he has—with people parking there to go gawping."

Robin gave Ben an encouraging nod. The constable had rapidly established himself as the team's king of the internet search. "Did you find anything else relevant?"

"Not sure. There's a definite feeling this is an unsolved crime. Most people don't buy the natural-causes verdict, despite the fact the doctor said the boy had an undetected heart abnormality that must have struck out of the blue and killed him outright."

"A bit like that footballer who nearly died on the pitch. Fabrice Muamba," Caz said.

Ben nodded. "Yes. Which is what some of the naysayers point out, but they get shot down in flames, most people being so determined that the medical report was either a cover-up by the doctor or sheer incompetence. I believe he retired not long after, which has been latched onto as being suspicious, although he was pretty old to start with."

"Both of which would be seen to support the incompetency theorists," Pru pointed out.

"You're right. Like most conspiracy theories, every aspect of what is definitely known about the case has been shaken out and turned upside down." Ben consulted his notes. "Once you eliminate the loony fringe—the boy was killed by aliens or ritual sacrifice and the like—the general view is that he was killed by suffocation, by somebody who was known to him, which is why there was no clear evidence of assault or him putting up a fight."

"Known to him and who had friends in high places, to be able to engineer the cover-up? Sounds like Jack the Ripper all over again." Pru was clearly unimpressed.

Robin leaped in to Ben's defence. "That sort of thing did happen back then. A cover-up happened with Wynter, remember, and that's not so long ago. Any names being bandied about for who they reckon did it?"

"Wouldn't naming supposed culprits online be libellous, sir?" Caz asked.

"Not under current law, although it's an area that keeps getting tested." Robin shrugged. "Most people assume you can't defame the dead. Is that the case here, Ben?"

"Yeah. Among the usual hints at politicians and minor royals—back to Jack the Ripper again, given the obsession with fingering them for that crime—two suspects crop up. One lived at Rutherclere itself. The Honourable Simon Greene. At the time he was the son and heir of the lord of the manor or whatever you'd call him."

"Why Greene?" asked Pru. "And if he was such an obvious suspect why did nobody investigate him at the time?"

Ben consulted his notes again. "He *was* questioned, but only in the general way that several people were. Whether they'd seen

Tommy and that kind of thing. What he might have been doing in the woods, which nobody seemed to have an answer for. The doctor was so adamant that nothing suspicious had happened and the inquest verdict so clear, that nobody took it any further. The fact that Culdover munitions factory was bombed the next day meant they had other matters to deal with, anyway."

Ben didn't need to elaborate on that story: everyone local had learned the story of the factory bombing when they were at primary school. Adam had included it as part of his pupils' World War II topic and he'd been telling Pru all about it a few months previously when they'd all met up for a Friday evening drink with her new boyfriend. The raid hadn't just obliterated the factory and all inside it—mercifully few workers at the time the raid had happened—but stray bombs had taken out a row of houses. Two children had died the next day, allegedly of delayed shock. For a town that had previously not been directly affected by the war, the bombing had been a bitter blow.

Still Pru persisted. "If it *was* murder, the killer would have been grateful to that bomb for deflecting attention. But the question remains: why are people putting Greene in the frame *now*?"

"Because he was a bit peculiar, for a start. Reading between the lines, I'd guess he was on the autism spectrum. He died quite soon afterwards too. Supposed to have been an accident with a gun he was cleaning, although inevitably people are calling it suicide. They even did at the time, according to some old letters someone turned up, but the inquest declared the death was due to the shock of the bombing, which Greene had become unhealthily obsessed with. He thought Rutherclere was the next target and decided to take matters into his own hands rather than leave it to Hitler. When Greene died, the direct line died too and post-war, the Greenes sold the place to an industrialist, Bowman, who was something like a second cousin. His family still own the place."

Robin noticed Chief Superintendent Cowdrey slip into the room; the boss gave him a nod, a mouthed, *Carry on,* and then leaned by against the wall, listening.

"Ben, you said there were two suspects," Robin said. "Who's the other?"

"This is where it gets like one of those clichéd television mysteries." Ben blew out his cheeks. "Gerald Edmunds. The local choir master. Never married. Lived not far from the estate. Knew Burley's family."

Cowdrey snorted and Robin thumped the desk he was perched against. "If the police charged somebody in on that amount of evidence we'd be all over the tabloids accused of harassment."

"Nah, sir." Pru grinned. "The tabloids would be the ones hounding Edmunds. Like pin the tail on the donkey. Pin the crime on the loner."

Robin took the point. "But *was* he a loner?" And why did that name ring a distant bell?

"Depends what you read. The Edmunds-did-it camp say he was a weirdo, whereas the Greene-did-it crew say he was extremely popular, and nobody had a word to say against him at the time. I bet some of the people on these forums have the safeguarding training, so they're saying that paedophiles build an image around themselves of being everyone's best pal. It doesn't ring true to me in this case." Ben spread his notes on the table. "Trouble is these two guys are damned in the conspiracy theorists' eyes, whatever they do. No hint of scandal means they've managed to get everything covered up. It's pathetic."

Pru gave him a sympathetic smile. "These things usually are. Like people who are convinced the world is flat and when you show them any evidence disproving the fact, they shrug it off by saying it's only a lie."

At last, Cowdrey spoke up. "This is all very interesting, but how does it get us any closer to catching Saggers's killer?"

The question struck Robin like a blow to the gut. They'd been so fascinated by Ben's account that they'd lost sight of the bigger picture. Best to be honest. "We don't know, sir. Not yet. Although everyone of interest—Saggers, Wynter, his mate Treadwell who threatened visitors to Rutherclere—all seem to be interested in Tommy Burley's death. The Surrey police have drawn a blank in terms of anyone local to Saggers who might have wanted him dead. The girlfriend seems on the level, and they're not aware of anyone threatening him. Wynter, on the other hand, is either scared stiff that someone's out to get him, or he's a very good liar."

"Do you think there's any mileage in his having been the intended victim?"

"That's what *he* maintains, but if Saggers was shot at close range, it doesn't square up."

Cowdrey shrugged. "No. But you'll work it out, although we haven't got forever for you to do so."

"I'm aware of that. Can I catch you about warrants, sir?" Robin waited for Cowdrey's nod of assent, then concluded the briefing, setting his team back to work before leading his boss into the corridor.

"Do you reckon you've got enough evidence on Wynter to justify forcing that box open?" Cowdrey asked, jiggling the change in his pocket restlessly. "What do you think he's got in there?"

"In reality, probably not, and no idea. I was thinking that with your average witness we could bluff him into opening it, but Wynter's too slippery for that approach. Ah, hang on." The distant bell from earlier rang clearer. "I've just remembered something else. May be a coincidence, but the vicar at St. Crispin's in Lindenshaw, the one who made sure all the problems with Wynter were kept hush hush, was called Edmunds. It might even be the same bloke if he was pretty ancient by the time he was incumbent here, although the Christian names don't quite match."

"Don't you remember him? He must have come to the school."

"No. We used to get the curate." Easy to remember *him*. Handsome bloke who'd stirred strange emotions in Robin's young breast. "I'll get Ben onto it."

Caz came into the corridor, hovered uncertainly for a moment before appearing to be on the verge of diving back into the incident room. Cowdrey hailed her. "Did you want us?"

"I thought you were finished. I didn't mean to interrupt." Caz twisted a bright yellow Post-it note in her fingers.

"We're almost done." Cowdrey gave her one of his rare smiles. "Out with it."

"I've been having a look at the Rutherclere website, because I didn't think we'd cross-checked that previously. There's both a list of staff and one of recent donors and a couple of names jumped straight out. Chris Curran's on there as a benefactor."

Cowdrey raised an eyebrow at Robin. "Well, well. Good work, Constable."

"There's more, sir." Caz's smile oozed waxing confidence. "Daisy Lockwood. Don't know if it's the same one as Chief Inspector Bright met at the village hall, but she's listed on the estate management team."

Robin's thoughts ran headlong. If Daisy worked at Rutherclere, she'd perhaps have access to things relevant to the Tommy Burley case. "Great job, Caz. Can you get back and see if there are any other connections?"

"Will do." She scuttled off, glowing with delight.

"Still not enough for a warrant, is it?" Robin said.

"No. You'll have to try persuasion. And *I'll* have to work the Curran angle again. That bloke's too closely connected to this for comfort. Especially as one of the cars in his possession is supposedly a black Jaguar F-Pace."

"Is it? You kept that quiet."

"I only just found out. It could have been a match for the SUV your witness saw, but what motive would a man have to kill his solicitor?" Cowdrey shrugged.

"Let's hope your contact has a suggestion."

"He didn't have half an hour ago when he told me about the car. Trouble is, they can't seem to pin anything at all on the bugger."

Robin was about to say something like, *They need us on the bloke's case*, but bit back on it. You should never tempt fate.

Robin decided not to waste any tyre rubber chasing loose ends, not until he was sure how they tied together. While Pru was deputed to ring Rutherclere to find out what trouble they'd had this past weekend—or in previous months—from Tommy Burley fanatics, he'd chosen to get on the blower to Treadwell, getting straight down to brass tacks.

"In our previous interview, you said you met Harry Wynter through the local Lions. Is that the truth?"

"Of course it is." Treadwell sounded both offended and puzzled at the question.

"Really? Would you give the same reply if your mate Jesus walked in the room and asked you?"

"Of course I would."

"But you've another connection. An interest in Tommy Burley. The Babe in the Wood."

The line went silent.

"Hello? Are you still there?" There was no chance this was the local mobile signal playing up; he'd rung Treadwell on his landline.

"You've caught me being economical with the truth, Mr. Bright. That's the old Adam coming through."

Robin, momentarily puzzled at the reference to his boyfriend, twigged that Treadwell must be referring to original sin.

"I *am* interested in that old case," Treadwell continued, "even if I tried to give the impression I wasn't. My vicar would say it was unhealthy and prurient. But I swear I was shocked to find Harry lurking about on the same forum."

Robin suppressed a snort. "As you said, you're very close to the part of the estate where the boy was killed."

"Yes. Not far down the road, the wall between the two bridges backs onto a wooded area."

"So, do you and your mates on the forum ever hop over that wall and visit the scene of death?"

"Technically, I'm only mates with Harry. The rest of them have the most ridiculous ideas. Ones I don't want to get involved with."

"Answer the question, please."

"Once. About six months ago. We're both a bit too old for going climbing over walls, although we managed it. To my shame I pretended I knew the exact place, but in reality I just took Harry to somewhere that vaguely suited the one old black-and-white photo of the scene. I expect I was miles away."

"What on earth did you hope to gain? Apart from putting your hip out?" So difficult to understand someone else's obsession, and what it might lead them to do.

"Harry said he had the notion that if he went there, he might better understand the case, but all we saw was lots of trees and bracken and what I suppose might have been the old icehouse in the distance. I think Harry simply wanted to get one up on all the others for having actually managed to get on the site." Treadwell paused. "He was being a bit mysterious all round. Said he had a theory but wouldn't share what it was."

"Did he say why he wouldn't share it?"

"No. He's the type who likes knowing something that other people don't."

Which accorded with his mysterious box and its contents. Time to get that bloody thing opened.

"Another thing. You lodged an objection to Rutherclere holding weddings on-site."

"You're damned right I did. It would be an absolute nightmare for us locals. Noise day and night, carrying for miles. Fireworks at midnight, music, bagpipers. And what about all the drunken drivers leaving the place in the wee small hours?" That had clearly struck a chord, one with which Robin could sympathise. People didn't seem to be content with weddings at the local church, a few snaps in the churchyard, and down the village hall for a shindig that ended at eleven.

"I thought they'd applied for letting rooms, as well," Robin said. "That would reduce the risk of guests driving when they'd had one too many."

"And raise the risk of more people using the place. What if they extended their business and opened up Rutherclere for conferences? No business would want the rooms left empty on days they're not holding weddings, not having put in all that investment. Imagine if they built lodges in the grounds. People staying there the year round. Swimming pools. Theme parks."

"Aren't you getting a bit carried away?" Robin rolled his eyes, despite the fact that Treadwell couldn't see him. "They've not put in any planning applications for any of those."

Treadwell snorted. "Yes, well, weddings today, holiday village tomorrow. It stands to reason."

Given that Treadwell seemed to be prone to exaggeration, Robin ended the conversation there and headed for the interview room again. While he waited for Pru to join him at the desk, he checked with the custody sergeant regarding Wynter's possessions. Among them—as Robin had expected—was a bunch of keys, including one for the car, a couple that must have been for the house and several others, of unknown purpose. One of these looked like it might fit the box's lock.

Wynter, who'd apparently been no trouble at all overnight and was quite biddable this morning, had been taken to the interview room a few minutes previously. Robin had guessed that he might have called a solicitor by now, but the custody officer had confirmed he'd refused all offers of contacting one. Wynter *had* made one phone call, to someone who might have been a girlfriend.

Pru, who'd arrived during the discussion, asked if this girlfriend was Daisy Lockwood.

"No idea, ma'am," the officer replied. "He was very cagey about it."

"Let's see if he's cagey about this." Robin signed for the bunch of keys, then set off to the interview room with them in one hand and the box tucked under the other arm.

Halfway down the corridor, Pru halted and said, "Got some interesting feedback from Rutherclere. Want it now?"

"Is it relevant to Wynter?"

"Might be, might not."

Robin, afraid that his courage might desert him if he dithered, said, "Surprise me with it, then. I want to strike while this iron's hot."

"Mr. Wynter," he said, as he burst through the door and plonked the box down onto the table. "Yours, I believe?"

Wynter leaped onto his feet, the most animated they'd seen him. "Where did you get that?"

"I think you know exactly where I got it. I was maybe ten minutes ahead of your friend Daisy in retrieving it from the village hall."

Wynter slumped into his seat, then straightened himself, clearly determined not to show defeat. Pru went through the process of setting up the recording equipment, the usual format of stating who was in the room, while Robin eyeballed his ex-teacher. *He's a pathetic old man. He can't hurt you.*

Once they were set to go, Robin, smiling as sweetly as he could manage, asked, "Is Daisy Lockwood your girlfriend?"

"She's my *lady* friend, yes."

"And you sent her to the hall to get this." Robin tapped the box.

"I won't deny that. There are some valuable things in there— valuable only to me, that is. Sentimental. Family items. I wanted to know they were safe, so I asked Daisy to retrieve them, knowing she had her WI key. She was extremely miffed that all she found was a box of old newspapers." He let out a snicker.

"There's nothing funny about this," Robin snapped. "If the box contains such important items, why was it under the stage at the village hall where anybody could have taken it? Why not at your house or in a safety-deposit box at the bank?"

Wynter sneered. "I think the bank question answers itself, given that all the local branches have been shut. And what if I wanted to access it out of Abbotston branch opening hours?"

"Most people would store valuable things at their own houses," Robin pointed out.

"Most people don't get burgled." Wynter sat back, arms folded again.

"Your house was burgled?"

"Yes."

"Why didn't you report it?" Robin would be spitting nails if Wynter *had* reported it and Caz had missed the fact during her checks.

"Because they didn't take anything. Didn't get any further than breaking the utility room window. Buttons saw them off. I hope he bit their backsides while he was at it." Wynter sniffed, rummaged out a handkerchief, and dabbed his eyes. "I miss the old idiot."

Robin experienced an unexpected pang of sympathy. *Idiot* was a term they often used for Campbell. "Why get Daisy to check on them now? So soon after you'd scarpered."

Wynter's eyes flicked up and to his right. Robin remembered older colleagues saying that was a sure sign of a witness being about to lie, although hadn't that now been disproven? "More evidence of what a state I'd got myself into. I was worrying about everything."

Robin tapped the strongbox again. "Perhaps you'd like to open this now and show us what you were so worried about? Rather than us have to apply for a warrant and attack the thing with bolt cutters?"

"Why should I? I've got nothing to hide."

"In that case, open it and prove it."

"No. You get a warrant, if you can. And let me tell you, if you damage that box or its contents in any way, I'll sue." Wynter sat back, arms folded.

Robin was suddenly nine again: Wynter sitting in his chair behind a desk in the classroom, about to launch into a sarcastic tirade about the state of Robin's handwriting. Robin swallowed hard, suppressing a wave of nausea. "Tell us about the time you and Treadwell went trespassing on the Rutherclere estate."

"Oh." Wynter waved a hand. "Only technically trespassing. We were doing some vital research into the murder of Tommy Burley."

"Really? You *do* know the site Treadwell showed you was nothing other than one he'd picked at random? He has no idea where Tommy died."

To Robin's delight, Wynter seemed as taken aback by that as by the arrival of the box. Eventually the man said, "Well, well. You can't trust anyone, can you?"

"Is that why Saggers went to Rutherclere on Sunday? To go poking around in the woods?"

"He wouldn't have been alone if he did. Plenty of interested parties intended to go. It's all very suspicious, this continued secrecy."

Robin shook his head disdainfully. Conspiracy theorists found everything suspicious that didn't fit in with their ideas.

Pru took up the attack. "They had a lot of trouble there. Several visitors were ejected for straying where they shouldn't have. Apparently marking off an area with ropes and putting up No Admittance signs doesn't deter people. They had to employ bouncers."

So that was the feedback she'd had from Rutherclere. Wynter appeared pleased to hear it. "See? That proves they're hiding something."

"Perhaps all it proves is that they don't want people trampling over their plants. It's woodland of national importance, I believe. A number of rare species."

Wynter snorted. "So they say. A matter of keeping people at arm's length."

"You believe Tommy Burley was murdered?" Robin asked, literally sitting on his hands as they ached to punch Wynter's nose.

"Of course. There is said to be evidence the boy might have been sexually assaulted first. Not very clear evidence, because forensic medicine wasn't as advanced then as now."

Robin leaped to his feet, steadying himself on the table. "How on earth do you know that? Or is this just another bit of airy-fairy speculation? A child died in the woods, therefore there *must* have been a sexual element? Or do you *want* there to be a sexual element?"

Wynter opened his mouth, then shut it abruptly. Robin, still leaning over him, waited for the man to continue: many witnesses felt compelled to speak, rather than endure a painful and threatening silence.

Eventually Wynter said, "I have to concede that's a valid point, and perhaps one that Saggers might have been guilty of at times. I had to put him right once or twice when he spoke of things happening as though it were fact rather than speculation. This was his pet theory, and he refused to tell me anything about where he'd got the evidence from. I probed him enough on the subject."

Had he really probed Saggers or was he only saying that to look smart in front of an ex-pupil? Several of Wynter's answers seemed to be produced for effect.

"Did that special knowledge get him killed?" Pru asked, while Robin seated himself once more.

"I doubt it. I told you yesterday: it was me being targeted, starting with Buttons being killed to scare me."

"But that can't be true, can it?" She leaned forward, confidingly. "Not about Saggers, anyway. He was killed at close range. Close enough for somebody to know it wasn't you."

"What?" Wynter jolted in his chair. "No. That's not right."

"It is. And the indications are that he might have known who shot him. No evidence of a fight. He knew you."

Sweat had begun to trickle down the witness's brow. "No. That's nonsense. I would never have killed him. Even if I'd thought he was the one who'd killed Buttons. I'm not a murderer."

"Then who is?"

Wynter, shrugging, clammed up again.

"Does Daisy give you inside information on Rutherclere?" Pru asked.

If Wynter was surprised by the change in direction, so was Robin. "What? No."

"Really?"

"Well, perhaps the odd bit here or there. Nothing vital."

"Do her employers know she does that?"

"All employees talk about their place of work. You probably do the same."

"Not when it comes to personal details about ongoing investigations. I'd be careful not to disclose any details, however innocent, to people who might put what they hear on some internet forum."

Robin tapped the table impatiently. This was getting nowhere. "If you continue to refuse to tell us anything of importance, then we have two choices. Keep you here for as long as we can or simply let you go, so I'm proposing releasing you, pending more enquiries. The usual restrictions will apply, so no travelling abroad or doing another runner." Robin motioned to Pru, who concluded the interview formally for the benefit of the recording, then switched the machinery off.

Wynter watched her, astounded. "You're letting me go? Just like that? Do I get my belongings back first?"

"Of course you do." Robin smiled, then gave the hammer blow. "Except the strong box. That we'll hold as evidence, pending obtaining a warrant. I can assure you we won't open it without one."

"I'll keep the key, then." Wynter, still seated, didn't act or sound like a man—innocent or guilty—yearning for release.

Robin pushed his chair back from the table. "Only the paperwork to do now. I bet you're delighted to have your freedom back, at least for the moment."

Wynter stayed rooted to his chair. "Only if I have police protection."

"Protection? Why do you need that?" Robin, eyes wide, wagged his head.

"Because someone tried to kill me. Remember?"

"But whoever shot Saggers got close to the victim. They knew it was him, not you." Pru pointed out.

"Then they were still trying to scare me, like they did by shooting Buttons. Poor Fabian was—what do they call it?—collateral damage."

That was the last straw. "How can we give you protection when we don't know who we're protecting you from? Why the hell won't you tell us?"

Wynter folded his arms again and kept his mouth shut.

"Then you'll have to stew in your own juice," Robin said. "But not at our expense. If you really are in danger, perhaps you'd be better off staying at Ms. Lockwood's house, rather than your own. Unless whoever it is you say you're scared of knows her too."

"Actually, they don't." Wynter's outlook appeared to brighten. "Good idea, Mr. Bright."

"Patronising git," Robin said, as he and Pru went back to his office, after leaving Wynter with the custody sergeant. "Would you act like that if you were truly frightened of somebody?"

"You might if you were having second thoughts about whether you were in danger, and were trying to buy time for some reason."

That didn't make much sense, but Robin let it ride. It had been a long few days and everyone was tired. "What if he killed his own dog and then killed Saggers? He's left trying to play the part of a scared man and failing miserably."

"Well, releasing him should stir things up. Mind you, I know he's a git, but I still wouldn't like to see him dead."

And even though Robin had wished the bloke dead years back, he wouldn't want Wynter's murder on his conscience now, but what choice did he have?

Chapter Eleven

Later that afternoon, Cowdrey rang to say he'd come up trumps with the warrant, having found a sympathetic magistrate and maybe having slightly exaggerated the strength of case the police were in possession of.

"So you'd better make sure this works," he'd murmured darkly, before ending the call, leaving Robin feeling extremely exposed. So far in his police career he'd done nothing to slightly stain let alone blot his copybook, so he didn't want to start now. He phoned Wynter on his mobile to tell him the good news, saying he and Pru would be straight round so the key had better be ready to put into action. As he'd suggested, Wynter was staying at Daisy's, which meant they could see her reaction too, and hopefully catch an expression of either guilt or some other revealing emotion when the contents were exposed.

Daisy Lockwood's house was the other end of Lower Chipton from Wynter's, and about three rungs up the social ladder. Robin's murmured speculation, as they pulled up outside, about whether it was the result of a spectacular divorce settlement was instantly countered by Pru's clipped remark that maybe the woman herself had been successful in the city, favoured with the sort of bonuses coppers never got a sniff at. Robin apologised for jumping to hackneyed conclusions, then got out of the car before she could give him a lecture about falling into the same traps he told other people off for stumbling into.

Daisy answered the door, insisting on seeing their warrant cards before ushering them in, despite the fact she must have known they were on the way. Part of a genuine fear on Wynter's behalf or simply a touch of sheer bloody-mindedness given that she must have recognised Robin?

After making sure they wiped their feet on the mat, she led them into a large, elegantly decorated lounge, where Wynter was standing in front of the hearth, moving from one foot to the other like a nervous schoolboy.

"Well, Chief Inspector," he said, with unconvincing heartiness, "still the nonsense with the strong box? I'm afraid it'll turn out you obtained a warrant in vain."

"We'll see about that." Robin looked around him for a suitable place to put the box down, afraid to mark one of the pristine surfaces.

"Bung it on this old table, Chief Inspector," Daisy said, pointing to an antique that would be beyond his and Adam's combined price range.

"Are you sure? The corners are pretty sharp."

She waved her hand airily. "Oh, don't worry about that. It's knocked about for two hundred years, I daresay it can take it." She turned to Wynter. "And stop fussing, Harry. Whatever you say or do, this box will be opened by the police. Perhaps it's better to have it all out in the open, given what's happened."

"I agree with you, Ms. Lockwood. Your friend Mr. Wynter has been far too economical with the truth." Robin directed a hurry-up gesture at his old teacher.

When that had no effect, Daisy said impatiently, "Do get a move on, Harry. Or I'll come and get your keys and open the damn thing myself."

Still muttering protests, Wynter slowly produced the bunch of keys, then went through an unconvincing pantomime of finding the right one and fitting it to the lock. He turned the key with surprising ease, but when he first pulled up the lid, he almost let it fall again. "What the fuck?"

"Harry! Language."

Wynter ignored Daisy's reprimand, too busy rummaging through the box's contents, which appeared to be entirely composed of newspaper cuttings, and not very old ones at that.

"Is there a problem?" Pru asked.

"A problem?" Wynter swung round angrily. "Have you been interfering with this?"

"Of course we haven't. *I* always follow procedures," Robin stated. "Are you saying these contents aren't what you expected them to be?"

"No. Yes."

"Harry, do stop being an ass." Daisy carefully shut the box, then pushed it towards Robin. "Whatever was in here clearly isn't what he was expecting. That's true, isn't it, you daft old sod?"

"Yes." Wynter slumped into a chair. "All gone. Replaced by a load of old tat."

"Are you going to tell us what should have been there?" Robin asked.

"No. What's the point? It isn't relevant, anyway."

"It's up to us to decide what's relevant." Robin felt he was continually banging his head against the proverbial brick wall. "I should do you for wasting police time, but I really can't be arsed." Catching Pru's astonished look at his having used such an expression, Robin made a mental note to wind his neck in. He couldn't keep letting Wynter get under his skin. "We'll be back."

He picked up the box, then turned on his heels without another word, Pru following in his wake. Once they'd headed down the drive, he halted. "Sorry about the abrupt departure. He gets to me. It was either leave or punch his supercilious gob."

"I'd happily slap him too." Pru gave Robin an anxious smile.

Time to get back to proper business. "I didn't notice how Daisy first reacted to the substituted box contents. I hope you did."

"She struck me as being amused, as opposed to old panic pants. I thought he was going to have a heart attack." Pru rolled her eyes. "Somebody must have got there before all of us, and swopped over the contents. That change must have been made relatively recently, unless Wynter hasn't checked his cache in ages."

I should have worked that out, rather than angsting. He shut his eyes briefly and took a calming breath before continuing. "That means they'd have to have known about the contents, known where he'd hidden it, and got access to his key. Who'd be best placed to do that?"

"What about Mrs. Croydon, popping in and making a copy in a bar of soap like they do in the old films?"

"That's as daft as some of Anderson's ideas used to be. And don't suggest we have the box fingerprinted."

"That *would* be daft. Anybody with an ounce of sense would wear gloves."

Robin weighed the box in his hands. "If only this bloody thing could talk. Whatever was in here must have been important to other people, not just Wynter. What about Saggers himself? If Wynter had been gassing on about what he'd got and where he'd hidden it, Saggers might have decided *he* wanted the stuff, especially if it related to Tommy Burley."

"I like that idea, sir. Maybe that was why he invited himself to Wynter's house. If he got here Friday or Saturday, he'd have had time to snaffle the key, then slip into the hall when Wynter was out walking the dog, or something. What he found got him killed."

"Hold on." Robin put the box on the ground, then glanced up at the house, where Wynter was watching from the front window. While logic said they should leave the rest of the conversation until they were in the car, their continued presence likely couldn't help but make the bloke feel more uncomfortable. "That's too tight a timescale, surely? To open the box and let somebody else know about the contents without Wynter becoming suspicious."

"Unless he met somebody at Rutherclere on the Sunday, told them—or showed them—what he'd found and . . . I'm not sure what. Need to think about it."

"Okay. Don't let me stop you. But it's always possible Saggers got that information earlier. Maybe he met up with Wynter before last weekend and found a sneaky way of getting a copy of that key. People do sometimes put down their bunch of keys when they're at a mate's house."

"Irrespective of where and when, how would he know the right one to copy?"

Robin shrugged. "If it were me, I'd eliminate all the obvious house or vehicle keys and make an impression of all the rest."

"What about Daisy herself? She would be in the best position to get a copy of the key, or even use the original, and she certainly knows more than she lets on."

Robin took a deep breath. It was possible: Daisy had spoken about things being better out in the open. "She's the smart one of the pair. Treats him like he's a silly boy."

"Maybe he likes it that way. Turns him on."

Robin didn't want to contemplate, not for an instant, what turned Wynter on, although he'd be pleased that it wasn't children. "Right, let's go back in there. Ask him about Saggers and keys." Bringing the box with them, they headed for the house once more but had barely got halfway there when Daisy opened the door.

"I'm glad you've come back," she said, with a bright smile. "I think I've persuaded the old duffer to be helpful for once."

"If you have, we'll be very grateful." Robin wiped his feet on the mat again, then made his way to the lounge, where he found Wynter leaning against the mantelpiece. "Did Fabian Saggers know about whatever you kept in that strongbox?"

"Tell him the truth, Harry," Daisy snapped. "Stalling will get you nowhere."

Wynter passed his hand over his brow. "Yes, he did. You see, what was in there is relevant to the Tommy Burley case. Fabian was bound to be interested."

At last they were making a bit of progress. "And would he have had the opportunity to get his hands on your keys, either this past weekend or previously?"

"Not this weekend. I made sure they didn't leave my sight."

"So you already had reason to mistrust him?" Pru cut in.

"I . . . I began to feel I may have been unwise letting him stay. He was too determined to see everything I had that was relevant." He gave Daisy a sheepish grin. "You were right, old girl. I shouldn't have trusted him."

Robin gave Daisy a quizzical glance. "Did you know something about Saggers to make you distrust him?"

"Not personally, but he'd been in contact with Rutherclere a lot. Made rather a nuisance of himself, really, wanting information about Simon Greene and about the Bowmans. The people who bought the property post-war," she added. "He was a total pain in the backside."

"Talking of information, did *you* feed Mr. Wynter here with relevant information from Rutherclere?"

"Only the odd bit here and there. Nothing earth-shattering, because there's nothing earth-shattering to share." She jabbed a finger at Wynter. "Don't argue. Just because you don't want it to be anything to do with your pal Edmunds."

"Edmunds?" Robin asked. "Is that Charles or Gerald?"

"Eh?" Wynter appeared shocked at Robin knowing both the names. "Charles has been a pal of mine for years. He's Gerald's nephew, and if ever a man was cruelly used, it's him. Too many people spout a load of old tripe about his role in the case. He wasn't a pervert and he didn't kill Tommy Burley."

"That's because Tommy Burley died of natural causes," Daisy said, with a sigh. "Didn't he, Chief Inspector?"

"That's the official view." Robin ignored Wynter's snort of disbelief. "Mr. Wynter, your friend Saggers seems to have been a determined individual. Could he have been in a position *before* last weekend to have made a copy of your keys?"

"You met up with him, didn't you? At his office?" Daisy reminded him.

"Oh, yes, but I—" Wynter halted, frowning. "I left my briefcase in his office and had to go back for it. I think my keys would have been in there. Do you remember I said there was something fishy about the whole episode, Daisy? That I couldn't believe I'd been as daft as to go and mislay it?"

"And I said you'd had too much red wine at lunch to know one way or the other." Daisy chuckled, giving Robin a knowing look. "Saggers could have his keys copied three times over when he's had a few."

So it *was* a possibility. Time to check another line. "Does the name Chris Curran mean anything to you, by the way?"

Wynter shrugged, although Daisy said, "Rings a bell. Might be to do with Rutherclere."

"One of your donors."

"Ah, that's why it's familiar, then. Don't think I've ever met him—or her—though."

"Him. Not the sort who you'd think would be donating his hard-earned dosh to support our country heritage."

"We don't judge, or ask questions, Mr. Bright. We simply smile and take the money."

"What about dealing with unwanted publicity, though?" Pru cut in. "There was an altercation at Rutherclere on Sunday."

Chapter Twelve

When Adam checked his phone at the end of the day, he found the usual message from Robin trying to predict what time he'd be in and, for once, saying that it might be earlier rather than later. Adam replied, saying he'd have a pasta bake ready to heat through, as the day was turning distinctly autumnal. Thank God he'd finished doing his interview-by-pub-garden stuff the last few evenings, as the forecast promised this would be a colder night.

Adam hadn't intended doing anything this Friday night but going home and staying home. The children would be back in school on Tuesday, so every chance to top up his energy reserves had to be grabbed with both hands. He'd curl up on the sofa with Robin—and if he wasn't home, Campbell—and chill.

When Adam pulled into his driveway, he spotted Neil Musgrave jogging along the road, which was no surprise given that the vicar had been told he needed to lose weight so was on a health kick. He'd shed half a stone and was determined to lose more, and one of his usual routes took him past Adam's house.

"Hello!" Neil stopped, clearly pleased to have a chance to get his breath back. "Any luck with your house purchase yet?"

"Not at the moment. Once bitten, twice shy and all that. We're leaving it to the new year, now." Moving house had become a bit of a nightmare. They'd given the tenant in Robin's flat adequate notice, but then the sale of the property had fallen through at the last moment, and they'd decided not to make a move until that was all cut and dried. They had another tenant in on a short let and would see where things went after that.

"I hear your Robin's trying to get hold of the last incumbent at Lindenshaw. I think the parish secretary will be able to find an address, but he'll need the devil's own luck to get through Charles Edmunds's door. The man's a bit of an oddity. Doesn't watch the television. Can't stand the police."

The television bit Adam could understand, but the mistrust of the police wasn't the usual sort of attitude for a clergyman to have. "Why's that?"

"Couldn't say."

"Does that mean *shouldn't* say?"

Neil produced his habitual throaty roar of a laugh. "You always were smart, and being with Robin seems to have made you even cannier. Yes, I do know why he's cagey but I wouldn't reveal it to anyone. Not quite sanctity of the confessional, although I'm sure you get the picture. He might talk to *you* though. He doesn't live far away. That retirement village outside Upper Chipton."

Which wasn't far from Lower Chipton. Did that signify anything?

Neil went on. "He's always had a genuine interest in education and giving him a little inside gen—nothing unprofessional but so that he felt special—might earn you a heap of information in return. If you're allowed to get involved with investigations, of course."

Adam grimaced, thinking of the chance meeting with Gary, and other stranger coincidences there'd been in the past. "They seem to want me to get involved with *them*."

"Life's like that, isn't it? Maybe it's a sign from the Guv'nor"—Neil jerked his thumb heavenward—"that he wants you to take a hand. I'll text you Edmunds's contact details, then you can decide how you want to play it."

"Thanks. I think."

Neil chuckled, cuffed his arm, and ran off, leaving Adam wondering how he was going to put this idea to his partner.

Robin was in at a decent time, looking lathered. He went through the usual procedure of changing his shirt and getting freshened up before wolfing down his dinner like he hadn't been fed in weeks.

Adam's granny always used to say that thinking was a hungry business, so Robin's brain must have been working double and triple time. Once the meal was done, they took a pot of decaffeinated coffee into the lounge, where he gave Adam a description of what the day had brought.

"So you think Saggers got his paws on this stuff, then somebody found out he had it, and for whatever reason that triggered his killing? I'll just about buy it as a theory," Adam said. "Where does the dog come into it?"

"No idea. Any suggestions gratefully received." Robin smiled wearily.

Adam shrugged. "I was thinking about coincidence, earlier. I know it happens, irrespective of people believing there should be a link between things. What if it was killed by a lunatic who simply didn't care? Wanted blood, like those kids who get hold of a gun and let rip in a school. They don't care who they kill, so long as somebody cops it."

"In that case it's probably even more urgent to get our hands on him. I say *him* because it's usually a bloke in those cases. It wouldn't be Gary, would it? He's never shown any inclination to go rogue?"

"No, that doesn't sound like him," Adam said, although how often had friends and family stood in the dock and sworn that their nearest and dearest wasn't the sort of person to do what they were accused of, and it turned out said person was guilty as sin? Gary fitted the profile of white male, skilled with guns, and he'd been up at the common. But Gary had always been the joker in the pack, not the usual loner, especially when he'd been spinning one of his yarns like the story of how he got his scar. "Anyway, his car had gone by the time we got back to the car park."

"Somebody could have moved it for him." Robin gave Campbell—who'd come over to give him a bit of affection—a rub along his back. "I know, boy. Clutching at straws. Things might be moving forward, though." He reached to touch a small wooden table with his free hand. "We've got a connection between the firm Saggers worked for and the Tommy Burley case. We had Ben ferreting around, and it turns out one of the partners of the firm came down during the war and made what might have been a guilt payment to Tommy's mother."

"Did Saggers know that, which prompted him stealing the box's contents, or was he asked to get his hands on whatever Wynter had?"

"I can't ask him, can I? Sorry, shouldn't be tetchy. We don't know. But it would make sense if he'd been going through his firm's records and found reference to the payment. Or if Wynter had mentioned the solicitor's name—it's an unusual one—as being cited in the crap he kept in that strongbox, then Saggers might have decided to nick the stuff, in case it was potentially incriminating for one of their clients." Robin yawned. "Not that I can make out much incriminating from what Wynter said, but he didn't make the connection we have, and I'm not sure he'd recognise something of value under his nose if it didn't accord with what he was looking for."

"I bet Saggers was stringing him along. Did you say Wynter talked about a foiled burglary? What if that was Saggers, or some scrote working for him, trying to get a copy of the key?"

"Could be. It could also be Wynter didn't report the burglary as he was genuinely scared he was being targeted and didn't want to make it worse. There's no use seeking logic with him, though. He didn't bother with a solicitor when we had him in custody."

"Who does he use? If it was Saggers's firm, it might make sense not to call them. Although he could call the duty solicitor."

"But he didn't know about the link between what the box held and Saggers, he—" Robin stopped. "Excuse me. Got to text Ben."

"Feel free. I assume either you've realised you love him or I've said something clever."

"Not quite, but you've given me an idea. Let me quickly give him a job to get started on in the morning." Robin's thumbs danced over the phone screen. "Done. Sorry about that. That firm has got at least one dodgy client, although we've got to keep our hands off him. He's got a link to Rutherclere in terms of being a donor. I want to know if he's got any other connections."

"But didn't you say you're supposed to be keeping your hands off?"

"Finding out information isn't touching anyone." Robin yawned once more. "Sorry, I haven't asked about your day."

"Oh, same old. I saw Neil, by the way. He almost ran into me as I got out of the car. These bloody runners and their iPods. Oblivious to everything."

"I keep seeing him around, playing at being Mo Farah. How are things in cassock land?"

"Interesting." Adam related the conversation concerning Charles Edmunds. "So off he ran, leaving new ideas in his wake as always. Given Edmunds's supposed hatred for the police, do you want me to go and talk to him? I could arrange something for tomorrow or Monday, if you feel he's got anything to bring to the table."

"If he could tell us what was in that bloody box, especially if he can remember a few of the names mentioned, he'd be loading the table with a feast. If we had some idea of what he knows by the time we go to Rutherclere on Sunday, all the better. You've not forgotten, have you?"

"How could I? Highlight of my week."

Robin yawned again. "Sorry, got to get to bed." He got up, then leaned over, giving Adam a kiss and ruffling his hair. "You're turning into that sidekick the detective always has in mysteries."

"Oi! I'm not as thick as Hastings is made out to be."

"Never said you were. I wish a few of the coppers I worked with were as smart." Robin gave him another kiss, tickled Campbell behind the ears, and headed for the stairs at the same time as Adam's phone pinged at an incoming text from Neil. He'd provided a mobile number for Edmunds, and confessed that he'd taken the liberty of contacting him in advance. *Just in case he thinks you're trying to sell him something. He likes salesmen less than he likes policemen.*

Adam thanked Neil, resisting saying that those sorts of attitudes were unbecoming of a clergyman and how pleased he was that Edmunds wasn't the vicar now. But he managed to create a polite enough text to send Edmunds, referring to Neil's introduction, and asking to meet over the next few days. He gave the excuse that he was conducting research into local stories, with a view to publishing a book. It was an innocent enough lie, and maybe once they'd both retired he'd actually be doing it. *Campbell and me: our lives as detective chief inspector's sidekicks.*

"You could have the starring role if they make it into a telly series," he said to Campbell, who gave him a withering look. "Yeah, I agree. Bad idea. You're above such things."

This time he'd be making sure that Campbell wasn't involved in any denouement to the tale. Twice the dog had come charging to the rescue, but the third time might prove unlucky; the thought of that dead Saint Bernard was going to haunt Adam for a long time.

Chapter Thirteen

Saturday, those in Abbotston police station not on duty were usually watching or playing sport, going round the supermarket, taking the kids to the park, or meeting up in some pub for a leisurely pint or two. That was what weekends were made for, not for sitting in an office. But when a big case was on, everything changed, and while Cowdrey always made sure his officers got a break—an exhausted team was no use—those breaks didn't necessarily work around the normal schedule.

At least they had a late start, the briefing being delayed because Pru had managed to get an emergency dental appointment first thing, and given the rarity of those at weekends, she wasn't cancelling it. When she appeared, still numb in the mouth, she was faced with a barrage of banter, until Cowdrey's arrival put an end to jokes about too many sweets or slurring her words because she'd had whisky on her breakfast cereal. The boss was in to give a media briefing on a nasty sexual assault which had taken place in Abbotston on Wednesday evening but which had been reported late on Friday because the victim had been left so scared. Robin's previous sergeant, Anderson, would be taking the lead on it, and holiday time meant the local teams would have to be flexible. At times like this you had to pool resources and work with who was available.

The briefing started, and as so often it was Ben, shifting uneasily in his seat at being the centre of attention, who got the informational ball rolling. "Just as well we were later meeting up. I found out this morning that Curran's related to the Bowman family, through his mum's side. His sister keeps a family tree on one of those heritage sites, and it's all detailed there."

That made coming in at a weekend feel better. "I bet that's why he donates to Rutherclere; he's probably better off than the owners."

"Might be a nice way to launder your money too." Cowdrey rolled his eyes. "Good work, Ben." He turned to Robin. "He was Saggers's client. They were both here this weekend. Is he linked to the murder?"

"He might be. Curran couldn't have killed the dog, because of the timing of the row in the Rutherclere car park, but he could have killed Saggers. Pru, you were looking into his whereabouts?"

"Yes. When the officer took his details at Rutherclere, he said he was staying that night at Langley Hall." Pru spoke carefully, given her numb mouth, taking her time over the treacherous sibilants. "Hotel confirms he was there from Saturday morning through to the bank holiday."

"Langley Hall. He's got to be loaded." Caz voiced what must have been everyone's viewpoint. Langley Hall was the most exclusive hotel in the county.

Cowdrey sneered. "Loaded enough to pay for the best brief, and to keep evading justice."

"Got any coppers in his pockets, up in London, do you think?" Robin asked.

"I'd like to say no, but we all know what happened at this nick, and corruption can creep in anywhere." Cowdrey shrugged. "Seems to be a history of that firm helping to cover up serious crime. You'd better tell the team what you discovered yesterday."

Robin related the tale of the box, the missing contents, and what they might have consisted of. "Logically, the next man to interview is Charles Edmunds, but I've heard he hates the police. I know." Robin raised his hand at his team's angry murmuring. "It's a murder case, so he's going to have to lump it, at some point."

"That'll take a miracle," Caz said. "I got in touch with the church secretary yesterday, and she said there'd be no point contacting him as he'd refuse to grant us an interview. I was about to tell the team that," she added defensively.

"Well, seems like we got our miracle." Robin grinned, wondering if Neil taking his exercise past their house hadn't been coincidental. "Came last evening in the form of a mediating vicar, and while Edmunds isn't ready to talk to us, he *will* talk to Adam. He's meeting up with the bloke and picking his brains over. I don't think the vicar's tipped Edmunds the wink on Adam's connection to us." He turned to the boss. "Unusual, I know, but it may save time."

Cowdrey murmured assent, then asked, "Are we working on the premise that Saggers found some connection between Tommy Burley's death and one of the present crop of Bowmans? They're related to the original owners, who might have visited Rutherclere during the war, if they were related to the Greenes."

"So somebody silenced him to help protect the family name?"

"Why does it have to be protecting the family rather than protecting a specific person, sir?" Ben asked. "Tommy Burley died seventy odd years ago. If his killer was a child themselves, they'd only be in their late eighties now. They could have murdered Saggers."

"I accept that children do deliberately kill each other." Pru didn't need to elaborate; everyone in the room could name an example. "But do eighty-year-olds go around toting guns?"

"Don't be ageist," Robin said. "You don't turn into a saint when you start drawing your pension."

"What's an old person got to fear, though? They can always plead they're too infirm to go to trial. We've seen that time and again." Pru had another valid point: that had been a blight on those trying to get justice for victims of historic sex abuse. "And given that the crime was committed so long ago, there'd be no reliable evidence against the accused, anyway. Wouldn't Crown Prosecution Service laugh it out?"

"It could still be a disgrace to the culprit's family," Ben pointed out. "Stain on their reputation being greater if the killer is alive."

Robin rapped the nearest desk. "Let's keep to what we know, rather than speculating. By Monday we might have more of an idea what was in that box. Anybody got any other updates?"

Shaking of heads all around the room. All the usual avenues—people spotted acting oddly near the scene of either of the shootings, independent evidence of threats to either Wynter or Saggers—seemed to be drawing blanks. Nothing had turned up in terms of Wynter's assumed name, either. He hadn't been given a new identity because of a witness protection scheme, and he had no previous criminal record under either name, apart from a conviction for drunk driving five years previously. Saggers was clean as a whistle.

Robin sighed. What if this case fizzled out without a solution? Shuddering, he had a sudden vision of future generations digging into the case of the Dog on the Common or The Man in the Cottage, *their* equivalent of the Babe in the Wood. Who would they put in the frame for it? Probably an ex-pupil, perhaps Robin himself, given his animosity towards Wynter.

Get a grip.

Pru, who seemed to be able to pick up when his confidence was waning, said, "What if killing the dog wasn't meant as a warning? What if it was much simpler? You know, if Wynter had kept the dog for protection, killing it would have made him vulnerable. And it would mean having a second attempt at burgling his cottage would be easier."

While Robin appreciated the time Pru had earned him to get his act together, it wasn't the brightest idea. "That's possible. But why not simply poison the thing? Chuck a contaminated piece of steak into the garden?"

"Robin's right," Cowdrey said. "Have you ever stalked an animal and tried to shoot it? I have, in the Highlands, and it's not easy. I know pet dogs aren't as tricky as a stag, but . . ."

They took the point. The shooting of Saggers was, in a way, pretty routine. The clichéd three points of means, motive, and opportunity would come together, and they'd have their man or woman. The shooting of the dog seemed to make little sense measured against any of those criteria, although they now knew for certain that it hadn't been the same weapon used for both shootings. Not even the same type, Saggers having been attacked with a sawn-off shotgun using a silencer, whereas the dog had been the victim of a hunting rifle.

A young uniformed officer—Robin hadn't seen her before, so she must have arrived when he was on holiday—popped her head round the incident room door. "Sorry to interrupt you, Chief Superintendent. There's a call for you."

"Excuse me." Cowdrey raised an eyebrow at Robin, then left.

"Might be as well if you all tidy your desks and then go home for a break," Robin said, once the boss had gone. "Get your minds clear and we'll see how things look on Monday morning. Unless we have any unexpected developments."

Sod being busy operating his law, one of those developments came before they'd finished clearing up, a hurried text from Cowdrey asking Robin to keep the team together as he had news to share once he got off his landline. The anticipation built, Caz glancing up at the office door every time somebody went past. Robin kept calm by an intriguing text from Adam.

Meeting Edmunds for lunch at Bosie's. No idea why he's chosen that particular venue. Will update later.

Was it relevant that Edmunds had chosen to meet at a gay bar? Bosie's—named after Oscar Wilde's lover, rather than a reference to the Australian name for the googly, which had confused at least one visiting cricket team—had allegedly gone upmarket. While it still catered to the rainbow flag trade, according to Trip Advisor the food had improved from better-end pub grub to decent bistro-type cuisine. Edmunds might have been attracted by the smashed avocado on toast rather than the clientele. And if it turned out the bloke preferred his own sex, why did that matter? There were plenty of gay vicars, hard-line Christians notwithstanding.

Robin replied with, *Will this be a case of exit, in pursuit of a bear?* He wasn't so depressed at the lack of progress in the case that he couldn't make a naff Shakespearean joke.

The reply of *Don't know whether to laugh or groan!* gave him his first chuckle of the day, one he swiftly suppressed when Cowdrey came into the incident room.

"You have news for us, sir?" Robin said, coming out from his own office.

"Oh, yes. That was my mate from the Smoke, the one who's got his eye on Curran. Apparently they've arrested him. But not for dealing drugs."

"For killing Saggers?" Ben asked, almost leaping out of his chair in excitement.

"No, although it's for possession of a firearm without a licence and in a public place. He's saying it's been planted on him." Cowdrey rolled his eyes. "And this gets better. My mate reckons it could be a hunting rifle, although whether it's the same type that was used to kill the dog, a Blaser R8, only time and forensic tests will tell."

"The firearm has to be a coincidence," Pru pointed out. "If Curran was in a fracas at Rutherclere, he couldn't have been shooting the dog. The times don't work—and we know when the scuffle was in the car park because we have no end of witnesses, including one who recorded it on his phone and had a time and date stamp on it."

"And the time when the dog was shot has to be correct, because you witnessed it, sir, and you weren't going to get that wrong, were you?" Ben observed.

"Hardly. Although we didn't actually see the dog go down. We heard a shot, then found his body—it was still warm and from the state of the bleeding, the wound appeared very fresh." Robin had been racking his brains, in case he'd missed some vital clue that would put the time in doubt. He and Adam had discussed the affair only that morning at breakfast, Adam certain he'd not seen the dead dog when he'd stood up to throw the ball from the top of the ridge. Although there must have been a live one in amongst the bushes.

"Could it have happened prior to you hearing the shot, and what you heard was a second shot, not the fatal one?" Caz asked.

"I don't think so. In that case, the first would have been a lot earlier, because we didn't hear any other shots all the time we were at the common. It would also mean Adam's blind as a bat, so blind he'd miss seeing a dead dog, and he's not." He turned to Cowdrey. "Curran could have shot Saggers, though. Is your mate going to find out what he was doing on Tuesday morning?"

"I've suggested he work it into his questioning. Although if Curran is involved in this, it means Abbotston will have to hand over the investigation. The officers dealing with Curran's case don't want us muddying their waters. If they can get to investigate him for murder, then it might give them an 'in' to the rest of the business." Cowdrey raised his hand. "I know, you won't want to let it go, but sometimes you just have to suck it up. We need to work together, not in competition. If he's guilty, he has to go down, and it shouldn't matter who pins the crime on him. Right?"

Caz and Ben muttered, "Right," while the rest managed—through gritted teeth—to sound a bit more respectful. They'd eventually learn to accept what you had to accept.

"We carry on working on it, though?" Robin asked.

"You do," Cowdrey said. "We're not jumping to any conclusions. Now go home. I'll let Chief Inspector Bright know if there's any news about Curran. In the meantime, this isn't the only crime I've got on my plate." With a rueful grin, he turned on his heels.

"I don't envy him his job, sir," Pru said. "Nor your mate Anderson. Give me murder any day rather than sexual assault."

"Are we sure the cases aren't linked, sir?" Caz asked. "Are we being a bit quick to discount that?"

Robin weighed the notion up for a moment. "If Mr. Cowdrey says not, then I believe him. Now, I'm ready to go and put my feet up. You lot go and do the same."

Although putting his feet up without Adam to snuggle them against wouldn't be much fun. Campbell would have to play substitute. The thought of the dead dog, though—and the dead man—reminded him not to take either for granted.

He'd got home, had a spot of lunch, taken Campbell for a walk, and was having forty winks when buzzing from his phone woke him. Not Cowdrey, but Anderson, who wanted to pick Robin's brains to make sure he was doing everything he should regarding the assault case. He had one lead, which was an unsolved case from late February which had an almost identical profile, in terms of the attacker threatening with what appeared to be a kitchen knife, the words he'd uttered, and the fact that he'd appeared to lose his bottle and run away before the assault became rape. That had happened up near Pitlochry, though. Robin tried to reassure Anderson that he was doing everything that *he'd* have done and sympathised that the delay in reporting, and the victim's natural desire to rid herself of any trace of the attacker, meant that forensic evidence had long gone.

No sooner had he put the phone down on that call than Cowdrey rang. Curran had been given an alibi for the morning by his girlfriend, who'd sworn they'd been together surfing the net for a new three-piece suite. Not an easy alibi to break if the woman kept to her story, and a browser history couldn't confirm who'd been doing the browsing.

Robin wished he could get Curran into an interview room, but that looked so increasingly unlikely that he felt a perverse yearning that the alibi would prove to be genuine, so they could have the glory of bringing the actual culprit in.

Assuming they could find out who the culprit was.

Chapter Fourteen

Adam drove into Stanebridge, grinning like mad at the notion of having lunch with Charles Edmunds in the only gay bar in the town. He'd made sure Robin knew the choice of venue, not least because if he was spotted coming out of the place, there was always a chance the person who'd seen him might want to cause trouble. While he had no doubt that Robin trusted him, such a report might rack up the angst given the bloke's current emotional state.

Glancing down as he came to a halt at some traffic lights, Adam realised he was wearing the same outfit he'd worn for his first proper date with Robin—proper date meaning not something that had really just been tea, sympathy, and brain picking. He remembered trying on no end of different combos of clothes before settling for grey chinos, a classic-style striped shirt, and a jumper slung over his shoulders. He'd had to appear attractive, but not tarty. That same style should do well today, helping to create the right impression. He had to get the information Robin needed.

Adam didn't see himself as a knight in shining armour, nor was Robin remotely like a helpless, feckless damsel in distress—how insulting was that comparison?—but if he could do anything at all to further help lay the demons of Robin's schooldays to rest, then he would. Short of beating the living daylights out of Harry Wynter and anyone else who'd caused Robin harm, naturally. That included taking whatever action he needed regarding Gary, if it turned out Adam was such a bad judge of character that he'd not realised his old mate was in this up to his neck. Still, if he could help solve this sticky case, then the sooner life chez Matthews and Bright would be back to something like normality. Which, of course, would mean tackling their partnership situation, but even that seemed preferable at this point to dealing with Wynter.

When Adam entered Bosie's, he found that the rumour mill hadn't lied about the extent of the makeover. He'd expected the floor not to be as sticky from spilled beer as it had once been, nor the walls to bear the odd spatter of unidentifiable, although probably vile liquid, but he'd underestimated the full treatment the place had received. It was right at the top end of the rainbow-flag market, now. Not that everyone who used the place would come under that umbrella—certainly the lunch trade appeared to be a broader mixture than it had previously been, which meant he could no longer read anything into Edmunds's choice of venue.

A dapper, sprightly looking elderly gent, sitting at a table with a glass of red wine, beckoned him over.

"Adam Matthews?" the man asked, once Adam was within earshot.

"That's me." Adam put out his hand to shake.

"I'm so pleased. I didn't want some poor stranger thinking I was on the pull."

Adam grinned, relieved to find Edmunds much more amenable than the character report from Neil had suggested. "You're never too old to be on the hunt for romance. Except I have to say I'm spoken for."

Edmunds returned the grin. "She's a lucky girl. Or is he a lucky boy? Whichever, it's nice to meet you."

"And you. Spoken for with a fellah, by the way, not a woman." Edmunds deserved that much candour. "Can I get you a drink? In return for picking your brains."

"Not at the moment. I'll cash the offer in when I've finished this." He raised his glass. "I'm glad Neil warned me you'd be in touch, otherwise I'd have ignored your text."

"Yes, he said that was a risk. You don't like cold callers."

"Does anybody?" Edmunds sipped his wine. "My sister lost half her savings to a con man. Is it any wonder I'm wary?"

"No wonder at all." Maybe his distrust of policemen would have an equally prosaic and understandable cause.

"But Neil says you're not a salesman. You want to know about local history for a book you're writing?"

"Just researching it at the moment. Writing it will have to wait for the Christmas holidays." Adam laid down the notepad and pen he'd brought. "I'll get myself a drink, then we can begin. I'm interested in World War II, and a couple of things related to it."

"I'll do my best, although I have no personal recollection of the time, obviously."

Adam sniggered—he was definitely being flirted with—then went off to the bar. As he waited to be served, he spotted a notice about a fun run being organised on Pratt's Common to raise money for the local Blue Cross. The poster featured a beautiful black Labrador, the innocuous juxtaposition of dog and location striking Adam like a blow and making the thought he'd kept suppressing blossom once more. What if Campbell had been the intended victim, rather than the Saint Bernard?

"Can I help, mate?" the barman said.

"Sorry. Miles away. Diet lemonade and lime, please." *With a side order of reassurance, although you probably don't serve that.*

"So," Edmunds said as Adam returned with his drink, "what are the couple of things you want to know?"

"How Lindenshaw school coped from 1939 to 1945, first off. I was hoping there'd be material in the parish archives or the school records, but they seem to have disappeared. Given you'd been chair of governors, and vicar, I wondered if you either knew where they'd gone or had any information about that era you could share with me."

"I'm afraid I can't. I know that most of the old church records end up in the Kinechester archives, so the school records might have made their way there too. That would be the place to go." Edmunds frowned. "Or get in touch with Doreen Drummond. She was school secretary for years."

"Great. Any idea where she is now?"

"I'm afraid not. You'll have to make that your next bit of research."

Adam jotted the name down, relieved that piece of distraction had drawn a blank; his bluffing could only stretch so far. "I've got my fingers crossed that we do better with the next thing. Victor Reed mentioned you as knowing something about it, so if we draw a blank, he's for the high jump."

"Victor. There's a name from the past. How is he?"

"Victor's Victor. He doesn't change." Adam gave a summary of the personal items Victor had shared with him, hoping that he wasn't being deliberately led down a blind alley.

Edmunds, appearing interested in the news, interposed with a couple of astute questions, then said, "I'm sorry, we're going off on a tangent. What did Victor say I could help you with?"

"Tommy Burley."

"Ah. Yes." Edmunds nodded, knowingly. "He didn't go to Lindenshaw, though. I don't know offhand which school he went to, if went to school he did as he may have been too young. I might be able to find out for you."

"Thanks, although this is a different strand to the project. The overriding arc is assessing the impact of the war on children. Like those killed in the Culdover air raid."

Edmunds nodded. "A good story to tell. Too easy for the present generation not to be taught how close to home conflicts can come. I know quite a lot about it, and some of that information isn't in the public domain."

"Really?" Adam feigned surprise. "I've struck lucky, then." He took up his notepad and pen. "I suppose I should be recording what you say on my phone, but that feels too intrusive."

"Too intrusive for me too. Pen and paper is fine." Edmunds shifted in his seat; Adam had seen that sort of movement in parents when they'd come to talk to him about their offspring. Sometimes it appeared shifty, and meant they were about to put a positive spin on some misdemeanour, but in this case it suggested there'd be candour ahead. "I don't want to be quoted as a source, by the way. Not until I'm long gone, so wait till you see my obituary and you can amend the second edition."

That was the first thing so far that had chimed with what Robin had said about Edmunds possibly trying to protect himself. "I promise to maintain your anonymity."

"Good. I don't want to be bothered by these awful people from the internet."

"Tell me about it. I've given up researching on the web. Too few facts and too many theories. For example, that Tommy Burley was murdered and the crime was covered up. And the list of reasons for why he was in the woods."

"If you've been on the internet, you'll have come across the name Edmunds as one of the suspects. He was my uncle, and it's a travesty that his name gets bandied about. He was nowhere near the area when the boy died." Edmunds waved his hand, as though dismissing all those who continued to libel his uncle. "Anyway, Uncle Gerald went to pay his condolences to the family a couple of days later, and Mrs. Burley kept saying how Tommy had been obsessed with the Rutherclere icehouse. He used to say there were fairies living there and they'd come out to play in the woods and drink the water of life. He liked to watch them."

"Fairies?"

Edmunds smiled, ruefully. "You're a teacher. You know how children have overactive imaginations. Perhaps he'd created a make-believe friend or two, or more likely seen some of the guests from one of the house parties the Greenes used to give. Beautiful ladies all done up in silk and lace. If you were a boy from a poor family, you might never have seen anything like them. It would be magical."

"Water of life sounds like they were drinking whisky. And if they were using the icehouse for a post-dram romantic liaison, that might lead to him thinking they lived there." Adam made a note, although he failed to see what a child's fantasies and a bit of nookie had to do with his death.

"Gerald was good friends with the Greene family too. He helped them no end when Simon killed himself. Do you know about that?" Edmunds waited for Adam to nod, then continued. "Suicide was illegal in those days, and people might have said he shouldn't have been buried in hallowed ground. Gerald made sure the story that it had been an accident with the gun was believed."

"Did he ever say whether he believed Greene had killed the boy?"

Edmunds slowly twirled the remnants of his wine. "There's a question. I've accumulated quite a pile of documents relating to the case, which I've handed over to an old friend who's interested, although I'm afraid he's one of those awful internet theorists so I haven't told him everything. I don't trust him not to blurt it out. Can I trust you?"

Adam laid down his notepad. "If you tell me something, I can keep it a secret, I promise. I won't put it into my book." But wouldn't he have to tell it to Robin, the cause of solving a murder overriding other considerations?

"Like the attribution, you can publish it when I've gone. I've left a letter with my solicitor detailing it, to be published after my death, so I'm afraid you won't have a scoop." Edmunds chuckled. "My uncle believed Simon Greene smothered the boy, when the balance of his mind was disturbed. I don't know how he could be so sure. I suppose Simon may have confessed it to him. It's always possible Uncle Gerald advised the young man to take the honourable way out."

"But why should he have killed the boy in the first place? Was there a sexual motive?" Why should any of this make Wynter scared? Unless he'd misunderstood the information he *had* been given.

"That my uncle wouldn't tell me. He said there were enough clues in the pile of documents he'd left for me to be able to work it out, although I haven't. I never was any good at cryptic puzzles, and I can't work the murderer out, though I read piles of mystery books so I should be able to."

"It's easier on the telly. I go for the most well-known guest star." Adam watched a flicker of disdain pass across Edmunds's face at the mention of the television; he'd forgotten that idiosyncrasy.

"Uncle Gerald would have appreciated that point even if I don't. He always had the box on." Charles made a dismissive gesture. "I'm not sure I want to solve this big mystery, anyway. Uncle Gerald warned me not to go prying locally as the danger hadn't died with Simon Greene. Hence my reluctance to share all I know until I'm out of harm's way."

"Very wise." Adam would have to hope that Robin's knack of solving crimes could be applied to the contents of the box. Assuming they ever turned up. He offered to get Edmunds the glass of wine he owed him, the bar visit helping him to prepare for changing the topic of conversation to Harry Wynter, although he could use the issue of who Uncle Gerald's information had been bequeathed to.

As it turned out, Edmunds gave him another cue, accepting the wine with a bright "Thanks!" and then saying, "Neil tells me you were a staff governor at Lindenshaw. Well done. Not enough young teachers want that extra responsibility. Good for your career too."

"So I believe, although that's not why I do it, honest. Staff governors get away with things lightly, anyway, given how many difficult things we can't get involved with." Adam patiently sipped his lemonade.

Edmunds took a large swig of cabernet sauvignon. "You're better off out of it, if you're thinking of staff disciplinary panels. Both time-consuming and emotionally draining."

Adam said a silent prayer of thanks for how things were going. Time to tell lies about his mother again. "I didn't go to Lindenshaw school, but my mum's in on all the local gossip, and she reckons there was a bit of a scandal with one of the teachers. Must have been around your time as a governor. Tell me to mind my own business if I'm overstepping the line."

"Not quite overstepping, although hovering on it. How much of this will end up in your book?"

Adam ostentatiously put his notepad and pen down on the spare seat next to his. "None of it, I promise. I'm just being nosy."

Edmunds rolled his eyes, grinned, then leaned forwards. "You're a very naughty boy. I'll tell you, though, because I like you."

"Thanks." Adam, squirming slightly, didn't know whether to curse himself for having been flirtatious or pat himself, or more correctly his parents, on the back for being attractive and thereby loosening the old man's tongue.

"There was a teacher—I won't say his name, but it'll be the one your mother meant, so ask her—who left the school under a bit of a cloud. I admit that I felt sorry for him and managed to keep it all quiet. You might say that was the wrong approach, but he was leaving education completely to work for a cancer charity, and we didn't want trouble for the school."

"Did he relocate for this charity job? Only Mum says she didn't see him around for years, then she reckons he was back again."

"Your mother should consider a career in espionage," Edmunds observed, drily. "He did move away but now he's living in one of the local villages. To be near his parents' graves, so I've heard. I also understand he uses another name."

"Does he? Mum's spy network didn't mention that."

"They're losing their touch, then. Slacking on the job." Edmunds, cheeks reddening as the wine took effect, slouched in his chair. "In fact, it's all this kind of careless gossip that's made him assume an alias. You wouldn't believe the rubbish that I had to stop circulating at the time he left the school. Naturally people assumed he was a paedophile, which he wasn't. I'd definitely have called that into the police."

"Neil says you don't trust them, either."

"I would in that case. But yes, Neil's right." He swirled the remains of his wine round in his glass. "Not the normal attitude for a vicar to have, but there's a story behind it. A friend of mine at theological college had a great deal of trouble. He was the sort of chap who would have appreciated this place, if you take my meaning."

Adam nodded.

"He was incredibly discrete, as many of us had to be in those days—still have to be, to an extent, depending on the parish and the bishop. Anyway, somebody started to spread awful rumours about him, involving little boys and what he liked to do with them. Not a word of truth in the stories, but the local constabulary believed it."

Adam tried to seem suitably sympathetic. Perhaps this friend *had* been innocent, but perhaps he'd also been good at pulling the wool over people's eyes. The police nowadays had to take such accusations seriously, although knowing the track record of such matters being swept under the carpet it was a surprise—given the time this must have occurred—that they'd taken action. "What happened?"

"He simply disappeared one day. I believe he took his own life, although a body was never found. He left a note to that effect. And while I have a Christian duty to forgive the officers concerned, who must have felt they were doing their duty, I have been left wary of the constabulary."

Any thought Adam had toyed with about mentioning his relationship to Robin got swiftly discarded.

"I can appreciate that." Adam could also appreciate that leaving a note and faking your own suicide would be a good way of avoiding arrest and disgrace, although maybe spending so much time with

Robin was making him over-suspicious. "Did Gerald have any problems with the police?"

"No. Nobody doubted that the child died of natural causes, because the doctor was well respected. However, Gerald reckoned he was a secret alcoholic who might not have noticed the signs of suffocation. Tommy *did* have a weak heart, poor mite. No doubt got mollycoddled and decided that's why he'd go and have adventures."

"Some of my pupils show the same tendencies."

"Children through the ages barely change." Edmunds smiled. "So nobody suggested Gerald was culpable, and anyway if things had come to a pinch he could have saved himself by calling on his lady friend to provide an alibi. She'd have done her duty by him." He almost drained his glass. "Somebody did their duty by Mrs. Burley, though. Apparently, a solicitor came down from Surrey and made a payment to her. Supposed to be on behalf of a well-wisher."

"Well-wisher? Was that conscience money on behalf of the Greene family?"

"I would assume so. They didn't offer it on behalf of a charity, because she wouldn't have taken it. Too proud. And perhaps feeling too guilty herself. For letting the boy go roaming."

Yes. The mother would probably blame herself even if she believed the death was by natural causes.

"So back to your mate. The teacher, not the theology student. Can I ask what he actually did that meant he had to leave the school?"

Edmunds gave him another *well, seeing as it's you* look. "He'd been a bit free with his hands. Lads trespassing in his garden got six of the best. Sixty years ago parents might have said they deserved it. Not so in this case."

That was disappointing. Nothing that Victor hadn't already told him.

"There was a bit more to it, though. He'd always kept a dog, and the current version back then was a brute of a thing. It savaged a youngster on the arm. What stopped them going to the police was Wyn—my friend having the dog put to sleep and agreeing to leave the school." Edmunds drained his glass. "I wouldn't be surprised to discover he'd also paid the sort of conscience money that the Greenes or whoever it was did during the war."

An attack by a dog? That shed a whole new light on the matter. A warm, comforting light that suggested Campbell might not have been the intended victim after all.

ponds and things. It splits either side of the wood, so all they had to do was put fencing between the two streams."

Robin recalled Treadwell mentioning the two bridges on the road past the estate. He gave Adam a shrug.

"But you managed to find a way through all that?"

"Yeah, well, I'd researched the site on Google Earth, and I was never really intending going down the main path, anyway. It would have been too busy." Gary sounded chuffed with himself. "Anyway, I'm not sure that gets you too near where the body was found. Nobody's very clear on that bit, by the way, although I'm fairly confident I've pinned it down."

Adam, who'd been patiently listening and obviously trying to make the right encouraging noises in the right places, made a *shoot me now* gesture at Robin, who had to suppress a laugh. Maybe he *should* go and knock the crap out of the brambles.

Gary blethered on. "I wanted to test my theory, so I'd planned to go down the far side of the left-hand stream and then stroll along innocently pretending I was interested in the trees. I was going to cross the stream farther down, away from where it runs wide and deep. There's a bit where it shoals, if that's what they call it. Goes over stones. You'd get your feet wet, but you'd make it across and you wouldn't be seen from the house. Might have been the way the original murderer got there. Hello? You still there?"

"Listening to every word." And evidently slowly losing the will to live. "What stopped you?"

"Nothing. Not at first. It was mostly quiet, because people kept to the main areas, and this was back of beyond. You also have to cross a boggy bit and people would have been put off by the signs they'd put there saying beware of the dangerous ground and keep away from the wotsit orchids. I wasn't anticipating that, but I had a quick shufti and nobody was about, so I legged it down to the bank."

"That's the trespassing bit, I guess."

"Yeah, so don't tell *him*."

This was getting nowhere. Robin shrugged, got off his chair, and was sneaking out of the kitchen when Gary's next sentence stopped him short. "You *can* tell him that I'd barely got twenty yards into the woods the other side of the river when I heard some bloke shouting, asking me what the fuck I thought I was up to. I legged it quick, especially as I thought I heard barking. I'm not that brave."

"Sounds like it was no holds barred to stop people snooping about."

It did seem a bit over the top. Maybe the notices about boggy ground and orchids were just to deter gawpers. Did orchids flower at this time of year?

"Sod me, I haven't run so fast for years. But that's not all." Gary lowered his voice. Robin edged closer.

"I can barely hear you, mate. Can you speak up? *He's* still up to his arse in weeds." Adam grinned, ignoring Robin's mouthed, *Up yours.*

"Can you hear me now? There's an old building in that wood. An icehouse, according to the Rutherclere Wikipedia page."

"That's bound to be right, then." Adam sniggered.

"Yeah. Except in this case I think it *is* right. You can sort of make out this place on Google Earth, through the trees, and there's some kind of a track running up to it, from one of the old gates at the back of the estate. I'd assumed it was all ruined, but I got the impression something might have been happening around there. A couple of people lurking about by the building."

"How did you see that with the hound of hell at your heels?"

"Ah. I didn't. I'd taken my binoculars, though, and I managed to find a place I could get a decent view. Nothing definite, only doesn't it seem odd that they were in the woods when the estate was taking so much care not to let people in there?"

"Maybe they still use it for storage. They didn't want people coming and nicking the Prosecco they've got in stock for when they start doing weddings."

"Yeah, could be."

Robin doubted it, although if the rumours were true and they were short of cash, then they might want to protect all their assets. Yet bouncers and fencing didn't come cheap, so there had to be a lot of Prosecco and smoked salmon to justify the outlay. And who would store stuff in a ruined building?

"Oh, before you go, was your mate Nick with you when this was going on?" Adam asked. His face had hardened and was getting grimmer the longer he waited for an answer.

Finally Gary said, "Ye-es. But I didn't want to drop him in any crap that I'm dropping myself in."

"I was simply wondering if he was also at Pratt's Common with you. The police want to talk to anyone who might have seen something suspicious."

"Right. No. Picked him up later en route to Rutherclere, save taking two cars. I'm sure he can verify that if you want him to."

Adam looked ready to wind up the call. "Thanks for this. I'll pass on the relevant bits of what you've told me. I guess if Rutherclere haven't made a complaint about trespassing, then you can breathe easy. I won't snitch to them."

"But you'll snitch to me," Robin said, with a stroke of Adam's arm after the call ended.

"Don't need to, do I? You had it all straight from the horse's mouth." Adam ran his hand across his forehead. "This links with what Edmunds told me. Tommy Burley may have been killed near there. He was certainly obsessed with that bit of the woods, and the icehouse in particular. I'm starting to think he may have had special needs, because I know nine-year-old boys and they don't tend to be infatuated with fairies."

"Fairies?"

Adam related what he'd had from Edmunds concerning what his uncle had told him about Tommy Burley's death. "Only hearsay, as you'd remind me, but I believe him. Or maybe I mean that he seemed to believe what he was told. Not quite the same thing."

"No, although I trust you if you say he's a credible witness. Simon Greene." Robin whistled. "Who'd be hurt if that got out? I know the Bowmans are related to the Greenes, but I can't imagine them killing anyone to protect his name."

"It did strike me on the way home that the people who'd be most upset are the conspiracy theorists, especially the ones who don't want it to be Greene. Or anyone who wants it to remain a mystery." Adam took a sip of tea, then pulled a face. "This is lukewarm. Any chance of another?"

"As you say, what did your last servant die of?" Robin made him another, though. "I can't imagine conspiracy theorists resorting to murder. Somebody's going to a hell of a length to stop people snooping in those woods."

"Perhaps Saggers fell foul of that. I wish I knew whatever was hidden in that box that's getting everyone's knickers in a twist."

"Quite a contrast to the Welcome One, Welcome All thing. And wanting to open the place up for weddings. They can't have bouncers strung around the woods while Tamsin and Timothy are having their pictures taken after tying the knot. Or Terry and Timothy." Robin handed Adam a fresh mug of tea. "Something for us to have a pry into tomorrow. Not that we'll get into the woods. I bet they still have the fencing up."

"It does seem odd, all round. But if they're in financial difficulties, they may have no choice." Adam blew on his tea, then took a sip. "I'm surprised they don't run Tommy Burley theme days. They'd make a fortune if people really wanted to get to walk round the place. Tasteless, I know, but plenty of places cash in on this morbid stuff. The icehouse he was obsessed with. The wall he hopped over on the day he died."

"The place where the son of the house killed him? That would go down a storm. No good for the wedding trade, either. I don't think you can run both horses." Robin went to the wine rack, selected a bottle of white, then stuck it in the fridge. "For later. Anything else crop up? Did you get to the bottom of why Edmunds hates the police?"

"Yep." Adam told him not only why the bloke wouldn't voluntarily talk to them, but why he mistrusted cold calls and—most relevant—provided some illumination on Wynter's departure and return. As before, Adam had felt he'd been supplied with the truth, and his estimate of character was usually spot on. "I've kept the best bit to last."

"You always do." Robin sniggered. "Hopefully tonight, after the wine and in the absence of me being called in, you'll be able to demonstrate your skills to their full extent."

"I'll disconnect your phone, especially." Adam left his seat, came over, and gave him a scorching kiss. "Deposit on payment to come. I need something to cheer me up. Anyway, Wynter wasn't drummed out for belting kids whenever he felt like it. He had a dangerous dog that bit one of them. All covered up after the dog was put down and Wynter—excuse the bad joke—left with his tail between his legs."

"I'll excuse the joke. Just." It put a whole new light on the death of the Saint Bernard. Could the person who'd been bitten have discovered Wynter was back in the area and decided to take an appropriate *letting the punishment fit the crime* type revenge? And was said person extremely long sighted? To the point they could stalk a dog and kill it, but not recognise their old tormentor over the width of a kitchen?

Chapter Sixteen

Sunday morning dawned with a bright sun in a piercingly blue sky, but when Adam let Campbell out for his first pee of the day, the first smoky, sharp hint of autumn was in the air. That always brought in him a mixture of regret at time passing and excitement for the months ahead. A new school year and the challenges it brought, the turning of the leaves, and then the whirlwind of nativity plays and pupils making Christmas decorations to take home; all this brought out the child in him.

He was already glowing in recollection of the night before—ten out of ten in the bed department—but he'd not anticipated feeling such a tingle of excitement for the Rutherclere event. At some point he and Robin really had to resolve this regularising-their-partnership lark and this might be the kick up the arse they needed. He offered to drive, so Robin could get a bit of rest, but no matter how pleasant the journey proved, and the personal aspect to the day, Detective Chief Inspector Bright got his work face on as soon as they pulled in through the castle gates.

"Are those the Tommy Burley woods?" Adam asked, nodding towards an impressive sweep of pine trees.

"No. They're too near the house. The ones where the river splits are right on the edge of the estate. Hence the unwanted guests legging it over the wall. They'll need to put fencing up there too."

"We'll never get down there to have a poke around, if that's what you're thinking of."

"I have no intention of doing that." Robin snickered. "Anyway I bet they have the bouncers and their dogs there today."

Adam made a swift left turn, where a sign directed them to the car park.

"Bloody hell," Robin said as they got their first glimpse of the marked-out fields and parking marshals. "I hadn't realised they'd be expecting so many of us."

While they hadn't been held up on the road, there'd been an increasing stream of traffic, albeit they'd arrived as soon as the doors to the grounds were open and before the event proper had begun. "Maybe the high-vis-vest mob are here to prevent further fights over parking places. Costing them a pretty penny again, though."

"They'll make that back with fees from exhibitors and profit from selling refreshments. Probably to the folk who are waiting to get in."

Any thoughts they'd had of taking a quiet snoop around under the pretext of *We got here early and so we're simply killing time* had to be discarded. "No wonder the locals are up in arms about this place expanding its business side," Adam said. "Imagine this sort of function happening every weekend."

"I wonder how many people here are only coming for another gawp, either at the castle or at the Tommy Burley woods?"

"Will they let us near the castle? Surely they'll hold the event in that marquee we saw on the way in?"

"According to my expert on all matters wedding-fair related, the trade stalls will be in the marquee, but there'll be organised tours around the house. He's booked us on the eleven o'clock one."

"How does Ben find all these things out? I didn't see that mentioned on the website."

Robin laughed. "He's been to so many of these fairs he's got pally with one of the female photographers. Possibly more than pally—I didn't pry. I'll save that for when we no longer need the inside influence."

"Better you than me." If Ben was like Pru, he wouldn't relish any questions about his private life.

"It's at times like this I wished I smoked. I could find a quiet corner to have a fag, then have a watch and a think."

"Couldn't you pretend? You haven't got a handy e-cig to hand or something that would pass for one? Do you still carry a police whistle?"

"Less of that. I'm incognito today, for as long as I can get away with it." Robin halted, halfway out of the car. "Which is probably about five minutes by the look of it."

"Why's that?"

"Daisy Lockwood off the starboard bow, fifty yards range. Wynter's lady friend and on the staff here. I was hoping this event would be beneath her."

"Maybe she won't notice— Ah. Too late."

An immaculately dressed and coiffured woman had given them a cheery wave, which Robin returned, producing his charming smile, the one that had knocked Adam off his feet.

"Chief Inspector Bright!" she said, although thankfully at a low enough volume that the name didn't ring along the rows of parked cars. "Are you here in an official capacity?"

"Not entirely." The smile turned sheepish. "Policemen are allowed private lives too. I'm trying to keep in mufti today. Are the flat feet that obvious?"

"No. You'll be fine. You come across as more ... human than some detectives I've encountered. We had a major fraud case at my company, and I'd quite happily tell any of the officers I met via that to sling their hooks if they turned up here." Daisy flashed them both a smile.

"That's the nicest thing I've heard said with my official hat on." Robin gave Adam an I'm-being-flirted-with-now glance.

"Well, I'll leave you to enjoy your day." She paused, then said—in an unconvincingly airy manner, "If you're around later, do come and find me in the estate office. I can run to a pot of proper coffee."

"We'll take you up on that." Robin waited until she'd gone before continuing. "What's that about, then? Summoned to the headmistress's study."

"Headteacher's," Adam replied, automatically. "Maybe she's going to confess to shooting Saggers."

"It doesn't work like the telly, I'm afraid. At least we'll get a decent cuppa out of it."

"Sounds good. Then we can avoid the instant muck they'll be serving. Let's go and gander at those trade stands."

Half an hour later, and with a good quality paper bag—courtesy of Ben's photographer pal—full of brochures and leaflets, and heads exploding with the volume of information taken in, Adam and Robin set off for their tour of the house.

They arrived in a good time, and just as well: the woman leading it looked like she'd take no nonsense. She—Debbie, according to her name badge—seemed friendly enough, in a businesslike manner, but she struck Adam immediately as being someone you'd want to keep onside. She checked off her list as couples appeared, in between checking her watch and making it apparent that this tour would be leaving on time. The older couple—second marriage, maybe—who arrived at one minute to eleven got a tight-lipped smile and as soon as they were ticked off the list, she closed her file, then led the group up the steps to the main entrance. One second past the hour was obviously far too late.

"Those people don't appear amused," Robin whispered.

Adam glanced behind them, where a group—two couples, perhaps—had been strolling up the approach to the house and had suddenly broken into a comedy run at the sight of the tour setting off.

"Excuse me," the lady from the older couple said to the guide. "Shouldn't we wait for them?"

Debbie raised an eyebrow, simply said, "Punctuality is the politeness of kings," then shut the door behind her, condemning the latecomers to the outer darkness.

Adam suppressed a snicker. While everybody else's sympathy no doubt lay with those who'd been shut out, he had a sneaking empathy for the guide. He couldn't bear unwarranted lateness—it usually came down to either a lack of planning or a lack of concern for other people. Robin felt the same, and one of the things they'd had drummed into them from childhood, and tried to drum into colleagues, was that a ten fifteen appointment meant ten fifteen, not half past. He shot a glance at Robin, who waggled an eyebrow, clearly seeing the funny side, as well.

"This is the main entrance hall," Debbie said. "Your guests will enter through here, in order to make their way to the great room, where the ceremony will take place. This space may also be used for photographs of the happy couple, although the grounds would be better for larger groups."

Murmurs and nods of approval broke out among the group, probably due to being too scared to argue, as the guide carried on with a tour which seemed mainly to consist of what would happen in a particular place and—perhaps more importantly—hints at what would be frowned upon.

Adam, who'd already decided that if Robin wanted to hold their ceremony here, then he'd have to employ every bribe to dissuade him, concentrated on gleaning information relevant to Robin's case.

After five minutes he'd concluded this was a waste of time. For a start, he couldn't see the Tommy Burley woods from the house, and the only painting featuring the icehouse showed it as a picturesque ruin, so was likely to be as much of a flight of fancy as Tommy's stories of fairies had been. Rutherclere was like any other stately home Adam had visited whether as teacher, schoolboy, or tourist. Handsome enough in style and with plenty in the way of impressive pictures and antiques. Although the fact that some of the pictures didn't quite match the marks on the wall behind them suggested the best ones had been moved out of the view of the hoi polloi, perhaps into the private wing which Debbie said the Bowman family kept for their own use. Or they could have been sold, of course, to keep the estate afloat.

Debbie at no point made any reference to Rutherclere's notoriety—Adam couldn't say he'd expected her to—although she did refer to the grounds being generally open to guests attending functions, apart from a particular area that the family wanted to remain sealed off because of the rare and scientifically vital flora to be found there. The poor thirtysomething punter who made an ill-judged joke about having met a rare Flora in his time and she'd been a chemist was met with a stony stare and a clipped, "Thank you."

When they reached the exit—not the main door but a less impressive portal onto a formal garden that ran the length of the building's back wall, Debbie asked if there were any questions. She fielded most of them deftly, often simply referring people to the relevant part of the website. She confirmed that there would be a number of "exclusive, boutique" bedrooms on site, and that favourable rates would be available at the nearest hotel, the Blue Boar. Adam knew the place. A pub that had expanded to provide accommodation and which was supposed to be every bit as good as its website alleged it to be. He and Robin had been there with their mothers for Sunday lunch, although the beef hadn't been a patch on the Sporting Chance, up near Kinechester racecourse. He had a feeling the Boar was part of a chain which itself was part of the Bowman family business. Given that the indoor smoking ban had been the last nail in the coffin for many hostelries, it was no wonder that the Bowmans found themselves short of cash.

"I hear you're thinking of a holiday village," said the partner of the man who'd made the unfortunate joke.

"A holiday village?" Debbie shuddered. "I can't imagine anything worse. I'm sure the owners would have no desire to see the estate transformed in such a common manner."

The inflexion on the word *common* and the peering down her nose put an end to any further questions and meant Robin and Adam could escape from Debbie's clutches to the relative peace of the garden.

"Please don't tell me you'd like this as a venue," Robin said, as soon as they'd found a seat in a quiet corner.

"Not in a million years. Might be some useful stuff in here, though." Adam jiggled the bag of brochures. "Got to say I liked Ben's pal. A photographer has to be a given, whatever the rest of the event consists of, don't you think?"

"I do."

The phrase—with all its connotations—hung in the air between them, before the impending arrival of bad-joke-man, whose moaning voice reverberated like a foghorn along the path, made them share a glance and decide to move on. They were a touch too late.

"Excuse me?" Bad-joke-man's fiancée's voice sounded behind them.

"Yes?" Robin said, as they swung on their heels. "Can we help?"

As the couple approached, Adam had a quick gander at the woman's left hand, noting a mark on the third finger which indicated a wedding ring had probably been removed from it. What subterfuge lay behind that?

"I'm going to sound extremely rude, here," she said, "but I think I've seen you on the television. Are you a policeman?"

"Yes. Although I'm off duty today."

Adam smiled at his lover's reply: Robin was never really off duty, unless they were hundreds of miles away with the mobile phone switched off.

"Are you investigating the shooting of that man at Lower Chipton? They had his picture in the paper, didn't they, Sam?"

"Yes, Sal." The man grinned, sheepishly. "Thing is, we're here under false pretences, I'm afraid."

Robin groaned. "Don't tell me. You're interested in Tommy Burley."

Far from having their thunder stolen, the couple seemed delighted at Robin's answer. "Yes, the Babe in the Wood. We were here last week too, trying to see what we could find out." Sam gave his partner an encouraging glance but before she could say anything, Robin cut in.

"We're aware of the case," he said jadedly, "although I clearly can't comment."

"We don't want you to," Sal replied. "You see, I have a photographic memory for faces, which is why I remembered you. Why I remembered seeing that dead man, as well. Last weekend."

"Why didn't you tell us? We've had an appeal out for information."

"Because it didn't seem that important. Then when I saw you here I thought I'd tell you anyway. You know they've got all the fencing and that down by the woods?"

"To stop the gawpers, yes."

Sam and Sal appeared oblivious to Robin's dig at them.

"Well, he was there. The dead man from Lower Chipton. We saw him when we went down to have a peek, through our binoculars." What with them and Gary, the place must have resembled a twitchers' convention. "Only he was on the *other* side of the fence, talking to somebody. A man we didn't recognise."

"Hold on." Robin rummaged in the bag of brochures, evidently searching for something to write on. Luckily they'd picked up a promotional pen too. "Let me take your details so I can get one of my officers to come and take a statement." Once he'd jotted down the address, he asked, "Salisbury Villas? Is that the row of cottages near here? I had to deal with a callout to one of those when I was a sergeant."

"That was the domestic two doors up." Sam nodded. "They've moved now, thank God."

"That's why we asked about the holiday village," Sal cut in. "We've enough problems with the traffic, and this is going to add more. The odd wedding will be fine—they'll likely come up the main road rather than use a rat run like ours."

Robin gave Adam an apologetic glance. "Do you get a lot of traffic, then? I seem to remember it being a quiet country lane."

"It used to be, but we get no end of stuff now, and at the most peculiar hours."

"Don't exaggerate, Sal." Sam rolled his eyes at her. "She's right about the peculiar hours, but I say it's probably to do with the quarry that's a couple of miles away. They'd avoid using the local roads during the day."

Adam couldn't see any logic in that but carried on listening, fascinated.

"Could you give my officer any details about when the vehicles come along and what sort they are?" Robin had turned on his charming smile again, although it hardly seemed needed with this enthusiastic pair.

Sal beamed. "We'd be delighted. We obviously don't keep a record, but we'll try our best."

"I have no doubt you will." Robin slipped the notes he'd taken into the bag. "If you'll excuse us, got places to be."

"Of course. Mustn't hold you up." Sam grabbed Sal's hand and whisked her off.

"Sorry about that," Robin said, once they were out of earshot.

Adam squeezed his arm. "That's okay. I noticed the lie, though."

"What lie?"

"The bit about being off duty. You rarely are."

Robin winced. "Sorry about that too. Is it a pain?"

"Only sometimes. Not when I can eavesdrop on a conversation like that. What the hell's going on?"

"Not sure. Need to have a think." He gazed up at the castle facade. "Did you notice anything when we went round?"

"Not sure. Apart from circumstantial evidence of the family being on their uppers."

"You noticed the missing pictures too?" Robin grinned. "You can always tell unless you replace them with one of exactly the same size."

"I suppose they might have hidden the best ones away. So the riff-raff can't spill their Prosecco on them. The replacements are okay but not top-notch."

"*I* assumed they'd sold them. Nothing else to notice, though, unless it's evidence by absence of it."

"Sorry?"

"Nothing featuring that icehouse, despite all the landscapes of the castle and its grounds."

"There was one old engraving that made it out to be a ruin. You can't get much off Google Maps because of the tree canopy. I checked last night, by the way." Adam smirked. "Took me a while to get off. You were out like a light."

"You'd worn me out, remember?" Robin leered.

"While you'd got me buzzing. Anyway, I found another pencil drawing of the Rutherclere site, with the icehouse in the background, and it didn't look ruined then. And if Tommy Burley said people lived in there, I guess it resembled a house."

"Unless he thought it was an old fairy grotto. Still, those woods are starting to bug me. Especially after finding out that Saggers was allowed inside the inner sanctum. I think it's time to go and get our free coffee."

It didn't take long to find the estate office, it being clearly signposted, no doubt for the benefit of tradespeople. Their knock was answered by a businesslike "Come in!" that metamorphosed into a friendly "Hello. I'll get that coffee on!" as they entered.

The office seemed much as Adam imagined it might be, with filing cabinets, two large maps of the estate, and a desk, bearing a none too up-to-date computer screen.

She ushered them into chairs on the visitor side of the desk. "This is my domain, at least for two days a week. Keeps the old brain cells busy. What do you think of it so far?"

"Really useful," Adam said. "We've got a bag full of info to plough through."

"What about the house?"

"Very nice."

To Adam's surprise, Daisy gave out a roar of laughter. "Well, that's damning with faint praise. No need to hide anything from me; I know it needs a bit of money spent on it and I keep telling them they should be investing in tarting the place up first, but it falls on deaf ears. One can only hope they use the first tranche of income wisely. Once people start traipsing around, it'll soon show signs of wear and tear."

As Daisy waited for the filter machine to finish brewing—from the aroma this was going to be worth waiting for—Robin casually mentioned the question at the end of the tour.

"Tourist village? That old chestnut?" Daisy rolled her eyes. "We've heard them all, Chief Inspector. Such nonsense people talk. Including Harry. Yes, I know he and his pals have lodged objections."

"Nothing escapes you, does it?" Robin said, not unkindly.

"I'd hope not, if it's Rutherclere business." Despite the heartiness of Daisy's tone, Adam caught a hint of uncertainty, as though she was thinking of some aspect of the estate business she couldn't quite pin down. Or maybe he was being over-suspicious.

"A few of the people on our tour appeared concerned about the likely increase in traffic," Adam said, feeling that he should say something or he'd resemble nothing other than the dumb sidekick. "They say there's already an abnormal number of vehicles on the roads, at all hours."

"I'm afraid the locals are prone to exaggeration, Mr. . . . ."

"Matthews."

"Then, Mr. Matthews, I'd take what they say with a handful of salt, not merely a pinch. They won't be estate vehicles if it's early or late." She turned to Robin. "I can officially state that our plans for expanding our activities don't include anything like that. We may not even repeat the Welcome One, Welcome All open day. Not that it wasn't a great success, and quite a money spinner, but it's been increasingly hard to manage. We could have done with additional stewards on the car park, for one thing."

"And at the Tommy Burley woods?"

"There too. Can you imagine the problems with the Tommy Burley obsessives? We're going to have a proper fence put in to keep the area sacrosanct. It's such an insult to that poor lad's memory to have people traipsing about."

A proper fence wouldn't come cheap, not if they wanted it to blend in with the surroundings and not spoil the wedding snaps.

"But people were traipsing about down there last Sunday. The other side of the temporary fence."

Daisy, whose back was turned to them as she poured the coffee, seemed to freeze momentarily. "Nothing escapes you either, Mr. Bright."

"It doesn't when one of them is now dead. Fabian Saggers."

Daisy turned, a coffee cup in each hand. Cups that were shaking slightly. Adam rose. "Here, I'll take those. You look like you've seen a ghost."

"Not quite. A voice from beyond the grave, maybe."

"You sit down and tell Ro— Mr. Bright about it, while I get *you* a coffee." Adam laid the cups down and went for a third.

"Have you met Kerry Holding, Mr. Bright?" Daisy said, voice still unsteady.

"Yes. Saggers's girlfriend."

"I got a letter from her yesterday. Oh, thanks—" she took the cup from Adam "—black coffee's fine. Anyway, that's why I was so pleased to see you. Saves me contacting you tomorrow."

"I didn't realise you knew her."

"I don't. Harry must have mentioned me to Fabian and he told her. It's easy enough to find my address given that I'm a director of a small charity." Daisy bent down, picked up her handbag, and produced an envelope, although she didn't pass it over. "Harry doesn't know I've received this. She doesn't like him."

"I got that impression, although she wouldn't say why."

"It's in here." Daisy laid the envelope on the desk. "It reads rather like an essay, but I expect she found it cathartic. Easier to talk to strangers sometimes. She says that at some point in the past few weeks, Fabian warned her about Harry, and she got on her high horse and said she didn't need protecting. I can understand that because that generation of men can be a touch patronising. I'm trying to knock it out of Harry, but it takes time."

Robin snickered. "Ask my sergeant—she'd agree with you."

"We've had arguments about it, so I can understand Fabian and Kerry ending up in a flaming row. She said she only really got back onto an even keel with him about three weeks ago, which had left her with a bit of a grudge against Harry. For once he's not done anything to justify it."

Adam could empathise. He worried all day on the rare occasions he and Robin parted on a tiff. If anything happened and it turned out that was the last time they saw each other, how awful would the memory of that last row end up being? He asked, "Did she write to you to pass on a warning about him?"

"In part. It's all rather bizarre." She went to smooth the envelope, but Robin interrupted her.

"Sorry. Can I ask you not to handle that any further? Perhaps you could place it in another envelope and give it to me? Unlikely there's any forensic evidence on it, but you never know."

"Oh, of course. I've got an A4 size here." She produced one from a drawer, then gingerly put the smaller envelope inside. "I'd better give you a rundown of all the contents, so you don't have to open it until you've got your gloves on or whatever you need. Fabian sent her a letter. He must have posted it on Monday, but it wouldn't have been collected because of the Bank Holiday. Despite the fact he'd stuck a first-class stamp on it, it only arrived on Thursday. Typical. He was reiterating a warning for her to keep away from anything to do with Harry—I wonder if that was prompted by his dog being shot—but also to keep away from anything to do with Rutherclere. It made no sense to her, and it makes no sense to me."

Robin frowned. "Did she know that you work here?"

"I have no idea. She doesn't mention it. Oh." Daisy's eyes widened. "Are you saying that she knows I work here and is trying to get information from me?"

"Not necessarily. It could be a coincidence. Although did she say why she contacted you in particular?"

"Only that now Fabian was dead she'd better pass the advice on."

Not to the police, though. Adam imagined Robin would be on the phone to the woman as soon as was convenient.

"I appreciate you'll want to be loyal to the estate, but can you think of any reason why she was warned off?"

"No. And neither can Harry. I did some gentle probing yesterday about why Saggers might have wanted the contents of that stupid box, but he couldn't say." She glanced from Robin to Adam, then back again, eyes narrowed shrewdly. "I can rely on your discretion, I'm certain. I know this family—or rather the extended family—has secrets, but they were buried a long time ago when Simon Greene was laid to rest."

"Well, if anything occurs to you, please let us know."

Adam recognised that tone of voice. He'd heard it from Robin when he wanted to end conversations. They knocked back the rest of their coffee, placed the envelope in the carrier bag, and were about to go when Robin said, "One final question. You mentioned the shooting of Harry's dog. Did you know that he had to leave the Lindenshaw area because of a previous dog and the fact it bit a child?"

Daisy nodded. "Yes, he told me so, although I also know it's not common knowledge."

"Except to the family involved. Do you know who they were?"

"Sorry. Harry won't tell me. All I know was the child was a boy and got bitten on his upper arm."

Adam flinched, at which Robin shot him a glance. Fortunately Daisy had been in the act of putting her handbag back on the floor, so hadn't appeared to notice the interchange.

When they emerged from the office, and were sufficiently far away, Robin halted. "What was that about? Your reaction to where the bite was."

"I know someone with a horrific scar in the same place. Right age and location too." Adam blew out his cheeks. "Gary Beaumont. My pal from uni."

have provided a better form of cover. Lorries from there drive past the lodge gates, stop and pick up hooch, go and drop it off wherever."

"Genius idea. I'm going to make custard creams compulsory eating for my team." Robin snaffled one for himself, then got to work again on his phone. "That quarry's been in use since the 1930s. Doesn't have to have been a Bowman company. Private arrangement would work."

"So, young Tommy starts to represent a threat to the business. Maybe he starts saying things that couldn't just be laughed off as the imaginings of a child. Simon Greene kills him before he says the wrong thing to the wrong person?"

"Something like that. Black market activities could incur a prison sentence, and a heavy fine. Might all be coincidence, of course."

"Okay, I'll buy it for the moment. Let's pretend I'm Cowdrey, though." Adam, putting on a sombre face, jabbed expressively with a digestive biscuit. "Nobody would have taken the lad seriously. All this crap about fairies."

Robin chuckled. "Cowdrey wouldn't say crap. If he was as angry as you make him out he'd say shit."

"You've not answered the point, though."

"Okay. Maybe people wouldn't believe the fairies bit, but they might become suspicious if the lad insisted he'd seen something and then proceeded to give descriptions. Imagine if posh women visiting the house were taken to see the still. Maybe they were customers. Tommy starts describing the fairies' dresses and that rings a bell."

"Right, but why fairies and not ladies?"

"Over-active imagination? There's another thing too. Have you ever been to a distillery? Where they process the malt they have to be really careful with sparks or naked flames because of the dust particles in the air. What if Tommy saw some of those, in the glow of light from the icehouse? He might think it was fairy dust."

"He might. But this all happened over seventy years ago. How can it be relevant now? Are they still making knock-off whisky?"

"I doubt it." Robin rubbed Campbell's back. "But I have an idea what they might be doing."

Monday morning's briefing looked promising. Everyone was brighter eyed, benefitting from their day of rest. Cowdrey himself, who'd got less of a break, appeared more energised, especially as Robin started to explain what he'd found out. The dog bite and the possible link to Gary caused surprise: Ben was assigned to follow that up, including finding contact details for Nick and getting his story of what had happened on Sunday. The account of the visit to Rutherclere brought a mixed reaction of snickers at Sam and Sal—Caz got assigned to probe them, and Treadwell, for information regarding vehicles passing through—and raised eyebrows at the mention of Kerry's letter.

Edmunds's account of events surrounding the child's death was greeted with gasps, and even the whisky theory got murmured approval.

"You *have* been productive," Cowdrey said. "Nothing proven, but it's a start."

Not the expected grilling, although it turned out Pru was ready with that. "If all that's true, and you do tend to hit the nail on the head, sir, what's it got to do with Saggers?"

"Okay, this is where it gets into pure speculation." Robin took a deep breath. "If the icehouse was used for illegal activities during the war, perhaps it's being used in the same way now."

"Distilling?" Ben asked.

"No. Although you gave me an idea. When we went to see Treadwell, you made a joke about him maybe turning out to be the local drug baron, growing cannabis in the loft. Turns out you may have been a genius."

That was the sort of compliment he used for Adam; maybe Robin was surrounded by people who made intuitive leaps yet were unaware of the fact and maybe *he* was the one who simply put the jigsaw pieces together. Whichever, it seemed to work.

Ben's grin threatened to crack his face. "Thanks, sir. Can you tell my mum that, please?"

"If this works out, you can bring her round and I'll buy her a cuppa."

"Playing devil's advocate here, sir," Pru said, "but why still use the icehouse now, given it's a target for loonies?"

Robin had an answer ready for that. "Hiding in plain sight. It's a genius way of having an excuse for keeping the area under wraps without raising suspicions. 'Why have you got all those heavies?' 'Because of bloody ghouls looking for where Tommy Burley was killed.'"

Pru nodded. "I'll buy that. Just. What hard evidence do we have?"

"Precious little, and most of that circumstantial, but there's a list." Robin counted the points off on his fingers. "Neighbours talking about an unusual volume of traffic. All that stuff with the bouncers and dogs and fences. Totally over the top for dealing with Tommy Burley obsessives. Warnings to keep away from anything to do with the estate, including a box of statements about an old murder."

Cowdrey cut in as Robin took a breath. "And a suspected drug baron who donates to the estate and is related to the owners. Whose manufactory and processing base the local coppers can't locate."

"Who's represented by a solicitor who was seen the other side of the fence," Robin added. "A solicitor who's now dead."

Cowdrey nodded. "Don't forget Curran being arrested on possession of firearms. Although I've got a horrible suspicion he might have been set up on that one. According to my contact—and it's not the lead officer on the case, so don't quote me—he doesn't make silly mistakes."

"That would make sense in the case of Saggers. Get in, do the killing, get out unseen. The work of a professional, maybe?" Pru asked.

"Could be," Cowdrey agreed. "A professional who also takes care to muddy the waters by making it superficially resemble suicide. It's possible the timing of the attack could have been prompted by the shooting of Wynter's dog rather than being linked to it. Opportune moment to divert our attention elsewhere."

Ben raised a hand, schoolboy fashion. "What was Curran's motive to kill him?"

"Knew too much and was no longer useful?" Pru suggested. "He'd got the material from the strongbox, then passed it over. Perhaps he'd had a gander at it, made the same deductions we did, and started to make noises about them. The letter to Kerry would suggest as much."

"Maybe he threatened to go to the police," Caz said. "Or wanted money not to come to us."

"If you think Curran got set up on the gun possession, do you think he might have been set up for Saggers's murder, sir?" Robin asked.

"Quite possibly. It's also feasible he's made it all look like a setup. As you know, he's got previous on that score." Cowdrey, who'd been in his usual pose of leaning against the wall, eased himself off it. "Right, well, that's plenty to be getting your teeth into. That's the good news. Bad news is this investigation now goes out of our hands. No use protesting, because we've had this out before. Robin, can you tie up any loose ends that aren't directly Curran related, then start assembling all the evidence to hand over?"

"Of course. You're happy for us to keep pursuing whoever shot the dog?"

"For the moment. I don't like trigger-happy people on my patch, whatever the target. Although Anderson might be nabbing some of you to help with the sexual assault case."

"Understood." Robin waited until the boss had gone before addressing the team. "I know you're disappointed, but that's the way things go."

"Sir," Caz said, "are we sure that Curran couldn't have killed the dog too?"

"Not unless the bloke's got a twin brother—which he hasn't, according to the family tree that Ben came across. He's on camera in the car park. You're right to be suspicious, though. Trust nobody, apart from this team." Best not to let her feel slapped down and stifle initiative. "Okay. Ben, can you hang fire on contacting Gary for a while? Pru, could you contact Victor Reed—I'll get his number off Adam—then try to track down this Nick bloke? I think I want his version of events before Gary realises we're on his tracks."

Because Adam was involved in training day—mobile phones allowed when no pupils were on site—he was able to supply Victor's number within twenty minutes. The rest of the trail ran just as smoothly: Victor giving contact details for Nick's dad, with whom he played bowls occasionally, then the dad providing his son's number. Through the open office door, Robin could hear Pru working her magic, reassuring each person as she called them that there was nothing wrong—being called by the police out of the blue was enough to scare anyone. She simply said they wanted to talk to Nick because he might have witnessed something important.

Robin decided to handle the call to Nick himself, and handle it straight away, before somebody told the bloke that the police were after him. Robin would have happily trusted Pru to do a good job talking to the bloke, but this time he felt the need to complete the task. His nagging Nick-related itch needed scratching.

Nick answered the phone within three rings and confirmed he had time to chat. More than happy to help, he said. *So why don't I believe him? Copper's nose?*

"Did you attend the Rutherclere open day a week yesterday?" he asked.

"Yep. With my mate Gary. Why?"

"He's told us that he was suspicious of what he saw there, and we wanted your account of events."

Nick sniffed, loudly. Not a pleasant sound to have coming down the line. "We saw something going on in and around the woods. Fences and what looked like guards with dogs. No idea what was up. That was the only thing. Apart from the burgers."

"Burgers?" What was that about?

"Yeah. They were suspiciously cheap for these sorts of captive-audience functions. Maybe they were horse."

Great. It seemed like this bloke was as much of a joker as Gary was supposed to be. "Maybe. Were you at the common with Gary beforehand?"

There was a pause and then another sniff. "No. Why?"

"Must be my mistake. There was a shooting there on Sunday. Gary says he went for a walk on the common around that time."

"Yeah, he'd promised his mum to visit. Did you know she got killed earlier this year? He was dead cut up about it. We both were. She was like a mother to me too." Nick's voice caught. "Some silly cow stepped out in front of her car, but *she* wasn't the one who got hurt."

"I bet he appreciated the support you gave him."

"How did you know about that?" The tone had instantly changed to clipped and wary. Interesting reaction.

"His uncle said." Best to leave it at that and not actually tell a lie about who it was said to. "That's why we wondered if you'd been at Pratt's Common. I know it meant a lot to both of them."

"Ah, right." Nick appeared to relax. "No. It was too personal, so I left him to it. I arranged to park in a lay-by, where he could pick me up. Turned out to be a good idea having the one car, given the queues when we got there. He was lucky—he'd been for a slash in the woods before he left the common, but I was having to cross my legs. I was desperate by the time we got to the loos."

That was a bit TMI. "Okay. One more thing. Has Gary ever mentioned the serious bite he got from a dog when he was young?"

"Dog bite? Is that what his scar is? He told me it was a shark. I knew it couldn't have been, but he wouldn't tell me. I never thought of a dog. Makes me look a total plonker." Nick laughed, self-consciously. "Sorry. Got to go. Work and all that."

"I understand. Thanks, anyway."

Robin was trying to work out where the investigation should go next when a text from Anderson—still no leads on the assault case and was he missing some vital step that maybe wasn't in the manual but might be in Robin's head—turned his attention elsewhere. He promised he'd have a quiet think and get back to him if anything sprang to mind, then closed the office door and went through what he knew of the case. A similar assault had taken place near Pitlochry: where even was that? Scotland, he had a feeling, although if his knowledge of geography was as bad as Adam's, then he could be hopelessly wrong.

He found it on Google Maps, and was about to shut the page, smug in the knowledge that he'd guessed right, when he was struck by one of the other place names shown. Aberfeldy wasn't far from Pitlochry, and wasn't that where Gary had been living until recently? His mother had been killed earlier in the year, around the time the assault had taken place. It was just conceivable that the bereavement had been enough to flip him over the edge and into committing a sexual attack, especially as it had been a woman who'd been implicated in causing the fatal accident. Was it simply a coincidence that he was now back in the area and had clearly been thinking of his mother—and presumably her loss—again?

Cowdrey had said the two cases weren't linked, but there had to be a chance he'd be infallible on occasions, so perhaps this was one of them. Except, as Robin remembered when he was about to ring Anderson, Gary had an unbreakable alibi in the form of Adam for the time the Abbotston assault had taken place. Robin cursed himself for making connections where there were probably none to be made, stuck his head round the door, and gave a brief summary of what Nick had told him, then retreated to get his head down over some paperwork that was nearing its deadline.

A knock on his door brought much-needed relief from admin duties. "Yep?"

Ben popped his head into the office. "Got a moment, sir?"

"Yes. You've rescued me." Robin got up from his desk and stretched.

"I've been on the phone to Gary. He confirmed he was the boy that got bitten by Wynter's dog although he says he doesn't like to talk about it."

That accorded with what both Adam and Nick had said about tall tales.

"He also said he used to be scared of dogs, after it happened, but he eventually overcame the fear. Said your Adam could confirm that."

"Yeah. Apparently, Gary and Campbell seemed to get on. Although Campbell gets on with everybody. Total tart." Robin sighed. "Thanks. I'll get back to the self-imposed torture. Remind me not to take holidays again."

"I don't envy you clearing the backlog, sir." Ben backed out of the door, leaving Robin to his paperwork.

He was halfway through adding up a set of figures for the third time because the first two hadn't tallied, when he had one of those sudden recollections of childhood that seem to spring from nowhere, triggered by some seemingly trivial occurrence. Once, when he'd been in Wynter's class, he'd covered for his mate, Jonny, who hadn't done his maths homework. He swore that he'd seen the wind—it had been blowing a gale that morning—snatch it out of Jonny's hand, and even though they'd chased after it, the work had gone. Wynter hadn't believed them, but because the school inspector was in that day, and the teacher had to be on his best behaviour, they'd got away with it. Wynter must have left soon afterwards, because Robin didn't recall being made to pay for the lie. He and Jonny had been thick as thieves back then, covering for one another.

Covering up. You've been a bloody idiot.

Robin pushed aside the calculator—the figures could keep—and emerged from his office. This was the sort of theory he usually put past Adam first, but there wasn't time today.

"Listen up. I've got an idea, and I need you to tell me if it's a pile of crap."

Pru got up from her chair to perch on her desk, her typical briefing pose, while Ben and Caz pushed back their chairs. "All ears, sir."

"Gary Beaumont was badly mauled by Wynter's dog and may have wanted to take revenge. I can imagine that ongoing unhappiness caused by the death of his mother may have prompted him into taking action once he was back here. He knows Pratt's Common and could have discovered that Wynter always walked the dog there on Sunday morning. Add to that the fact he's been living in Scotland, was taught to shoot there, and that he's a competition-standard marksman . . ." Robin spread his hands, awaiting comment.

"Doesn't sound like crap so far, sir," Pru said. "Maybe we should all start doing admin if that's the effect it has on the brain cells."

"It's the power of the subconscious working while you're doing something else." Caz should know—she'd studied psychology at uni. "Like when you can't think of somebody's name, then you wake the next morning and you've remembered it."

"How much of what you've said is fact, though?" Pru asked.

"About sixty percent. I'm also speculating when I say that he might have had the opportunity to learn how to stalk when he was younger. At present, however, he's the best option we have for the person who killed the dog."

"I looked up the type of rifle—Blaser R8—and it's supposed to be pretty versatile," Ben said. "According to the Shooting UK site, anyhow. I had no idea how many different sorts of hunting rifles there are. An experienced hunter would be in the frame."

"He's been very helpful, though." Caz pointed at the board where the evidence for the Saggers case was displayed. "You heard Gary telling Adam about the dog patrols at Rutherclere."

"Perhaps he thought if he was forthcoming on that, he'd escape our notice for the other thing," Pru said. "Only what about his car? He couldn't have got back to the car park to move it."

Robin nodded. "I haven't forgotten about the car. If Gary *did* learn to stalk, and he's good at it, he could have stayed unnoticed until the three of us had gone. We didn't take more than a quick glance around before we legged it, so once we'd turned, he could have scarpered, heading for the other car park, where somebody could have been waiting with his car, having moved it there after we'd arrived. Then they set off for Rutherclere as planned, job done."

"Do you think this other person might have been waiting for your arrival?" Ben asked.

"I doubt it. They might have hoped another car would arrive so that the green monstrosity could be seen, but the blackberry pickers might already have spotted it, so that purpose had been served."

Pru asked if Robin had any idea who had moved the car.

"His pal Nick. The one he went to Rutherclere with later. The one I've just spoken to and who was a bit on edge. They've been best mates since school days." Robin gave Ben a grin. "Didn't your best pal at school cover up for *you*?"

"All the time. But there's a world of difference between saying your mate was nowhere near Church Street when he'd really been playing Knock on Ginger, and covering up for your mate shooting a dog."

"You're right. But if your mate knew something about you that you didn't want known, you might be inclined to do anything he wanted." Robin paused, but his team simply looked at him blankly. "This might be stretching credulity, but the place Gary lived in Scotland wasn't far from Pitlochry, where last Wednesday's similar assault took place. I know *not far* in Scotland doesn't mean what we'd call *not far* down here—just bear with me. Gary's got a cast-iron alibi for Wednesday, so we can discount him, although Nick was up in Scotland staying with Gary's family at the time that other assault happened, and he's here now. What if that's what he wants to keep secret and Gary's making Nick pay for his silence? You cover up my crime and I'll keep shtum about yours."

Pru, who'd been listening intently, nodded. "It's worth having a word with Inspector Anderson about it. Is there any forensic evidence from the first assault?"

"A bit. Stuart says they tested it against the usual suspects in the Pitlochry area, but no matches turned up. He'll have to work out how to persuade Nick to give a DNA sample, but that's his problem." Robin rubbed his hands. "Right now I think we need to talk to Gary again. Pru, are you—"

Robin's phone ringing interrupted him. Sandra, their domestic help, rarely contacted either of them at work unless there was an emergency.

"Excuse me while I take this." Robin returned to his office. "Hello. Sandra?"

"Yes. Sorry to ring you at work." The voice was shaky, quite unlike her normal confident tones.

"No problem. What's up?"

"There's a man, in the garden. With Campbell. And I think he's got a gun."

Chapter Eighteen

By the time Robin had reached his car, he'd managed to get Sandra calmed down and established that she'd got out of the house and was staying out. He'd called for an armed response team and had decided to wait until he arrived at the scene to get himself togged up with protective gear. The fact Sandra had reported there was a bright-green car parked along the road suggested the man with the gun was Gary, and the brief description she'd given seemed to fit.

He'd already asked Pru to get over to Culdover School pronto and make sure Adam knew what was going on, so he texted her with the information on who the man with gun was likely to be.

As he drove home, he went through what he'd learned. Sandra had let the dog into the garden while she'd been upstairs changing the bed and having a bit of a spring clean. She'd happened to glance out of the window to make sure the hairy horror wasn't digging where he shouldn't be digging, only to see a stranger sitting in one of the garden chairs with the dog sprawled happily at his feet, wagging its tail.

Robin knew Campbell would trust Gary, having met him before, and would no doubt have assumed that Adam's pal was simply visiting. If dog biscuit bribes had been applied, then probably no thought at all would have been involved. Gary must have got in through the side gate, which although bolted was simple enough to unfasten when standing on tiptoe.

Robin's mind raced through a catalogue of wild thoughts. From the laughable—they'd *have* to move house now, given that this was the second time somebody had come round there threatening life and limb with a firearm—to the ridiculous—he and Adam would have to tie the knot soon, while they still had Campbell to share the big day with them and before anything could split up their special threesome. His mother and Adam's could have a hat-off to see who got the privilege of bringing Campbell down the aisle bearing a bag with the two rings in his slobbery jaws. Funny how the mind went to strange places in times of stress.

More pertinently, he recognised that Campbell had saved both of their lives, on separate occasions. He'd even rescued them from a domestic nightmare, but this time Robin had to save the Newfoundland.

He found the armed response unit parked along the road from the house, with a cordon already in place. The same green car that he'd seen at Pratt's Common was pulled into a lay-by, confirming his suspicions about who he had to deal with. He was grateful for that, because if he'd rushed gung-ho into the situation and found that it wasn't Adam's old mate he was faced with but some disgruntled ex-con that Robin had banged up, it might have turned into a bloodbath.

Sandra was talking to an armed officer, gesturing as if explaining the layout of the property. Robin quickly joined them, insisting that it was his house, his dog, his case, and his suspect, so *he'd* get a protective vest on and go in. No amount of argument was going to persuade him otherwise.

"DCI Bright?" the officer said. "I'm Cassie Burns." She didn't need to add that she was in charge.

Robin shook her hand, then gave Sandra a smile. "If it's the guy I think it is, I don't suppose he really poses a threat. Let's face it, if we were the targets, he had easier ways of attacking us. He could have taken out me, my partner, and the dog a week ago at Pratt's Common and nobody would have been the wiser."

Except Nick, and if Robin was right about him, he wouldn't have been saying anything. Gary would have got clean away with it.

"I'm not happy about this," Cassie growled. "He could be waiting to lure you in there, ready to take a pop at you."

"He could, but as I said, he's had better chances. He's an old pal of Adam's, so there was nothing to have stopped him coming round to our house and doing the deed anytime he wanted." Robin raised a hand. "My decision. I take responsibility if it goes wrong, not you. Sandra is witness to that."

Cassie shook her head but seemed resigned to the plan. "If you are going in, here's the situation. One of my officers has got the suspect under observation from next door." Before she could brief him further, Sandra's phone sounded.

"Hello?" she said, then mouthed, *It's Adam.*

Robin glanced apologetically at Cassie, then gestured for the phone. "Hi, mate. Pru's told you what's up?"

"Yeah." Adam's voice shook. "Is he okay? Campbell?"

"I think so. Hold on." Robin turned to Cassie. "What's happening in there?"

"The target's not made any threats, in fact, he's not done anything except sit there with what appears to be a hunting rifle, stroking your dog. And feeding it biscuits," she added, with an unexpected grin.

"Did you get that?"

"Yeah. Do you want me to come home, now? Gary will talk to me."

"I know he will, but I've had training for these sorts of situations." Not a lot, but please God enough. "I'll get Sandra to keep you informed by text. It'll be fine."

"Okay. Just don't be a hero." Adam paused, neither of them wanting to make a spectacle of themselves. "Being fed biscuits? Useless bloody guard dog, eh?"

"He needs retraining." Robin left it at that, the catch in his voice already betraying him. Handing back the phone and taking a radio, so he could be warned if Gary moved and so Cassie could listen in to developments in the garden, he crossed the cordon and strolled towards his house. He decided to take the side gate, because going through the house meant he'd be both unsighted and unable to hear if Gary got on the move. Before he opened the gate, he shouted, "Gary! It's me, Robin. Adam's fiancé."

He'd never described himself as that to a third party, but analysing why he'd chosen to use the term now would have to wait. A scramble of canine paws and a thump against the back gate announced the arrival of Campbell and brought a wave of relief. If Gary had meant to shoot the dog, wouldn't he have done it already?

"I'm coming into the garden. I'm not armed."

"Okay. Bring the dog, will you? He keeps me calm."

"Right." The wave of relief broke and faded. Robin had intended to send Campbell across the road to Sandra, getting him out of harm's way, but that option had gone. He opened the gate, gave Campbell a pat and a "Good boy!", then led him back to where Gary sat, seeming for all the world like someone who'd simply dropped in for a friendly beer.

Apart from the rifle at his side.

So was that what a Blaser R8, or whatever the thing was called, looked like? Nasty bit of kit, not like the old-fashioned rifles they probably used up on the moors. Robin took the seat next to it.

"I got your address from Uncle Vic," Gary said.

"I guessed you had." When they moved, *Uncle Vic* wouldn't be among the select band of people who'd be given their new location. "How did a nice bloke like you get into a mess like this?"

"Harry fucking Wynter, that's how." Gary offered Campbell another dog biscuit, which the hound took enthusiastically, clearly overjoyed at the special treatment he was receiving. The other hand kept a grip on the gun.

Robin, trying not to show he was watching that gun like a hawk, nodded towards the Newfoundland. "We'll be needing to put him on a diet. And talking of Wynter, you have my sympathy. He was my teacher too, and I hated him with every part of my being."

He hadn't meant it to come out quite so strongly and so personally, but the confession seemed to strike a chord with Gary.

"Right bastard, wasn't he? I think you might have been in the year below me, though. You didn't have to have three terms of him. You know why he left?"

"Yep. His dog bit you. It got covered up." Robin didn't have to put on an act; he could guess how Gary felt. "Even as a child you must have been fuming."

"Tell me about it. Wasn't only this." Gary rubbed his arm. "It led to the breakup of my parents' marriage. Mum was all for having the bloke prosecuted while Dad said we should keep quiet. Wynter had been made to move, the dog was being put down. *I* shouldn't have been climbing over his garden wall to get my football back or else I wouldn't have been bitten."

Victim blaming to add insult to injury. Mr. Beaumont sounded a right charmer. "So you thought you'd get your own back?"

"Yeah. I'd been thinking about it for years, although never seriously. Revenge fantasies, you know?" Gary glanced up, got a nod—Robin knew all about those—then stared at his feet again, turning the gun within his hands. "When Mum died, I wanted to punish Wynter. It wouldn't have been so bad if she'd got heart disease or something, but if we hadn't had to move to Scotland, she'd not have been involved in that crash. When I discovered he liked to walk his dog in one of Mum's favourite spots, it felt like a sign."

Robin had heard that sort of self-justification before, although with Gary it sounded plausible. Maybe he'd been searching for signs, blinded by his grief.

"How did you find out he walked his dog at Pratt's Common?"

"By accident." Gary, smiling, stroked Campbell's ear. "I'd been up there the previous weekend, visiting the place and thinking of Mum. Honest. I had a hell of a shock when I saw him in the car park, but he didn't appear to recognise me. Beneath his notice."

Very likely. Wynter would surely have mentioned any encounter he'd been suspicious of. "Go on."

"He was talking to a pair of young women—nice-looking girls. I think he was trying to chat them up—so he was oblivious to me listening in. He told them he always walked the dog there on Sunday mornings so maybe he'd see them again." Gary snorted. "I'd have said they'd avoid him like the plague. They weren't there the next week. Obviously."

They were coming to one of the crunch points. No matter how sympathetic Robin felt, it had been inexcusable to shoot a defenceless pet. "So you decided to stalk the dog like you'd stalked deer?"

"That's right. Damn sight easier, to be honest, because they don't tend to leg it when they get wind of you." Gary stroked the Newfoundland again. "Bit thick, dogs. Sorry I gave you such a fright. I was so intent on the Saint Bernard I didn't see this lad running around."

"We thought it was him that had been hit." The words stuck in Robin's throat.

"I know. I really am sorry about that. I never meant for anyone else to be involved. It was only Wynter I wanted to hurt. I didn't really want to kill *him*—Mum would be turning in her grave if I'd done that—only scare him. Eye for an eye."

"You certainly managed that."

Gary sniffed. "Yeah. I'm going to sound like a total bastard, but it's a shame, in a way, that the dog had escaped. I didn't realise Wynter had legged it home—I meant him to see it be killed. Have that image live with him like my scar's lived with me."

Robin, certain that the mental image of the dead Saint Bernard would never leave his mind, kept focussed on the case. "Your mate Nick moved your car, so it'd look like you'd left the scene before the shooting started?"

"Yep. I was going to drive there, then swop drivers so he could pick me up later, but there were a couple of old biddies by their vehicle in the car park. I thought it would look odd to drive in then away again."

"So your plans changed?" Robin had puzzled over why so distinctive a car had been left in plain view.

"We had to make the most of the car being spotted." Gary studied his hands. "I got Nick to duck down so he wouldn't be seen, then I parked at the other end of the car park. I told him to make sure the car was there for ten minutes or so then to drive off, but not to let anyone see him. I didn't realise it would work out so well."

Luck had been on his side, all right. "Nick agreed to do all this because you were aware that he'd attacked the woman near Pitlochry."

Gary twisted to face him, eyes so wide that Robin worried he'd got his facts all wrong. "I didn't realise you knew."

"I've only recently worked it out. He's been fortunate."

"Maybe. I don't agree with what he did. You need to know that." The wide-eyed expression became pleading. "He said what happened in Scotland was a one-off. Mum's death hit him really hard, and there was the one particular day he reckons he hardly knew what he was doing. He'd screwed himself up into such a state of anger against the woman who'd stepped out in front of Mum's car that he must have taken that out on the victim. Only afterwards he realised that he must have done it. I hardly knew what I was doing myself, around then, so

I kept quiet. I told myself it was for Mum's sake, although I doubt it was. I found I had too much on my plate, and the longer it went on the harder it felt to come clean."

Was that the real explanation or one Gary had created to ease his conscience? "So you thought you'd make use of him?"

"Yes. You're going to tell me two wrongs don't make a right, but at the time it felt like I was completing an act of justice." Gary studied his feet again. "I didn't realise Nick was going to make a second attack, I swear. I'm guessing that was him at Abbotston, although he's not said anything and I ain't asking him direct."

"We have to consider that possibility."

Gary was going to have to put all this down in a statement too, and the sooner the better. Robin was about to suggest they go to the station and do that over a nice cuppa, when a burst of static from his radio made them both jump.

"Someone approaching the house," Cassie advised him. "He's hiding behind one of the cars and we've got him covered if he makes a move. I don't know if he's aware we've clocked him."

"Is he armed?" Robin asked.

"Can't confirm or deny that."

"It might be Nick," Gary said, voice hoarse. "I told him I was having second thoughts about things, after your constable rang me. Said I wanted to talk to you. He went apeshit. Said Mum would turn in her grave if she knew. I told him to piss off."

"Did you also tell him where I live?"

"No. I said I'd be going down the station. I promised I wouldn't mention him—just say he did me a favour—but he still tried to talk me out of it." Gary blanched. "Said if I wasn't decent enough to keep quiet for Mum's sake, then maybe I needed something stronger to persuade me. Asked me if I remembered how useful he was with a hunting knife."

Great. "So why didn't he go to the station to find you?"

Gary, still ashen-faced, glanced towards the gate. "We've got each other on the Find Friends app. He'll have used that to see where I am. Sorry. I should have guessed he could follow me here."

Trouble was Gary didn't seem to have really thought through the outcome of any of his actions. Bringing the gun with him was a case in point. Oblivious? Self-centred? Or simply so impulsive that he acted first and dealt with the fallout afterwards? "Can you check on your phone that it *is* him? And does he have access to firearms?"

"No. He hates the things. Chance he'll have that knife, though."

"How dangerous is he? Gary. How dangerous?"

"I don't know." Gary put his head in his hands. "God, what a fucking mess."

Robin spoke into the radio. "The bloke by the car's likely to be armed with a knife. Have you got that?"

The radio crackled again. "Yes."

Gary, who'd at last had the sense to check his phone, pointed at his rifle. "It *is* Nick outside. You take this, to be on the safe side."

"You think I'll need it? Or are you preventing yourself using it?"

"Bit of both." Gary smiled, sheepishly. "I thought I'd best carry it round with me after speaking to Nick, in case his threats were more than hot air. But I only brought it in here because it makes me feel brave."

What was it with some blokes that they didn't feel like real men without a weapon to hand? "You're a better shot than I am."

"Yeah, but I don't want to find myself in court for murder."

Robin's mind flooded with thoughts of murder versus allowable force in self-defence, and whether he could even work out how to use the hunting rifle let alone wing Nick with it. It would look threatening to the bloke, though.

Cassie's voice sounded over the radio. "Leave any shooting to us, Mr. Bright. Do you have the situation under control?"

Robin glanced at Gary, who nodded. "Gary's given me his rifle. I'm less concerned about him than the other joker. What's he up to now?"

"Trying to get to your house, I'd say. He's got too large a gap to run across at present."

"Right." Robin quickly assessed the situation. He wasn't going to risk Campbell flinging himself at Nick, and if *he* had his hands on the dog's collar to hold him back, then he couldn't also manage the rifle. "I'm going to put my dog in the house. He has a habit of thinking he's a superhero, and I don't want him rushing some loony with a blade."

One hand on Campbell's collar, the other on the rifle, and eyes on Gary—Robin wasn't so stupid as to risk being jumped—he backed towards the kitchen door, opened it, and pushed the dog inside. Next step was tricky. He and Gary could also go in the house, lock the doors, and leave it to the armed response unit to sort out Nick, which was no doubt the strategy Cassie would suggest, although that stuck in Robin's craw. Illogical and unwise to think it, he knew—and possibly immoral, as it dragged Gary's safety into question—but Robin wanted to confront Nick himself, probably because he hadn't had the opportunity of confronting Curran.

He told himself not to be such a prat, then lifted the radio to his mouth, hissing, "If he ends up in here, listen in but keep your end silent. I'll shout for help if it's needed."

"Hmph," Cassie whispered. "I'll decide if you need help."

"Now hold on—"

A rattling from the garden gate announced the arrival of Nick. Robin laid down the radio out of sight at the same time as Nick rounded the corner of the house, bearing two hubcaps that he must have been using as shields in case he was fired at. The sight was so ridiculous, Robin started to laugh, stopping abruptly as Nick dropped his makeshift armour and produced a large kitchen knife from a shoulder bag. Irrespective of Robin having a rifle, which he raised to cover the intruder, the danger Nick posed wasn't to be underestimated. He could throw the knife, or dive in quick and stab Robin before he'd sussed how to use his own weapon.

"Put the knife down," Robin said, as calmly as he could manage. "This is pointless."

"Is it?" Nick weighed the blade in his hand, then pointed it at Gary. "If I take you out, I'm taking out the only person who can dob me in before you've had the chance to do it. What have I got to lose?"

"Part of your life, for a start. A longer chunk of it spent in prison." Robin sounded a lot calmer than he felt. "Don't forget, we'll have your DNA to match up for the assaults. That'll speak as loudly as any testimony in a witness box."

Gary cut in. "Anyway, I've already told Mr. Bright what I know."

Nick wheeled round, facing his friend. "You fucking idiot. I told you not to tell the police anything. You could have left it at saying I was helping out a mate, giving you an alibi."

Gary, still as pale as the late-blooming white roses in the flower bed behind him, stammered, "I c-couldn't. I'm tired of having to lie about things. I just want this all over."

"I can arrange for that." Nick waved the knife. "Reckon the flatfoot here has no idea how to use the rifle, given the way he's holding it."

Shit, was he so obvious? Thank God the radio was catching all this, so Cassie would be able to hear and make a call on what to do next. Nick didn't give the impression of acting rationally—trying to negotiate calmly with him and Gary was like tiptoeing through a minefield.

"Better still, I'll take the gun. I can shoot you, then shoot Gary. Make it seem like murder and suicide." Nick's eyes blazed.

"Don't be so stupid," Robin said. Would Cassie get whoever was observing from the house next door—and doing it so effectively that Robin hadn't spotted him or her—to try a shot at winging Nick? Or whip out their Taser to temporarily disable him? Assuming they could get a shot of any sort away, given the angle, the way the windows opened, and the fact that Gary might be in the line of fire. Whatever the action, it had to be necessary and proportionate, a phrase that was all very well in a manual of good practice, but which felt pretty meaningless when you were faced with somebody determined to hurt you.

"What would Mum have said, Nick?" Gary said, slowly rising from his seat. "About you and that knife? She'd have done her nut."

"Don't you bring your mum into this." The question had hit home, though. Nick had turned as pale as Gary.

"She treated you like a son, and look at the way you're repaying her. You're right, she *will* be turning in her grave." Gary took a step forward, while Nick took one away from him. "Put the bloody knife down, you wanker. Cos if the rozzer here can't use the rifle *I* sure as hell can, and even if you run, I can take you down."

Nick's grip on the knife didn't waver as he pointed it at Gary and Robin in turn. "Maybe I should simply kill *him* and say you did it. Or there was an accident. It'll be your word against mine what happened here. I don't know if the team out there saw me come in here, but I'll tell them I only came to talk you out of being such a stupid tosser. I'll be the hero."

"No, you won't." Gary put his arm out towards Robin for the gun.

Robin shivered. The Gary he'd been talking to had so far been largely bumbling and apologetic. Now the cold-blooded deer stalker had come out. Still, Robin had no intention of giving him the weapon. "Nick, there's a radio here. The head of the armed response team has heard everything. You can't hide anymore."

"I don't believe— Shit!" Nick slumped to the ground, like a felled stag, knife clattering from his hand. Robin pounced, retrieved it, then glanced up to see an armed officer peering over the neighbour's fence.

"It's all under control," Robin said, still not quite convinced it was. "Gary's going to come quietly. Your boss can get across here and take over. Her scene now."

Robin texted Adam as soon as was practical to let him know that everyone was safe, getting a swift reply—the bloke must have been glued to his phone, and who could blame him—saying that he was glad to hear it and had the neighbours started a petition yet to force them out of the area? Thank God that Robin was in his own car where nobody could see him, because *Soppy detective sheds a tear over gay lover's text* didn't appeal as a headline. A second text said they'd speak later, as if Adam rang now, he'd end up a sobbing mess.

Gay teacher weeps in playground at useless guard dog situation.

Back at Abbotston nick, he was relieved to find his colleagues appeared to be more worried about Campbell's welfare than his. Robin suspected that might have been Pru's doing, knowing that he hated any sort of fuss at the best of times—and where the combination of home, dog, and Wynter were concerned, the time was far from the best.

They had a brief mop up, Robin relating what had happened, including what Gary had told him related to the assault case, concluding with, "Plus point to all this is that he'll have to give us a DNA sample now Gary's spilled the beans."

"Anderson won't be happy that you solved his case for him, sir," Pru said. "Although maybe that's the universe balancing things up because we had to pass the Saggers case on."

"Got news on that too." Cowdrey, who'd been listening from his usual place by the door, broke into a wry grin. "I've heard that Curran's girlfriend has said she'd lied about being with him on Tuesday morning."

Pru beamed. "That's good."

"Good and bad. Bad news first, it seems she'd heard he's been knocking around with another woman, so the chances are the defence will call her evidence sour grapes. On the positive side, they've got Curran's car caught by the newly installed speed camera on the dual carriageway not far from the Lower Chipton turn off. Better still, the back end of the Rutherclere estate's been in lockdown since not long after this morning's briefing ended."

"You don't hang around, sir." Robin hadn't realised he'd be quite so quick off the blocks.

"Yeah, well we didn't want them having any time to dispose of the evidence." Cowdrey headed for the corridor, reminding the team that the case was no longer their issue and encouraging them to get home and recover from another difficult day's work.

Robin echoed his boss's viewpoint on both counts, although his brain wouldn't be able to put this case to bed until Curran—or one of his cronies if he'd employed a hit man—was safely convicted. Fabian Saggers couldn't become another Tommy Burley.

Chapter Nineteen

Neither Robin nor Adam felt like cooking, although the prospect of leaving the house—and Campbell in it—felt too raw at present so a pub dinner was out, as well. Adam suggested nipping down to the Chinese takeaway, which Robin did while he laid the table and made a fuss of the dog. The Newfoundland seemed a bit perplexed as to why everyone was being so nice to him today, although he lapped it up.

When Robin returned, bearing a bag from which mouth-watering aromas emerged, Adam asked if he'd by any wonderful chance got prawn crackers in the plastic bag, because he'd forgot to ask for them.

"I do." Robin hesitated, then put the bag on the table. "We'll eat them with the spare ribs while we keep the rest warm."

When they finally sat down with their starters and a glass of beer each, Adam remarked, "You said it again, earlier. Like you said it at Rutherclere. 'I do.'"

"I know. I didn't mean it to be awkward, either time. It was just . . ." Robin reached across and took Adam's hand, a tender gesture none the worse for the spare rib sauce on their fingers. "It made me think of us saying it. Not at Rutherclere, but . . . wherever."

"A bit of déjà vu?"

"Yeah. And it seemed such a private, joyful moment, it wrong-footed me, when Sam and Sal steamed up on us."

"I get that." They went back to eating. "So Rutherclere's off the list. What about eloping to Gretna Green, and getting married with nobody but the blacksmith and his wife for witnesses?"

"Do they still do that? Not quite my cup of tea, though having a really small ceremony, with only the people who really matter to us appeals." Robin sucked some sauce off his thumb. "To hell with anyone whose nose gets put out of joint."

"I tell you what, these last few days have helped clarify my mind. No way that I'd want to get married at anywhere like Rutherclere, so I'm glad that's not a problem."

"Hell, no. I was going to suggest a civil ceremony at the registry office and a knees-up at the village hall would be perfect, but given the Lower Chipton hall's link to this case, I'm off that idea too."

"Have they found those missing documents yet?"

"Ah. No chance of that happening now. I got a text about it while I was waiting for the food. Curran's destroyed them, or so his girlfriend says."

"Shame. I'd love to know what Gerald Edmunds had put in there that was so cryptic that Charles Edmunds couldn't figure it out but was so obvious that it managed to incriminate Simon Greene and the rest of his family." Adam, another prawn cracker halfway to his mouth, paused. He recognised that expression on Robin's face. "Come on, what do you know that I don't?"

"The fact that Saggers snaffled some of those documents and posted them to his girlfriend, Kerry." Robin, grinning, licked some sauce off his fingers. "Silly sod sent the envelope so it had to be signed for, and she only picked it up today. She e-mailed Pru scans of the documents—they arrived just before I left the station."

"And . . .?"

"And nothing much that we hadn't already worked out. A couple of things did strike me, though, where somebody—Gerald, I guess—had made additional notes. One was a statement from Tommy's mum where she described him talking about the icehouse and fairies and the water of life. That bit had been annotated with the words 'Like Walker. Still happening?'"

"Walker? Who— Oh, you've got to be kidding. The spiv from *Dad's Army*?" Adam broke into laughter.

"That's my guess. Hinting that black-market activities were involved."

"No wonder that left Charles baffled. He doesn't watch the telly, but his uncle did. All the time. Anybody else might have made the connection after a bit of thought, although perhaps not if they hadn't started thinking black market beforehand."

"Yep. Stupid, isn't it?" Robin picked up the last rib from his plate. "You know what's stupider? There's another page, with a report of a confession to the murder. Tommy Burley was killed because he knew too much, it says, and the family had to be protected. No signature, only a note at the bottom of the page. 'Robin Hood.'"

"Robin Hood?" Adam couldn't think of anyone connected to the case called John or Marian.

"Ben, the king of Google, had the bright idea of searching for actors who'd played the character."

Nobody called Costner to do with the case, either. "You're going to tell me he found a bloke called Greene who acted the role on telly?"

"Yep. Black-and-white days."

Adam pushed his plate to one side. "How bloody ridiculous. I'm ready for my main course and a change of subject."

Once they'd got the food out of the oven, onto their plates, and enough of it into their stomachs, Robin resumed an earlier part of the conversation. "We were talking wedding venues and how neither Rutherclere or Lower Chipton works. Got an alternative?"

Adam, savouring a succulent piece of salt and pepper chicken, said, "I do, actually."

"That phrase again. We need to keep it for the big day. What's your genius idea?"

"Remember going for Sunday lunch at the Sporting Chance? That roast beef?"

"I'll never forget it. Nor the Yorkshire puddings and those roast parsnips." The most direct route to Robin's heart was always through his stomach. "Thinking of there for a reception?"

"Thinking of it for the whole show. They have accommodation—enough rooms for a little do—and according to the newly qualified teacher who's recently joined our staff, they've recently converted the old barn at the back and got themselves a licence for weddings and civil partnerships. I wasn't sure I believed her, so I had a gander at their website. Seems very nice, although these places always come across as impressive in their photo galleries. The website says they cater exclusively for the smaller, classier kind of gathering. Dog friendly, with it."

"It's a deal." Robin held out his hand, not for finger fiddling this time but to seal the agreement with a handshake. "Although have you solved the problem of what we do with the bigger list of people, or do we just say that if they're offended, they can lump it?"

"I've a suggestion on that front too. Let's say we're having a small celebration because we need to move house as well, but we still want them to be part of our big day. At which point we tell them we're making a donation to one of the charities for the homeless on their behalf. Some poor soul will get a meal at Christmas in their name."

"I like that. If they complain, it'll make them look miserable sods."

"Absolutely. I wouldn't actually say that the homeless deserve to fill their stomachs more than a few of the potential hangers-on need to fill theirs, but I can think it." There were a couple of Adam's cousins whose faces would be a picture at the proposal.

"Yeah. This is about us. The Matthews-Bright household." Robin nudged his head towards where Campbell was snoring in his dog basket. "He'll be the star of the show. As usual."

"That's what I like to hear. It'll take the attention off us."

Robin sniggered. "Our mothers' hats will do that. We'd better check that the Sporting Chance is big enough to accommodate both."

"We'll give them a maximum allowable size." Adam gave Robin a smile. "Feels right, doesn't it?"

"More right than anything has the last few days." Robin took a draught of beer. "I owe you a ton of gratitude. Not only for helping put your mate in the frame. I couldn't have faced Wynter if it wasn't for you."

Adam resisted saying something like, *Daft bugger*. This was too important to joke about. "You know I'll always have your back."

"Yeah. I know. You're a diamond." Robin put his glass down, and nestled up closer. "I'll always have your back too. I'm sorry about Gary."

"Not your fault, is it? Mine for taking so long to believe he could be involved." Adam rubbed the top of Robin's head. "Shooting the dog was bad enough, but covering up for someone who'd committed that sort of assault . . . it turns my stomach. Neil would say I have to find it in my heart to forgive, but it'll take a long time."

"Gary never forgave Wynter, did he? Right, that's it. I'm banning all talk about murders or weddings for the rest of the evening. Tell me what you think Harlequins' chances are for the new season, or what box set we should watch next weekend."

"Can I try talking you into an early night, instead?"

"Sounds good." Robin bent down, picked up his beer glass, then raised it, encouraging Adam to do likewise. "To us."

"To us."

The chink of glasses must have roused the dog, because he lifted his head to give them an accusatory look.

"All right," Adam said, saluting the Newfoundland with his beer glass, "to all three of us."

Campbell gave a happy bark, wagged his tail, then lay back down.

Normal life restored.

Explore more of the *Lindenshaw Mysteries* series:
riptidepublishing.com/collections/lindenshaw-mysteries

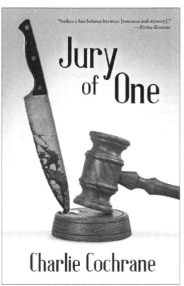

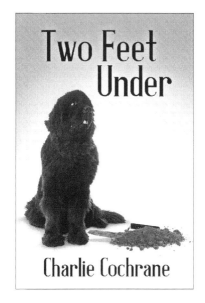

Dear Reader,

Thank you for reading Charlie Cochrane's *Old Sins*!

We know your time is precious and you have many, many entertainment options, so it means a lot that you've chosen to spend your time reading. We really hope you enjoyed it.

We'd be honored if you'd consider posting a review—good or bad—on sites like **Amazon, Barnes & Noble, Kobo, Goodreads, Twitter, Facebook, Tumblr,** and your blog or website. We'd also be honored if you told your friends and family about this book. Word of mouth is a book's lifeblood!

For more information on upcoming releases, author interviews, blog tours, contests, giveaways, and more, please sign up for our weekly, spam-free newsletter and visit us around the web:

Newsletter: riptidepublishing.com/newsletter
Twitter: twitter.com/RiptideBooks
Facebook: facebook.com/RiptidePublishing
Goodreads: tinyurl.com/RiptideOnGoodreads
Tumblr: riptidepublishing.tumblr.com

Thank you so much for Reading the Rainbow!

RiptidePublishing.com

Acknowledgements

Many thanks to those who contributed to this story, especially Caz, my editor, and L.C., the cover art whizz.

Also by
Charlie Cochrane

About the Author

Because Charlie Cochrane couldn't be trusted to do any of her jobs of choice—like managing a rugby team—she writes. Her mystery novels include the Edwardian-era Cambridge Fellows series and the contemporary Lindenshaw Mysteries.

A member of the Romantic Novelists' Association, Mystery People, and International Thriller Writers Inc., Charlie regularly appears at literary festivals and at reader and author conferences with The Deadly Dames.

Where to find her:

Website: charliecochrane.wordpress.com

Facebook: facebook.com/charlie.cochrane.18

Twitter: twitter.com/charliecochrane

Goodreads: goodreads.com/author/show/2727135.Charlie_Cochrane

Enjoy more stories like
Old Sins
at RiptidePublishing.com!

.

Printed in Great Britain
by Amazon